"Smart and witty."
—*Library Journal*

"A delightful romp! Dry and breezy wit . . . a delightful, funny read for pugs and humans alike."
—Wilson the Pug with Nancy Levine,
authors of *The Tao of Pug*

"*Pug Hill* is all at once touching, witty, and so very smart. I love this nervous and self-deprecating narrator who makes low self-esteem not only funny and endearing but enviable. There's a terrific comedic eye at work here and a tender heart—a most satisfying combination."
—Elinor Lipman, author of *My Latest Grievance*

"Playful, funny . . . *Pug Hill* is the story of a woman confronting her fears and the adorable pooches that can help her do it."
—*Pages*

"Pitch-perfect and deftly written . . . a funny, charming, and touching novel."
—Robin Epstein and Renée Kaplan,
coauthors of *Shaking Her Assets*

"Alison Pace isn't afraid to tackle serious subjects, even as she delivers a wry and witty portrait of growing up and growing into herself at long last."
—Joshilyn Jackson, author of *Gods in Alabama*

"To paraphrase Woody Allen, love is too weak a word to describe how I feel about this novel. I loove it!"
—Melissa Senate, author of *See Jane Date*

continued . . .

Also by Alison Pace

IF ANDY WARHOL HAD A GIRLFRIEND
PUG HILL

through thick and thin

Alison Pace

BERKLEY BOOKS, NEW YORK

THE BERKLEY PUBLISHING GROUP
Published by the Penguin Group
Penguin Group (USA) Inc.
375 Hudson Street, New York, New York 10014, USA
Penguin Group (Canada), 90 Eglinton Avenue East, Suite 700, Toronto, Ontario M4P 2Y3, Canada
(a division of Pearson Penguin Canada Inc.)
Penguin Books Ltd., 80 Strand, London WC2R 0RL, England
Penguin Group Ireland, 25 St. Stephen's Green, Dublin 2, Ireland (a division of Penguin Books Ltd.)
Penguin Group (Australia), 250 Camberwell Road, Camberwell, Victoria 3124, Australia
(a division of Pearson Australia Group Pty. Ltd.)
Penguin Books India Pvt. Ltd., 11 Community Centre, Panchsheel Park, New Delhi—110 017, India
Penguin Group (NZ), 67 Apollo Drive, Rosedale, North Shore 0745, Auckland, New Zealand
(a division of Pearson New Zealand Ltd.)
Penguin Books (South Africa) (Pty.) Ltd., 24 Sturdee Avenue, Rosebank, Johannesburg 2196,
South Africa

Penguin Books Ltd., Registered Offices: 80 Strand, London WC2R 0RL, England

This book is an original publication of The Berkley Publishing Group.

This is a work of fiction. Names, characters, places, and incidents either are the product of the author's imagination or are used fictitiously, and any resemblance to actual persons, living or dead, business establishments, events, or locales is entirely coincidental. The publisher does not have any control over and does not assume any responsibility for author or third-party websites or their content.

First edition: August 2007

Library of Congress Cataloging-in-Publication Data

Pace, Alison.
  Through thick and thin / Alison Pace— 1st ed.
    p. cm.
  "Berkley trade paperback"—T.p. verso.
  ISBN 978-0-425-21561-6
  I. Title.

PS3566.A24T47 2007
813'.54—dc22   2007008010

PRINTED IN THE UNITED STATES OF AMERICA

10 9 8 7 6 5 4 3 2 1p

to my sister

acknowledgments

For the myriad and vast ways in which they contributed to this book, many, many thanks go to Susan Allison, Joe Veltre, Jessica Wade, Lisa Mondello, Leslie Gelbman, all the great people at Berkley Books, Sarah Swidler, David Corcoran, Andrea Strong, Joanna Schwartz, Cynthia Zabel, Jennifer Geller, Christine Ciampa, Robin Epstein, Sarah Melinger, Lynda Curnyn, Wendy Tufano, Mom and Dad, and of course, Carlie.

part one

get into the zone!

one

blurry vision

It wasn't always like this, Meredith thinks, as different towns—towns she has never been to and, truth be told, has no great interest in ever going to—all pass by, all in a blur. If you don't pay attention to it though, anything can be a blur. Can't it? Can't all of New Jersey be a blur, just like all the houses passed by, and the picket fences? And then, maybe even the distance, and the marriages, and the babies. They could be a blur, too. Except, actually, the babies don't seem to know how. Babies, though so soft by their very nature, refuse to be a blur. They are sharp and in focus, solid, completely and utterly defined. They leave everything else, everything less important swirling around them.

But, right, yes. Meredith tries to go back a few steps in her thoughts, to make it so that they, her thoughts, don't branch out in the ever forward-thinking way they have always liked to do. She tries not to think about blurs, and suburbs, and the babies who bring people here. And she tries not to think the thought that is bound to come next, the one that is not going to crown her "World's Best Aunt." She is, she imagines, not the best aunt. But maybe that's just because she's so new at it. Maybe all she needs is more time. It's only been six months after all. Could be that in the seventh month, or even the eighth (the eighth would be okay, too), she'll be better at it. It's not that she doesn't love her still-new niece, Ivy, because she does, she just feels so completely removed. From Ivy. From Stephanie. From all of it. She thinks that it might have a lot to do with New Jersey. She thinks that so much these days, that it, all of it, might have a lot to do with New Jersey.

Right as the train approaches the Ridgewood station, right as the announcer is earnestly and helpfully, though also more or less unintelligibly, reminding her to gather her belongings and to double-check that she hasn't left anything behind, Meredith finds herself back at her initial thought. She thinks again, *it wasn't always like this.* And it really wasn't.

She gets up and gathers her things; she does not double-check for her belongings. Meredith is tired of earnest and helpful suggestions that fall under the category of What She Should Do Next. She stares down at her feet, at her more functional than stylish Nikes, the type of sneakers that a person would run in, if she were so inclined to run. If running didn't make her knees hurt, her lower back ache, didn't always put her in mind of an overweight hamster on a never-ending Habitrail wheel of despair. If only running made her feel as if she were leaving all her troubles behind, if a journey once around the reservoir in Central Park made her feel as if she were on a path toward the ever-

elusive adjectives, *slender, thin, fit* (ever
use these very sneakers.

She keeps her gaze fixed on the sn
train, over the subtly scary space bet
form. Subtle, because it would in fact be qu
actually take some maneuvering, to really fall down to
tracks. Scary, because even though it would take some doing,
you could get down there. And then she looks up, and right as
she does, she sees Stephanie waving.

"Meres! Over here," Stephanie calls out. Meredith waves
back and smiles. She smiles mostly at the "Meres," because it's
only Stephanie who ever calls her that. She hitches her bag, a
cream-colored canvas tote with navy blue handles and a logo
from the Aspen Food Festival, higher on her shoulder and quick-
ens her pace. Stephanie is half-hidden, well, slightly less than
half-hidden, behind Ivy's stroller—one of those bright green
Froggy things that Meredith has learned from Stephanie are very
important. And she's sure Ivy must be in it somewhere, swaddled
under all those blankets, and as she gets closer, she can see a little pink fleece hat sticking up. She wonders, with all the swad-
dling, why Stephanie didn't just wait for her in the car. And then,
she sees that standing next to Stephanie, there is another. Another with a Froggy stroller, too.

And yes, by the way, Meredith does in fact know that it isn't
technically called a Froggy, but something else that sounds like
that. She's also pretty sure that she should never call it, out
loud, a Froggy. And she definitely should not say it in front of
this other one, because it will, as probably so many things do,
reveal her to be childless, urban, career-driven, and possibly

spinster. All things, except for maybe the part about
ng a spinster, that Meredith has long maintained as not nec-
ssarily bad things. All things perhaps long maintained in
Ridgewood, New Jersey, as not necessarily good. She makes a
mental note to steal a closer look at the prized stroller, an informative glance. Because, and it's not just people in Ridgewood
who think this, it's Meredith herself who thinks this, too: it's
one thing to be without your own child, it's quite another to not
be head over heels in love with and to not know every last thing
about your new (still fairly new) niece, Ivy. The offspring of
your sister, who isn't just your sister, isn't just a run-of-the-mill
sibling, but your best friend in the world, the person with whom
you shared everything. Until you didn't.

For the last few steps of her approach, Meredith takes quick
stock of this other one standing next to Stephanie. Both she and
Stephanie are in sneakers, too, but they're both in the kinds that
are expressly not for running; Velcro is involved. They're both
wearing identical ski jackets, two-toned shells in black and
royal blue, hitting mid-thigh, the kind that always puts Meredith in mind of snowboarders or men who live on the Upper
West Side. They're both wearing hats. This other one's hair is all
tucked up into her hat, no wisps or strands escape to frame her
angular face, which is quite red from the cold. Stephanie's hair
hangs down, out of her hat. Stephanie's hair, so recently thick
and shoulder-length and dark brown, exactly the same as Meredith's, is now thick and shoulder-length and dark brown with
blonde and red highlights. Meredith thinks the highlights were
a mistake, but has not said so. Meredith wonders if this other
person has highlights, too.

"Meres. Hi, love," Stephanie says stepping out from behind the stroller. They reach out to each other and hug, holding on for a moment. Meredith looks down over Stephanie's shoulder into the froggieboo and smiles at the tiny slice of Ivy, just two tiny closed eyes peeking out.

"Hi," she says, once she and Stephanie have separated, turning her attention, extending her hand, "I'm Meredith."

"Hi, Meredith," comes the reply, very happily, very perkily. "So great to meet you. I'm Caryn."

"Caryn's in my New Mommy Group and lives just a few doors down," Stephanie explains.

"And since it's not even ten minutes, we power-walked to get you!" Caryn volunteers helpfully, and Meredith thinks, *Annoying.* "Stephanie's told me all about you. That's so cool that you're the restaurant critic for *The NY* and you know, I used to read your reviews first thing every week. Every Monday, *New York* would arrive and *The NY* would arrive and I used to go right to *The NY,* right away, to read your reviews. Loved them. Always used to go to the places you wrote about."

"Thanks," Meredith says cautiously, thinking to herself, *Why used to?*

Caryn continues, "I mean, we still get the magazines but it's just so much harder to get into the city for dinner these days."

"I can imagine," Meredith says and follows Caryn's loving gaze down to her own little blanketed bundle in her own important stroller. "This is Ashley," Caryn says joyously and Meredith smiles in the direction of the other baby, a purple-hatted one, who is not Ivy, whose eyes are wide open, and who is peering up into the brisk air looking mildly horrified.

"Hi, Ashley," Meredith says, and then turns slightly and motions to Ivy in her stroller, and mouths to Stephanie, "Is she asleep?"

"She is. Finally," Stephanie says, without any sound coming out. Ivy has not been big on sleep lately. To be fair, Ivy is not completely against sleep during the day, she has in fact dabbled in it, but she has not at all warmed up to sleeping at night. Meredith thinks that if she had a baby who didn't ever sleep at night, she'd probably drive to the train station, she doesn't think she'd "power-walk" there. "You can say hi to her at home, she'll no doubt be up when we get back," Stephanie offers.

"God," Caryn says next, her eyes darting quickly from Meredith to Stephanie and back again, perhaps more for effect than anything else, "you two look *so much alike.*" And Meredith thinks that the *God*, it really does come out sounding like *Gawd.* "It's like you're twins!" she exclaims.

"We're only eighteen months apart," Stephanie answers proudly. Stephanie had taken, throughout their adult lives, to informing people of this fact, happily, sweetly, even when they hadn't inquired. It was only recently that Meredith had started to hear this statement as something of a declaration of victory, as if Stephanie was pointing out that she had accomplished so much more, had acquired so much more—the husband, the house, *the baby*—and yet she'd only had a relatively short head start.

"Oh, that's so cool," exclaims Caryn, as she and Stephanie both pull back on their strollers and maneuver their froggieboos through graceful one hundred eighty degree turns. Their movements are almost perfectly in tandem; they look to Meredith so much like a practiced skill, like a water ballet, only on land and with strollers. Once everyone is turned and facing away from the station, the three (or, wait, make that five) head slowly, so as not to jostle, in the direction of Linwood Avenue. Meredith is in the middle, thinking she'd rather be on the outside of Stephanie. Stephanie takes one hand from the handle of her froggieboo and slips it through Meredith's arm.

After a moment, Caryn leans forward, almost across Meredith, and says, "See, Stephanie. You guys, you two, so close in age and everything and so close. There's an argument right there for having your second baby right away." Meredith raises a subtle eyebrow at Stephanie. Perhaps the eyebrow is too subtle though as Stephanie, as far as Meredith can tell, seems to have missed it altogether. Once Stephanie and Aubrey's white brick house is in view, Meredith remembers and focuses her gaze on Ivy's triumphantly green stroller.

It's called a *Bugaboo*. A *Bugaboo Frog* to be exact. She was close enough.

two

lasagna

Once they're standing on the sidewalk in front of Stephanie's house, just in front of the gate, Caryn thrusts her arm out to shake Meredith's hand again.

"Meredith," she says, "it was a pleasure to meet you."

Meredith takes the offered, gloved hand, shakes it, and says it was a pleasure for her, too. It was not a pleasure. It was a ten-minute walk in the cold during which Caryn talked mostly to Stephanie.

Meredith tries, with a certain though not complete degree of success, not to take Caryn personally, not to see her very existence as an affront. But it's not like there wasn't an occasion or two during the walk when Meredith didn't consider how much nicer it would have been if Caryn weren't there.

"Stephanie says you come out to visit all the time," Caryn says, and Meredith nods in agreement, says yes, even though she doesn't. Visit all the time. She should, or at least she should visit more than she does.

"So, I'll look forward to seeing you again," Caryn adds on.

"Yes," Meredith says again, and maybe the way she says it, maybe it's a little blankly.

And with that, Caryn turns to Stephanie, tilts her head to the left and then to the right. "See you Monday for lunch after music class?" she sings more than says.

"See you then," Stephanie says, smiling broadly, happily, and the way she says it, it's not even a little bit like she secretly hates her. Stephanie has always had a much greater capacity for love than Meredith has. They have both always thought so. Even when the term "a greater capacity for love" was used euphemistically, in college, when Stephanie was going through her recreationally slutty phase, they still believed it.

"Here, Meres," Stephanie says once they've walked through the gate and she's backed the stroller flush against the stoop and climbed up the few steps, "Just grab that end, and help me get this up the stairs and inside?" Before Meredith has even made a move for the stroller, Ivy, sensing an imminent cosmic disturbance, wakes up and starts to cry. Meredith looks to Stephanie, unsure of what to do next, amazed, as she has been before, at how Ivy manages to put her entire being, her heart and soul, into her crying.

"It's okay," Stephanie says, to both of them, Meredith thinks. And then, as she grabs the back of the stroller, Ivy's crying ceases, just like that. Meredith, again, is amazed; even though peace is so fleeting for babies, so fragile, and so tenuous, so is despair. Which is nice, she thinks; it almost makes up for the peace being so fragile in the first place.

Together, Meredith and Stephanie maneuver the stroller—or let's call it the *Bugaboo* now that we know not only its importance, but also its name—up the side steps and into the small laundry room that leads through to the bright and airy country French-inspired kitchen. The air smells like Bounce, and like something else, too. Air maybe, the air you can't ever smell in the city because there's always too much else. Everything here is open. Beyond the kitchen, through an archway, is the living room—family room rather—and it all looks so effortlessly perfect. This house, where Stephanie and Aubrey and Ivy have only recently arrived, already feels so lived in, stretched out in, but not cluttered. Organized and neat but not sterile or stifling. Stephanie's rooms have always been nice rooms, inviting rooms, the rooms you might see in the background of a J. Crew catalog: natural and fresh, clean with a preppy flair. Meredith is so often reminded of a J. Crew catalog when she is at Stephanie's, because of things like the white-painted hooks where she is presently hanging their jackets, and because of Aubrey. She's always thought of Stephanie's husband, Aubrey—and she means this, really, in only the complimentary way—as being from the J. Crew catalog of husbands. If only, she has thought on occasion, there actually was such a thing.

"Okay," Stephanie says authoritatively as she unsnaps Ivy's down onesie, the one that Meredith has admired from afar. On colder days in New York she has thought the world would be nicer if she had her own down onesie to swaddle herself within. "Someone is going to watch her *Baby Mozart* in her bouncy seat!"

As Meredith watches the swift transfer of Ivy, through the kitchen and into her bouncy seat in the family room beyond it, she almost says, *Are you sure?* But she catches herself, and is glad she did, because she thinks it wouldn't have come out the way she means, which is more along the lines of, *Is there something else that I'm supposed to do?* more, *Am I supposed to be better at this, to want to play with Ivy more before she is relegated to the baby bouncy seat?* Meredith opts for saying nothing and follows Stephanie's lead through the kitchen and into the family room and watches as Ivy is once again snapped, secured into the bouncy seat. Two deliriously chubby arms stretch into the air toward Stephanie.

"Da Da!" Ivy says.

Stephanie looks annoyed, just for a flash, before saying, "Yes, Da Da."

"Da Da Da Da Da Da! Da Da Da Da!"

Stephanie picks up the remote and aims it at the flat screen TV mounted on the wall. She talks to Meredith without facing her as she scrolls through the DVD menu options on the screen. "I'm sure you want to play with her and all, but I think the *Baby Mozart* is good for right now. I think she's wound up and the *Baby Mozart* works wonders at chilling her out."

The lava lamp shapes and soothing colors of the opening scenes of the *Baby Mozart* DVD fill the screen and Ivy's vision, and she is instantly mesmerized, becoming almost as globular as the images on the screen.

Meredith and Stephanie, from where they have finally sat on the couch, both sigh exaggeratedly, loudly, in unison. Ivy turns to look at them, her eyes momentarily wide, perhaps perplexed, and just as quickly returns her complete and utter focus to her *Baby Mozart.* As she stares at the screen, she opens her mouth and keeps it that way.

Meredith, from her reclining position on Stephanie's couch, is suddenly very aware of how her body feels, the way she sometimes is whenever she isn't busy. It happens sometimes when she comes here, or even when she's home alone, whenever it is that she sits down, relaxes, stops for a minute. She notices how strange it feels, so foreign, it's almost like it hurts. She wonders if staying home, as Stephanie does now, if being a mom, not going to work anymore, feels anything like this? Or is it the exact opposite? Is it in fact so much busier, busier than she ever could have imagined, in her most frenetic dreams? Everyone stares at the screen.

"Thank God for *Baby Mozart,*" Stephanie says.

"It's like a baby tranquilizer," Meredith marvels.

Stephanie adds, "It's a whole series, *Baby Einstein*, there's a ton of them, did you know that?"

Meredith shakes her head, *No, I didn't.*

"Right, no, I mean why would you?" Stephanie says quickly, "But really, thank God for them, for all of them." Stephanie pauses for a moment, marveling at the screen, before adding in a slightly different voice, a higher tone than the one she usually speaks in, "And thank God for the blonde, very skinny, not freaked-out-at-all mom who pops up at the end of each DVD and talks about how she developed the whole *Baby Einstein* series. The one who doesn't make you feel like a tremendous underachiever just because you can't imagine finding the time for a shower that lasts longer than forty-five seconds, let alone find the time to start an educational media empire."

"Yes, thank God for her," Meredith says even though she's never seen this blonde, and skinny, and apparently rather unsettling woman at the end of the DVD. She wants to say, *Are you okay?* Because something like that, that's an okay thing to say, right? That's not making a *thing*, that's not making the drama that Stephanie insists not be made. Stephanie does not like *things,* does not subscribe to what she thinks is the drama people can make out of stuff, out of anything. Even if a lot of other six-month-old babies are already quite settled in to a sleep schedule, a nighttime sleep schedule. Stephanie says she has heard of these babies who sleep from seven to seven, and for the life of her, she just can't imagine that it could be true.

"Aubrey thinks it's like baby pot," Stephanie continues. "Baby crack. I try not to let her have too much TV, especially with the way this zones her out, but I just get so tired, and especially since you're here and I don't get to see you, I think it's fine."

"It's educational," Meredith assures, and then for a while, for a full five minutes or so, they watch the soothing colors and shapes and sardonic sock puppets on the big screen; Meredith wonders if maybe she should get a *Baby Einstein* video for herself, or whatever the adult equivalent is. Though actually the adult equivalent is probably, as Aubrey says, pot, or crack. Probably not the best idea. Probably.

"Speaking of Aubrey, where is he?" Meredith asks.

Stephanie stares at the screen for a second more. "Oh, I think he's in his workroom," she answers vaguely as she glances briefly in the direction of the door across the room.

It could be the inherent 1970s implication of a finished basement—like the one they never had growing up in their house in Washington, the District, not the state, because the house was too old, the basement wasn't the type that could be finished. It could be that. Whatever it is, something always makes Stephanie time-travel back a few decades and call Aubrey's corner of the basement a workroom, as if there's a toolbox in there, and a saw, some drills, a wooden sawhorse perhaps, as if it's the site of various and sundry manly man crafts. But it's not that at all. It's just a different part, a sectioned-off area of the basement. Aubrey has a desk set up there, and his seventeen-inch MacBook Pro that Meredith has on occasion felt lust for, having the fondness she does for shiny new things. Aubrey also has about five million CDs down there, and his golf clubs, and both his and Stephanie's skis and snow-boards that were never used this winter, for the first winter ever. He has all these *Sports Illustrated* magazines, hundreds of them, and for some reason, a mini-fridge.

"I should get him," Stephanie says after a moment, and the way her voice turned before, becoming higher when she talked about the woman who pops up at the end of the *Baby Einstein* videos, her voice gets that way again, as if an anxious glaze has just been painted onto it. "He should say hi. I didn't even think. So rude, I'm sorry."

"Oh, no, it's fine, Steph," Meredith tells her, "don't be sorry."

"I guess he thinks if it's just, you know, *you*, and not an ac-tual guest, he doesn't have to come up and say hi," Stephanie explains. "But he should. I'll get him." The only movement she makes is flipping her hands up and making quotes in the air around the word *guest*. Normally, Meredith would want to address the subject of air quotes with Stephanie. Meredith has long thought of the use of air quotes as a matter of concern. But right now, it doesn't seem important.

"No, don't, it's fine," she says, with some manufactured urgency. She extends a flexed palm, as if to quite physically stop her sister's mad dash to the basement door. She wants Stephanie to think it really does seem like she's about to go down there and get him. She has no idea why, but she thinks that it's necessary. "It's fine," she says again, "I'm here all day. It's fine, it's nice to see just you for a little bit." And it is, even if there might be something about it that's lonely.

"I just don't want you to think he's rude," Stephanie adds, still concerned.

"I don't think he's rude," Meredith assures.

"No, I know, and it's nice to see just you, too." Stephanie brightens as she angles herself on the couch until she is completely facing Meredith, the door to the basement/workroom now out of her line of vision. The sounds from the *Baby Mozart* hit a crescendo and then settle down again.

"So," Stephanie says, reaching out, touching Meredith's knee, "Tuesday? Big day." Tuesday is Valentine's Day. *Big day,* Meredith thinks, and smiles; possibly it is closer to smirking than smiling.

"Josh is still coming up?" Stephanie double-checks.

"Yep, still is," Meredith replies, noticing how they both felt it necessary to use the word *still*.

"Where are you going?" Stephanie asks, now beaming a little bit. The beaming, just so you know, isn't because she's a fan of Josh, Meredith's vanished and now reappeared ex-boyfriend, but because she is a fan of Meredith having a date for Valentine's Day again. She is a fan of Meredith giving romance a chance again, even if it is with Josh. She is a fan of Meredith finding her happy ending, even if with Josh, the ending was not so happy at all.

"Bouley," Meredith says with more restraint than Bouley would normally be said with. Yes, she's been there four, even five times before, as she's been to so many wonderful restaurants four, even five times before. But the restraint in this instance is less because she's jaded and more because she thinks restraint is important to have with Josh. Restraint, really, is the only way to play it. Especially with Josh.

"Oh, I do love Bouley," Stephanie says dreamily. She sighs and looks a little wistfully off at nothing in particular, some point above Ivy's head, past the flat screen. "I miss coming with you." And something in Meredith surges, and she wonders if it's just that she misses her sister so much, even if they are sitting less than two feet away from each other, even if there's really no way to explain what it feels like when things, husbands and babies and suburbs, happen to everyone around you but not you, when everyone changes, when everything changes, and you just stay the same.

"I miss you coming with me, too," she says, "You're my favorite dining companion, hands down."

"I miss the wigs, too." Stephanie says, still wistful, perhaps even more wistful. Stephanie always liked the secret agent aspect of Meredith's job, the disguises and the aliases and all the different credit cards, almost as much as the food. Stephanie used to come over beforehand and disguise herself, too. And Meredith would always happily accommodate; she understood, she's always liked the disguises very much, too.

"You can always come, whenever you want."

"Right," she glances at Ivy, "tell me when you get switched to the New Jersey beat." Stephanie does have a sitter for Ivy, or maybe the correct word would be nanny since it's the same person who comes every Monday, Wednesday, and Thursday afternoons and is available on Saturday nights, too; something that Stephanie had, at one point, been quite pleased about, so representative it seemed to her of freedom. But Meredith isn't sure when a person stops being a sitter and starts being a nanny, or if she is in fact technically either since Stephanie has yet to let her stay alone with Ivy. At some point, freedom stopped being at the top of the list of things Stephanie got pleased about.

"Steph," she suggests, treading lightly, "you should really come in one night. I have to go back to 66 in the next few weeks, twice probably. You know, it's Jean-George Vongerichten's Chinese-themed outpost in Tribeca?" Meredith asks, and Stephanie shakes her head, as in *No, Meredith, I didn't know,* because really, how could she, out here in Ridgewood, not living, breathing, and sleeping (poorly) the New York City restaurant scene? Or maybe she shakes her head, no, as in *No, I'm not coming with you.* Meredith continues on quickly, "You'd *love* it there, he does this soy-cured salmon with Asian pears and a crème fraîche that is just exceptional. He uses cilantro in it, in the crème fraîche. You should come," Meredith says invitingly, and when Stephanie looks a bit more wistful, a bit more like she'd really quite like a nice night out at a restaurant, Meredith adds on, "You can wear the red wig if you'd like."

"The long red one?" Stephanie asks longingly, just a hint of elasticity in her voice. Meredith considers it for a moment, braces herself, and then ever so cautiously adds the thing she's been thinking should have been added onto almost every sentence for the past few months.

"Steph," she begins, in a tone she hopes strikes only the right level of impassioned, "at some point you need to be okay with letting Ivy stay with her sitter, or even just with Aubrey for the night." (Was it impassioned? Impassioned enough?) Stephanie stiffens. Meredith isn't sure when exactly Stephanie stiffened, when the 66-long-red-wig glimmer went out of her eye; if she lost her at *sitter*, or at *Aubrey*. Surely it was at *sitter*. She reapproaches, "Steph, lots of people, lots of really excellent mothers, almost as dedicated as you, use sitters. Nannies."

Stephanie tucks a new highlight behind her ear, and repeats the motion on the other side. She considers the lava lamp shapes on the screen for a moment and then she glances at the door to the basement before turning again to Meredith, her forehead slightly clouded. "It's not just that. I can't go to a big dinner, I'm starting a new diet on Monday," she explains. "I haven't lost hardly any of the baby weight."

Meredith doesn't say anything for a second, she hates the word *diet*, always has, and wonders how the topic changed so quickly away from 66. Stephanie is looking at her expectantly. "You look great," she tells her, and she thinks so, she does.

"No, I don't. I've lost none of the baby weight."

"Steph, that's an exaggeration."

"But it's not a big one. I'm a cow."

"You are absolutely not," Meredith protests. Sure, Stephanie's been thinner before. Sure, she could be thinner than she is now. But who hasn't, who couldn't? Meredith looks quickly at Stephanie's middle, first at her stomach, then at her thighs, and then, even more quickly, down at her own. She reminds herself that thighs, just by their very nature, look a lot bigger when sitting down on a couch, stomachs do, too. She tries not to compare. Comparing herself to Stephanie has never worked out well for her. Stephanie had always been the nicer sister, the sportier sister. She'd always been the prettier sister even though they looked so much alike; people had never noticed that because Stephanie had always been the thinner sister. She tries not to judge herself or her sister. And then she does anyway. She's still heavier than Stephanie is, and she remembers (how could she forget?) that Stephanie, for all intents and purposes really, should probably be the heavier one. Stephanie has a new baby. Meredith just has *The NY*, and ten thousand restaurants in New York City, so many of them needing to be reviewed. But she shouldn't compare. She tells herself it's not a contest. She tells herself that a lot.

Meredith sits up a bit straighter, tucks a thumb into the waistband of her jeans, and pulls them up a bit, up and over her stomach, which she will only call her stomach. She will not say *roll* or *pooch*, because it might actually be more than that, and also, attributing the words *roll* and *pooch* to one's body parts can't be considered productive. She will say, however, that low-waisted jeans (a fashion trend she can now see she was wrong to have tried to embrace) are not friends. She has seriously begun to contemplate the very real possibility that low-waisted jeans are in fact the devil's playthings.

"What diet?" Meredith asks. Just to be polite.

"The Zone," Stephanie tells her. "Caryn lost twenty-five pounds on it." Caryn, Meredith thinks, could very well be one of those annoying women in Manhattan, the miniature ones whose numbers are legion and vast, who actually look good in Seven, Citizens of Humanity, Hudson, Rock & Republic, True Religion and all the other myriad brands of low-waisted jeans that are *everywhere*. Meredith knows all their names (the names of the low-waisted jeans, not of the miniature women). She would bet right now that Caryn, even when she was pregnant, has never actually seen the other side of size six. Meredith does at times see how it's wrong to hate people on sight. Now is not one of those times.

"Caryn actually did the thing where they deliver it every day to you, three meals and a snack. But I'm just going to do it with the book. I have the book," Stephanie says authoritatively, and Meredith worries for a moment that she's going to jump up and get the book and brandish it at her. But that doesn't happen. Stephanie only adds hopefully, almost as wistfully as when she remembered Meredith's wigs, "People say it's complicated, but I can't see how it can be that complicated. I mean, it's just a diet."

Just a diet. Meredith doesn't think there's any such thing. But Stephanie doesn't know that, how could she? She doesn't have the advantage of accumulated years of knowledge that Meredith has. Stephanie hasn't spent her entire life feeling fat.

"See, how it works is . . ." Stephanie begins to explain something, something about the ratios of fats and proteins and carbohydrates, but Meredith isn't really listening. She's thinking that she's heard it all before and she doesn't want to hear the intricacies of this particular diet, doesn't want to know why it's easy to follow, why this one will work. She's thinking that even with everything they used to have in common, before there was Aubrey and Ivy and Ridgewood, before everything changed but Meredith didn't, now the one thing they have in common is this. Weight. Weight that needs to be lost.

She turns her attention back to Stephanie. She tries to focus, because she thinks she might see a little bit of a glimmer in her sister's eyes again, and she thinks that right about now, Stephanie could use a bit of a glimmer.

"Jennifer Aniston swears by it," Stephanie concludes triumphantly, both as summary and as further proof that clearly the Zone must be very effective indeed.

"Jennifer Aniston doesn't count," Meredith says, in spite of the glimmer, and really, in spite of herself.

"Love Jennifer!" Stephanie answers back quickly, as much a protest as an urgent request.

"No, I do love Jennifer," Meredith says, because it's not that she doesn't love Jennifer Aniston, and it's not that she doesn't agree with Stephanie's wholehearted assertions that Jennifer Aniston needs everyone's love and support what with all the absolute awfulness with Brad and Angelina. "I just think Jennifer Aniston is too skinny to be a dieting touchstone," Meredith explains.

Stephanie's cheeks puff momentarily, her hair moves up in

the air as she exhales. She shouldn't have done that with the highlights, it looks too different, weird different.

"Well, Meres, right about now, I could use a dieting touchstone, and Jennifer Aniston is as good as any."

Touchstone, Meredith thinks. They used to be each other's, on everything, and now they're not, on anything. Not even on this, the new thing that Meredith had just decided they had in common, even if the new thing was only weight that should be shed, lost, evaporated, and forgotten.

"I think she lost thirty pounds, you know, before she was even on *Friends,*" Stephanie continues. "That counts. And we love Jennifer."

"Yes, we do," Meredith says and thinks, *Maybe it is something, maybe it does count,* and after a moment asks, "So, when are you starting?" It's a question she stopped asking herself a long time ago because, pretty much, it's a *very big* question.

"Not this week," Stephanie says, "the week after." Meredith nods. She doesn't ask why the delay, because there is always a perfectly good reason, always has been. She looks at the alligator hand puppet on the television screen, his puppet face all scrunched so that he looks a bit annoyed, and she tries not to think about it.

"Do you know how much weight I actually have to lose to get to where I want to be?" Stephanie asks.

"How much?"

Stephanie takes Meredith's hand and holds it; she always does this during moments she feels are important. Quickly, she blurts out a number. The number. Meredith nods, and thinks she could lose that much, too. More even, except for the fact that she doesn't want to do this. She squeezes Stephanie's hand.

"You can do it," she says, and is it, the way she says it, maybe a bit wistful? Does she sound a little bit how Stephanie sounded when she was talking about the wigs? Surely not.

"Thanks, Meres," Stephanie smiles appreciatively and lets go of her hand and they turn their attention back to the puppets and blocks on the TV screen and to the occasional bounce of Ivy's head. Meredith thinks of Jennifer Aniston and of Caryn the power-walking neighbor who did or did not lose twenty-five pounds. She thinks that Stephanie didn't ask her to do the Zone with her. She doesn't want to wonder why.

She thinks instead that if Stephanie's going to go on a diet, then she needs a good send-off. She thinks maybe she'll borrow Stephanie's car and run to the store and get the ingredients for a lasagna and she and Stephanie, and Aubrey, if he ever comes up from the basement, will have lasagna instead of going to the Village Green Café. Going out as much as she does, Meredith sometimes loves a home-cooked meal. She loves the layering of the noodles, and the meat sauce, and the three different kinds of cheese, mozzarella, Parmesan, ricotta. Meredith has often thought that there might be no better freedom than lasagna. Freedom from complicated recipes, and reservations, and too much importance placed on spices. Freedom from measuring, from searching for perfection, from having to always be somewhere, from having to always be someone else.

They say that even bad pizza is good, but Meredith has never thought that to be true about pizza. She thinks bad pizza is bad, but she's never thought that about lasagna. She doesn't think a bad one has existed or will exist in the future world, ever. And if you think about it that way, what is there really that is better than lasagna?

three

a little more about josh

Okay. He did call, there's that. But, just so you know, there are plenty of other things, too.

There'd been—what was it—a year, in which Meredith had waited for him to call. (It was in fact closer to two years if a person was inclined to be honest about it.) And then, after that, there'd been a shorter period of time in which she hadn't waited, but had occasionally thought, *Now he'll call because I don't want him anymore, and they know not to come back until you don't want them.* She was sure she'd heard that somewhere, but then she was also sure that thinking something like that could very well cancel out the whole "I don't want him anymore," in the first place. And then she didn't think it, or want it, she really didn't, and he still didn't call.

And then he called.

"I was wondering if you were free on February fourteenth?

It's a Tuesday," he'd said the second time he called, as if the greatest relevance of that day was that it was a Tuesday. "Because I'll be in New York," he'd added on, and there was something in the tone of his voice that made Meredith think of the drawings in her high school French textbooks, the cartoon figures with names like Marie-Claude, Pascal, Jean Christophe, who would point and exclaim into a bubble above their heads, *Quelle Coincidence!*

"I'm free," she'd told him. And she didn't have to hang up the phone and rearrange her busy Valentine's Day schedule so that she could nonchalantly see him. She was actually, come to think of it, free. In fairness, Valentine's Day wasn't a good night to review a restaurant, what with all the tourists and the special Valentine's Day menus. She had briefly toyed with doing a Valentine's Day survey. (Meredith loves surveys, like the one that Frank Bruni, the critic at the *New York Times*, did on fast-food restaurants across the country; she still wishes she'd thought of that.) She had briefly considered dashing from restaurant to restaurant, having dinner at each one; she could probably fit in four if she started early enough, five if she planned on staying out very late. A survey always appealed, but then there was something about the thought of racing around New York on Valentine's Day, without a Valentine's Day date, that made the idea of putting pins in her eyes hold a certain appeal, too.

And to be fair, she was free on Valentine's Day because it had been quite a while since she'd come across anyone she liked. To be honest, it's not as if she's really come across anyone else, met anyone else, in lo these many years since Josh had been gone. (And in this case, "lo these many" is equal to three.)

"Guess where I made reservations?" he'd asked her on the third time he called, "it starts with a *B*."

And she'd thought they'd done an okay job of getting past the awkward moment when she'd said, with quite a lot of enthusiasm, "Babbo?! How great! Babbo, hands down, is my favorite restaurant in New York!" and he'd said back, with less enthusiasm, "No, Bouley."

For the record, had she been given the opportunity to lie, she would have. She would have had no problem saying, "My favorite restaurant, the best restaurant in New York, is Bouley." Bouley, Babbo, though very different, in Meredith's opinion they both fit the criteria to be the best: beautiful atmosphere, impeccable food, outstanding service, originality, creativity.

The phone rings and Meredith jumps. She's not startled by the ringing itself, or even by the interruption of her thoughts; she's just trying to get to it on the first ring. She always tries to get to the phone on the first ring, her logic being that if she always picks up the phone on the first ring, then maybe so will everyone else. Eventually, it'll have a domino effect. Everyone will pick up the phone right away, it will be what people do, and she won't ever have to sit idly waiting, listening to a ringing phone. And maybe next, if people start picking up their damn phones on the first ring, inspired by her good example, if she ever manages to improve the world in that way, she thinks she'd like to tackle being put on hold. Call waiting in general. She always feels as if there is so much to do, and she likes that feeling; sometimes she feels bad about it though, sometimes she feels as if she'll never accomplish enough.

"Hello?" she says. She hears a new sort of urgency, an acceleration in her voice, and it occurs to her that she's worried, worried that it might be Josh calling to cancel.

"What are you wearing?" Stephanie asks. Their conversations have never been hindered by the need for introductory "how are you?"s and "what's new?"s, since there used to be so many of them. Meredith looks down at her painstakingly selected but resultantly uninspired ensemble. It seems almost too boring to describe, she's disappointed at that.

"What do you think I'm wearing? I'm wearing black," she says.

"Snappy," Stephanie observes. Stephanie's right, she's snappy. She should be more excited than snappy. Shouldn't she be more excited? Shouldn't she be, frankly, head over heels excited that the man with whom she used to be head over heels in love with (at least she'd thought that's what it was) has called and asked her out for Valentine's Day?

"Yeah, no. I'm fine," Meredith says,

"Are you nervous?" Stephanie inquires.

"No, I'm just . . ." Meredith begins but doesn't finish because she doesn't know what should come next. She doesn't know *what* she is right now, and hopes maybe this small feeling of dread that's in the place of where the excitement should be, could actually just be nervousness after all. *Nerves*, she thinks. Nothing at all to worry about.

"Look, if nothing else, it's dinner at Bouley," Stephanie offers cheerfully, the time-tested consolation to daters. If nothing else it's dinner at, insert name of admired/sought after/artfully selected/hard-to-get reservations at/expensive restaurant here.

People, even Stephanie it seems, forget that it's not the same for Meredith, who can go to any restaurant she'd like, and pretty much does.

"Right, dinner at Bouley is always nice," Meredith agrees, because right now she wants to agree with Stephanie, wants to be of the same mind-set as Stephanie, for whom things so often work out nicely. She'd like, as she embarks on her evening, to bring some (if not quite a lot) of Stephanie's goodwill, and good luck, along with her.

"But, Steph," Meredith says next, because she thinks maybe she should check, "how does it work?"

"What's that?"

"How does it work?" she repeats. "I mean, can people really just come back?"

She asks because she really would like to know, even though she doubts that Stephanie could be the one to tell her. Stephanie, who has been with Aubrey for so long, and who Meredith doesn't think has any idea what it feels like to be left. As she waits for Stephanie to have a good answer—to say something along the lines of *Sure, of course, look, they have, right?*—she wonders about people coming back, and if you can in fact believe the things they tell you when they do.

"Just see what happens. Really. Try not to think about it all so much," Stephanie says, with a certain degree of earnestness, and Meredith considers it as an option, though not seriously. Meredith never listens, Stephanie knows this. Meredith thinks instead about what can and can't be forgotten. "Really," Stephanie adds, wanting to make her point, "it's as good advice as any."

"Thanks," Meredith says, and then, trying to move on from the topic that isn't going anywhere, at least not right now, she asks Stephanie, "Are you guys doing anything?"

"Oh, you know, I don't know," Stephanie says, and she says it so quickly that Meredith wonders for a second if it's coy—dare she say smug. Though, more likely, it's probably more protective than anything else, more, *Meres, love, don't trouble yourself with thinking about my Valentine's Day with my cute, sporty, outdoorsy husband whom everyone loves, even those not so outdoorsy. You have to think less, like I just told you.* Maybe, most likely, that's what it is. But the thing is, and this is what bothers her, is that she just can't be sure.

four

trouble sleeping

The evening's special menu is made from pink handmade paper, with marbled lines of white running across it, speckled with dried and flattened flower stems. *Valentine's Day Menu* is printed across the top, without flourish, in what could even be Times New Roman, twelve-point font.

"You know what we should do?" Josh asks, looking up from his menu.

Yes, I know! Meredith thinks. *We should perhaps start by acknowledging the fact that this is actually a date, and a big-deal date at that, it being Valentine's Day and all? Let's, let's do that. Let's not call today "Tuesday, the fourteenth" anymore. Let's call it a Valentine's Day Date. A rekindling of a long-ago and quite effectively doused fire. Let's call it what it is, a date at Bouley, on Valentine's Day because you are, as it turns out in*

the end, sorry that you left me, and because you see now, so
clearly, that it's all been a big mistake?

"No, what's that?" she says, in lieu.

"We should go, section by section, through the menu and make sure that we don't order any of the same dishes. For example," he says, angling his menu so she can see it, even though, clearly, she is in possession of her own menu. "Well, the first is just Chef's Canape, so we'll both have that obviously," he explains, actually pointing to that line with his index finger. "But here, look," he continues, index finger following suit, "for the first course, why don't I get the Phyllo Crusted Florida Shrimp, Cape Cod Baby Squid, Scuba Dived Sea Scallop, Sweet Maryland Crabmeat in an Ocean Herbal Broth, and *you* get the Sashimi Quality Tuna, Nantucket Bay Scallops and Osetra Caviar Tartar with Organic Micro Greens and Lavender Olive Sea Salt?"

Josh nods his head authoritatively, right after *sea salt*, beaming as if it was he who gathered every ingredient on the entire menu and presented it in such an appetizing fashion. It feels like waking up from a strange and confusing dream, as she remembers, hazily, a bit fuzzily, Josh's disinclination toward shorthand or summary. With menus. With some other things, too. It would, she now recalls, be quite impossible for him to say, I could get the first thing, and you could get the second. She'd forgotten that.

"And then . . ." he continues, continuing also to beam with what Meredith can only still identify as pride, "I could get the Cape Cod Monkfish Stuffed with Asparagus with Jerusalem Artichoke Puree and Garlic Coconut Cloud, and you could get—"

"The salmon?"

"Yes"—he nods—"with the Coulis of Roasted Tomatoes and Raspberry Vinegar Dressing." He pauses, perhaps for a gulp of air and also to take a sip from his glass of water. Meredith sits politely in her chair and listens to him read to her from the menu in a festival of emphasis, *"Swiss Chard Leaves, Squid Ink Tagliatelle."* She listens to the very long version of the Seared Foie Gras with its accompaniments, Rosemary Apple Puree and Armagnac Sauce, and onward to the Maine Day Boat Lobster with the White Asparagus and Sweet Peas. And she tries (really she does) to look patient, and interested. And as she listens, at one point she's even able to hear beyond Josh and only hear the details of the dishes. *It's this,* she thinks, *food, prepared so lovingly, so perfectly, so exceptionally, that makes so many things worthwhile.* And maybe that's exactly what people mean when they say things like, *If nothing else, it's dinner.* It's not about the dinner being free of charge, it's just about the dinner.

As she listens, she thinks that the food at Bouley has always been so exquisite and maybe now that she thinks of it, she does prefer it to Babbo. Listening to the menu, looking across the table at Josh, she is seized so suddenly with a fleeting but almost overwhelming wish about her future meals. She wishes not that she could eat so many of them with Josh, but that she could eat them at Bouley.

Josh's next declaration, "I've had the Pennsylvania All Natural Chicken Baked in Buttermilk with Seasonal Rapini and Mitake Mushrooms," snaps her out of her reverie, and she stops thinking about a world in which every night was spent at Bouley, but rather thinks, *Oh, have you?* She has to remind herself that tonight, she's not reviewing. She's not judging. And she shouldn't judge Josh. She should only, like Stephanie said, see what happens.

"And it really is outstanding, so maybe we should both get that," he says, and even though she just reminded herself not to judge, to be open-minded, to see what happens, she can't really see why she should do that. For a moment she can't think about the chicken or anything else. For a moment, all she can think is, *You broke up with me. And you told me that it was because I wasn't smart enough or ambitious enough or thin enough.* He'd called it *fit,* not thin, but he'd actually said that. Of course she hadn't forgotten that, but she'd thought for all the time she'd missed him, maybe she could have, by now, forgiven that. Only now she's not so sure.

"I think I'll have the venison," she says, trying to maintain an adventurous eater's emotional distance from any thoughts of Bambi.

Josh purses his lips. Josh, it seems, does not care for venison. "I don't care for venison," he says, "though I'd be interested to try the Sliced Almonds, Grilled Radicchio, Quince Puree and—"

"Great then," she says, "you can try some of it," and he purses a little bit more, and she can tell he's a bit taken aback by his soliloquy being so rudely cut off. She would like to ask him, out loud, *Were you always like this?* She thinks that if she were to actually ask him this, he would nod and say quite seriously, *I believe so, yes.*

The waiter is here now, as is the bread. Meredith has never, in her entire career of eating, ever had bread that came anywhere close to comparing to the bread at Bouley. It is, she feels, beyond comparison. It is, and she truly believes this, perfection.

"Will you be enjoying the wine pairing with your meal?" the waiter asks. Meredith thinks she sees the glimmer of recognition in his eyes.

Josh says, "No," right away, and Meredith thinks that she would have liked the wine pairing. Though, the wine pairing takes the dinner from one hundred and fifty dollars per person to two hundred and forty. No matter how unaccustomed she is to paying for her own dinner (a close second would be how un-accustomed she is lately to having someone across the table from her buy her dinner) she's well aware how extravagant, how very over the top a price tag on a meal like this is.

"I'll have a glass of the Cabernet, please," she says, thinking it will go well with the venison. She looks up, across the table at Josh, and smiles. He smiles back. She still finds him, his salt-and-pepper hair (very straight and maybe thinning a significant amount more than it used to be), his gray eyes and fine features, so handsome. She watches the way he takes a piece from his bread, the subtlety of his movement, the delicacy of his hands that always seemed aristocratic to her, and still do. She imagines she'll always think of him as handsome and something about that makes her feel a little bit tricked. She wonders if he missed her. Not now, not from whatever it was that led him here, to Bouley, but when it was over, when it was done, for three years, the years she turned thirty-one and thirty-two and -three. She wonders if he missed her during the years that she got noticed and recognized and published and promoted until she got the call from *The NY* (and it was, she thought, the best phone call she had ever answered on the first ring) and she got so busy that it started to hurt when she wasn't. Did he miss her then? And

she wonders if she asked him, if he'd be honest, if he'd say, *No,
I didn't miss you then. It wasn't until recently.* She wonders if
having an important job at an important magazine, as important as *The NY,* is what makes her no longer not smart in his
eyes, and no longer not ambitious, and that's why he's here.

This isn't a night to judge, not food or Josh, she tries to remind herself again. It's a night just to enjoy and experience, to
step back and see what happens. See what happens. It has never
been her special skill. She smiles and savors the perfection of the
food that is brought to them, the presentation perfect, the tim-
ing without flaw. And it's not until they're more than halfway
through the hot Valrhona chocolate soufflé that she realizes
with absolute certainty that she doesn't miss him anymore.

* * *

As they are leaving the restaurant, they pass a couple, sitting
at a table right by the archway that separates the maître d' station from the dining room. It's not the best table in the room by
any means, but they look happy; the woman, especially, she
looks very happy. She's very thin, petite, and she's wearing an
intricate, delicate, top: black silk, spaghetti straps with sequins
arranged all across the front. She leans forward and Meredith
sees that the spaghetti straps tie together at her neck, in a bow.
Meredith imagines the straps being untied later, in just one
quick motion. She imagines herself as the type of woman who
wears strappy, shiny shirts that say, *Look!* rather than always
wearing ones that say, *Don't.*

They walk through the vestibule and are completely enveloped for a moment in the soft, sweet smell of the fresh apples

that line every inch of the wall space, and Meredith says to Josh, "Thank you."

When they are standing on the street, the apple smell somehow still surrounding them, Meredith takes another look through the dome-shaped windows, one last look at all the Valentine's Day diners still enjoying the last of their meal. It's so beautiful, every single thing. Her eyes refocus in the window, and then instead of being focused through the glass, she catches her reflection. She sees Josh in the reflection also, standing next to her, holding her hand, and she thinks maybe it's a bit presumptuous of him to be holding her hand. Or maybe, holding someone's hand after you've just bought her dinner at Bouley isn't really a lot. But that's not what stops her, not what stops all her forward motion, everything racing around in her mind along with the apples she can still smell, and the chocolate soufflé she can still taste. What stops her, what puts it all out of her mind, is what she sees when she looks at herself. It's the first time in a long while she's been out to dinner without wearing a disguise, and there's something about that that makes it so much worse.

Earlier, inside Bouley, she had worried that someone might recognize her, dining out without a disguise. And here, now, only a few hours later, she doesn't quite recognize herself.

She sees someone so much bigger than the person she thinks of when she thinks of herself. She sees someone who looks so much worse than she could have ever thought of herself. And she hates what she sees. She wants to look, and to be able to see accomplished, competent, driven. She sees lumpy, she sees looming, she sees so much more than she wants. It is only right here, right now, that the word *substantial* has become a bad one. She wants to look and to be able to see herself and think any number of things, but all she can think is, *That can't be me.* She has told herself so many times that it's a job requirement to indulge, to have everything. But it didn't prepare her.

She turns away from the reflection, but she lets the image linger in her mind, because she does things like that, because when she has made a career out of judging everything else, it is quite impossible for her not to give herself a hard time, too.

She's facing Josh now, and he smiles. She thinks he smiles a lot. Maybe it would have been different if they'd gone somewhere less romantic. Like the Modern. Even though the *Times* only gave it two stars, Meredith actually thinks they were so off the mark about that. She thinks it's beautiful and elegant and special, but she would never describe it as romantic. It's one of her favorite new restaurants in New York, and she wonders if that must speak volumes about her.

She smiles back at Josh, and she thinks that smiling itself has almost lost its meaning. When she looks at him, it's true: he's still the guy who left her. He's the guy who told her, it wasn't him, it was her, who said in the spirit of honesty, because he thought honesty was so important, that he thought she wasn't ambitious enough, and not successful enough, that she could be smarter. She could be more interested in politics, and international affairs, and she could be more *fit* and maybe take up running. He worried that she used to smoke when she was in college and when she'd lived in France and that she'd go back to that should times ever turn tough, as smokers often do. He's the guy who left. He really left, he moved to Philadelphia to be a lawyer there, even though it seemed to Meredith at least that there were plenty of opportunities to be a lawyer in New York. And everyone told her that would make it easier, that he was in Philadelphia. But it didn't, not for a long time.

"Do you want to come back?" he asks her, and he means his hotel, the Plaza Athénée, a hotel she has always thought of as beautiful. When she looks back on this night, it'll probably be true that he was talking about more than the hotel. She doesn't let herself look in the window again, at the reflection, and she looks right at him. She thinks that the people who really hurt you, who really truly left you with a hole in your heart, that maybe they kind of have to stay that way, as the people who left you, that maybe they don't get to come back.

"I don't know," she tells him.

"Why not just see what happens?" he says. See. What. Happens. Apparently, it's all the rage. And the only answer she can think of is that she doesn't want to. She wishes for a moment, for longer than that, that she'd known this all along, that he would come back, even if it was three years later, and that when he did she wouldn't want him. And she wishes she knew this not because it would have made any of it a victory, it has nothing to do with victories, it just would have made it so much easier.

"No," she says, "No, Josh, I don't think I do."

And he nods, thoughtfully, and looks right at her and says, "I can understand that you might be ambivalent." She wonders for a minute if she should just go back to his hotel with him, and sleep with him, and then bow out gracefully (though of course the bow-out would be perhaps slightly less graceful than had she not just used him for sex). She can see that there would be some merit in that, there not having been any sleeping with any-one for longer than she'd care to admit. But, no, she thinks, it would do more harm than good. And she longs for a moment to be the type of person who'd just go back with him and not think twice about the repercussions, and she longs for the mo-ment after that just to be with him, and she imagines that's ex-actly what he means by ambivalent.

"I don't think," she says, meeting his gaze, a gaze she thinks she'll try to remember as steely, "I don't think *ambivalent* is the exact best word."

And he doesn't seem compelled to argue, or at least if he is compelled, he doesn't. He only nods and he hails her a cab and they say goodbye really quickly like they'll see each other two, three weeks from now, the next time work just happens to bring him up to New York. Saint Patrick's Day maybe.

It doesn't take long at all to get home; it seems actually like it has taken a lot less time than it usually takes to get all the way up, from all the way down in Tribeca. Meredith nods at her doorman, heads up twelve floors in the nondescript elevator, to her nondescript floor. She turns the key in her door, and once she's inside she smells her hair conditioner, Frederic Fekkai Technician Conditioner for Dry, Damaged, Color-Treated Hair. Her hair isn't any of these, but she really likes the smell. And the smell, it has a way of lingering in her apartment after she's washed her hair and she likes that, too. She'd washed her hair tonight, wanting to be sure it looked nice for Bouley, for Josh, right before she left.

Before she even takes her coat off, she fishes her iPod out of her bag, and puts it in its Bose iPod dock. She hits *Play,* and the song she's been listening to a lot lately, the Perishers' "Trouble Sleeping," starts to play.

"I'm having trouble sleeping," fills the room, and Meredith thinks how, lately, she really has. She listens to a line or two more, just standing there, still in her coat, her keys still in her hand, her eyes on her cuticles, until the line when the Perishers implore whomever it is they are singing to, to leave. She slowly takes off her coat and lays it over the back of her couch: purple velvet, sectional, from the 1960s she thinks, stunning.

For a long time after Josh had left she'd recorded every rerun of *The West Wing* on the Bravo channel—they aired all the time—and she would watch an episode each night before she went to sleep and it was because she missed him, because she'd always felt that on his better days, Josh reminded her of Josh Lyman, White House deputy chief of staff. Not Bradley Whitford, the actor who played him, but actual Josh Lyman, as if he really existed, as if he were indeed an actual man. And for perhaps even longer, she thought that it wasn't really going to happen this way, that really, it couldn't and that in the end it would all work out. She'd move to Philadelphia, too, and they'd live in a townhouse, and she'd review restaurants there, because there were so many good restaurants in Philadelphia, some of the all-time great ones, even. Le Bec Fin so often popped into her mind.

Meredith turns and heads into her room. She gets undressed in the dark, gets her pajamas from the hook on the back of the bathroom door, and brushes her teeth, quickly, unconscientiously, in the dark, too. She splashes water on her face, and feels a tiny twinge, because she knows she's just asking for a breakout by not fully washing off her makeup, but she doesn't want the light on, and she thinks maybe she's just too tired. And she's too aware right now that no matter how busy you are, no matter how completely you fill up every day, you can't fill it all up. There's always time left at the end of it to feel lonely.

She pulls back her covers, and gets under them. She reminds herself that in the end, what actually happened was that *The West Wing* got canceled, and Le Bec Fin lost its fifth star.

five

what would jennifer do?

Stephanie is sitting in their office, on her side of their desk. "Our desk" is what they called it. And before that, when they first saw the white brick house on Linwood Avenue, with the beautiful front porch and the open downstairs, they'd referred to the small room in the front as "our office." "This room, here," they said smiling, standing in its doorway, "it can be our office." When they'd found the great partners' desk at an estate auction in Far Hills, they said, "Look at this fantastic desk, we should get it for our office." And when their partners desk arrived, at their new house, they'd placed it in their office, right under the window with two matching chairs from Pottery Barn on either side. They added their laptops, their papers, their things.

Even after Stephanie had left her job in PR and no longer had any work to bring home, even after Aubrey carried his laptop down to his workroom, where it remained, with all his papers and God knows what else, on what was turning out to be a permanent basis, Stephanie had continued to think of it as "our desk." Even now that it is only her laptop, her papers, her things, even now that his side of the partners' desk looks extremely empty, glaringly so, especially in the mornings when the sun glints across its surface like a spotlight, she still calls the desk "our desk." She still calls the office "our office." She thinks that even if it is not reality-based, it is important to continue to call them that. She thinks that maybe somehow it could help.

Stephanie startles slightly, snaps back to attention as she hears the familiar rustling through the baby monitor, the one that precedes Ivy's waking up. Through the monitor, Stephanie can see Ivy stirring. A fist slides into view over her little face and is just as quickly gone. Ivy. She is so beautiful, even through the baby monitor that lends a green pallor to her skin. The convex angle of the baby monitor makes Ivy look as if she were looking through a peephole, the kinds they have in the doors of apartments, as if Ivy is just a guest visiting, coming to the door of the apartment she and Aubrey had on Seventy-third Street between Columbus and Central Park West. Aubrey loved that apartment, because of the outdoor space (he had a grill) and the close proximity to the park.

And you would think, wouldn't you, that if those were the things that were among his favorite things about their apartment, that he'd be so happy here in New Jersey. They still have a grill. And what are the suburbs about really other than outdoor space? Are they not just one great land of proximity to the park? But Aubrey is not happy in New Jersey. She wonders if he would have been different, less catatonic, less subterranean, less completely changed, had they moved instead to Connecticut.

Ivy's fist is back on the baby monitor's screen. She watches as it waves in the air, side to side like maybe Ivy thinks she's at a rock concert, the rock concert of her mobile. She looks through the motion of her daughter's fist at her peephole face, and thinks in a way that's what happened; Ivy, the promise of Ivy, stopped by. Her promise rang the doorbell of their New York City apartment and they decided it was time to go.

The phone rings, and Stephanie looks at it. She thinks that if she doesn't answer it, then whoever it is—most likely some New Mommy Group person calling to announce that *her* six-month-old can recite the alphabet—will go away. Or it's Aubrey calling to monotonously personify disappointment and disillusion-ment, "Hey, Steph. I'm working late again tonight. I have a client meeting tonight. Uh, actually, it's not really either of those things, it's uh, actually, something else that neither of us will ac-knowledge and maybe if we keep refusing to acknowledge it, then by virtue of that, it'll all go away. Okay?"

She wonders if it's entirely possible that she simply no longer has the energy left in her reserves to participate in either of those conversations, regardless of how minimal her participation would actually have to be. She wonders when it was that she stopped applying her Approach Everything With a Positive At-titude philosophy to Aubrey. She thinks it might have been a while ago now. She wills the phone to stop ringing, wills the en-tire piece of plastic and battery and antenna to magically disap-pear, go away. Except that she never used to be the kind of person to not want to pick up the phone. And it could be Meredith calling to tell her about last night; she wants to talk to her.

"Hello?"

"Hey." It's Meredith, sounding annoyed, though it's impossible to discern if that's because of last night with Josh or, rather, because of Meredith's irrational peevishness about everyone picking up the phone on the first ring.

"How'd it go?" Stephanie asks, because that's the most important, that's more important than pointing out, as she sometimes would like to do, that getting annoyed about listening to a ringing phone, about other people's flip-flop straps being flipped (yes, Meredith had gotten annoyed over this once) is not going to make the world a better place, is not going to do anything actually, other than make her life a bit harder than it really needs to be.

"Okay, just tell me, have you ever once thought of me as not ambitious?" Meredith asks. *Josh*. It's not ringing phones this time, or even flip-flops, it's Josh. "I mean, you remember why he broke up with me, right? You remember what he said?" There's a spark to the question, a flare, and by the light of the flare Stephanie can see clearly that it's not really the Josh of last night, the one who came up from Philadelphia to take Meredith to dinner at Bouley, but the one who left her.

"Yes," Stephanie says, of course she remembers why. And even though she says she remembers, Meredith repeats it anyway.

"He broke up with me because I wasn't smart enough, or ambitious enough, or successful enough," Meredith says a bit blankly, almost as if she's reciting it. Stephanie doesn't try to stop her; she imagines in some way it might help. Though it does strike Stephanie as a bit odd that these are the reasons she's repeating, because of all the reasons that Josh gave Meredith, three years ago, before he went to Philadelphia, the last one, the only one she isn't saying, was the only one that was true.

"I mean," she continues, "I have to say I'm among the more ambitious people I know."

"You are, Meres. You always have been," Stephanie agrees. She smiles to herself, remembering a scene from their childhood; one that's always there in her memory, easily accessible, continually replayed. "Remember how excited you used to get whenever anyone would ask you what you wanted to be when you grew up?"

"I do. Exactly," Meredith says defiantly, and Stephanie can see it again, so clearly: a seven- or eight-year-old Meres. Whenever anyone would ask her what she wanted to be when she grew up, she would always jump up and clap her hands and announce loudly, "I want to be an astronaut! A writer! An actress! A chef! A famous chef! I want to be famous!" The job titles would occasionally change, astronaut was a staple, as was chef, but doctor made an appearance sometimes, too; the President of the United States popped up on occasion, as did scientist, rock star, and Olivia Newton-John. It was always something Meredith felt was very important. Meredith was always excited to be something very important; she always couldn't wait.

"Remember," Stephanie says, "you always said chef, and you always said writer, and look at you now."

"Yeah, but I'm not an astronaut. Or Olivia Newton-John," Meredith says, but she sounds happier, and Stephanie's pleased to hear that. "And what would you always say?" Meredith asks, joining in, "you wanted to be an ice-skater, right?"

"Hmm, yeah, I think it was that," Stephanie says nonchalantly. She thinks of herself as a child of eight or nine, when the grown-ups would look at her and ask her that same question. "And, Stephanie, what do you want to be when you grow up?" And with Stephanie, there wouldn't ever be the great flurry of jumping and clapping that always accompanied Meredith's answer. Stephanie would generally stay seated and smile a bit shyly, and her answer would always be one of two things. More frequently, Stephanie would say, "I want to be an ice-skater," and she really did believe that to be true. But every now and then, if she thought someone was really paying attention, if she thought someone really wanted to know the truth, she would look up and tell them, quite seriously, "I want to be happy."

"But, Steph?" Meredith asks her.

"Yeah?"

"You remember he also broke up with me because I was fat?"

"I remember," she says. As unkind and off-base as the other things he said had been, they just didn't make sense. But the other thing, that Meres was fat, she wondered for a long time how Josh could have said that. It wasn't really fair, she'd thought, because it wasn't as if Meredith were any fatter when they broke up than when they had met. Which she thinks in a way made it so much worse.

"Okay, see, what I've been mostly thinking about," Meredith begins "is that if I'm going to be thirty-five and single, then that's fine. I can handle that. It can be because I haven't met the right person, it can be because I'm not ever going to meet the right person—"

"Meres, you're going to meet—"

"No wait, listen. It can be for all sorts of reasons, it can be for no reasons, it can just be. But it can't be because I'm fat."

"Okay, okay," Stephanie says, agreeing, reassuring.

Meredith says, "Okay," too.

"And, Meres?"

"Yeah?"

"You're not thirty-five and single, you're thirty-three."

"You know I like to plan ahead," Meredith says, and Stephanie laughs, she knows that all too well.

"So I guess you're not taking him back?" Stephanie says, even though the answer is obvious, and she thinks the obvious answer is the good one. She wants Meres to be happy and she'd like it if Meres could be happy with someone, but Josh is not the guy. And being with the wrong guy isn't good. Nor, she thinks, is being with the right guy who later turns out to be wrong. She tries not to linger on that.

"No," Meredith says, "I'm not."

"Good," Stephanie says, "And, you know, if you think of all the great breakups, I don't think they ever end with anyone getting taken back. I just don't. I mean would Jennifer have taken Brad back? What with Angelina and Maddox and Zahara and Shiloh Nouvel and now Pax Thien? And beautiful Brad carrying their baby bottles around in his jeans for all the world, or at least all the world that reads US Weekly, to see?"

"No," Meredith says.

"Right," Stephanie continues, "think of a post-Brad Jen in

Chicago. All those pictures of her running, all those clips about her staying at the Peninsula Hotel on Michigan Avenue," and as she says that, an article she read about Jennifer Aniston pops into her mind, and a lightbulb goes on above it. "She wouldn't have taken him back. Not ever. Or at least we need to believe that. She would have held her head high and she would have eaten grilled lamb and vegetables and goat cheese!" she says excitedly. "I read that exact menu in *People* magazine!"

"You know, I think I read that, too. I thought I read it somewhere else, but maybe it was in *People*?" Meredith answers, and Stephanie's pretty sure she sounds a bit enthusiastic, even if she is taking the opportunity to subtly announce her preference for magazines other than *People*.

Stephanie pauses and pictures Jennifer Aniston, in the early days right after Brangelina was unleashed onto the world, and she's sure Meredith must be picturing it, too. "You know," she adds on temptingly, "Jennifer would have balanced out her good fats and good carbs and lean proteins."

And they pause, and they don't say anything, and then Meredith says softly, "She would have gone on the Zone."

"I think so," Stephanie agrees, smiling.

"Steph?" Meredith says, "I want to go on the Zone with you. And it's not just because of Josh. Well, maybe it's a little because of Josh, but it's also my reflection, and I've been thinking about it a lot, and I don't know if this makes sense, but I don't see myself when I look at my reflection, and I think when you look at your reflection you should be able to see yourself."

"I hear that," Stephanie says, and she does. She listens as Meredith takes a breath.

"And, Stephanie? Also, it's because of you. I want to do it with you. I want us to do something together again."

"Oh, Meres, that's so great!" she exclaims, instantly excited at the prospect, at the camaraderie, at something that they can share together and talk about other than Josh coming back, or restaurants that she can't go to anymore, or Aubrey, who they can't really talk about. And just like an eight-year-old Meredith destined for certain fame, Stephanie can't wait to do this together. "We'll succeed at this," she adds on. "I just know we will if we do it together."

"Go team!" Meredith says, and Stephanie thinks that's a good sign that she says that, even though she was never the sporty one. Stephanie was always the sporty one, even her initials were sporty: SI, for Stephanie Isley, the same as *Sports Illustrated.*

"Go team!" Stephanie says back to her, and thinks how her last name isn't Isley anymore anyway, how it's Cunningham now. "Okay, how much do you want to lose?" she asks next, her tone unmistakably upbeat.

"Um, I'd say around what you said you wanted to lose. Maybe a little bit more?" Meredith answers.

"You can totally do it, Meres," Stephanie tells her, and hopes that she isn't already thinking of the next time she's going out to dinner. She grabs the book, *The Zone Diet* by Dr. Barry Sears, PhD, which has been sitting right next to her laptop, and opens it up. "Okay, listen," she says, and begins to read out loud. "According to Dr. Barry Sears, the Zone is 'that mysterious but very real state in which your body and mind work together at their ultimate best.' "

"That mysterious but very real state," Meredith repeats, almost dutifully.

"Sounds possible, right?"

"Yes, it does," Meredith says, pausing before she adds, "along with not possible." Stephanie pretends not to hear that last part.

"Yes, and look," she says, holding out the book, and pointing to the very next line, even though Meredith isn't right there to read along with her. "It says the premise is simple. Calorie counting doesn't work. Maintaining the correct ratio of fats, proteins, and carbohydrates is what works. Simple." Stephanie concludes and then for a few minutes, Meredith doesn't say anything, and there is only silence on the phone. But she'd have to say that the silence, maybe, it's hopeful. Ivy pipes up again through her monitor, no longer on the verge of waking up, but now very much awake, and it's time to go.

As they hang up the phone, as Stephanie heads out of their office to go get Ivy, she really does feel hopeful. At the doorway, she turns around and glances at the Zone book, where she's left it on Aubrey's side of the desk, a red, yellow, and white striped beacon of hope.

six

a rose by any other name

"Aubrey?"

Silence. She says his name again, "Aubrey."

She used to like the sound of his name so much. They used to play back the messages he left on their answering machine. She and Meredith did, when Meredith first got back from Paris, and they lived together, in a railroad apartment on Eighty-fourth Street, right by the river, when she'd just met Aubrey. "Hi, uh, Stephanie? It's Aubrey calling," he'd say, and they'd hit *Stop*, and *Rewind*, and *Play*, and he'd say it again. And they'd laugh as if they were a lot younger than they were, and Stephanie would swear she got butterflies in her stomach just from the sound of his voice.

"Hi, uh, it's Aubrey," they'd repeat. And when they read the cards that always came with the roses he always sent to Stephanie, Meredith would say, "They're from Aubrey," and they'd both smile, widely, completely, and say, "*Aubrey, Aubrey, Aubrey.* He of the excellent name."

Meredith had once confided that she felt it was both unfortunate, and perhaps indicative of something worse, that she'd only ever been with men who had boring names. Rob, Matt, Dave, Jim. Josh. Stephanie, on the other hand, in addition to her greater capacity for love, had what Meredith believed to be a far greater capacity for attracting men with much more interesting names. Men with Celtic names, last names as first names, names that sounded like somewhere foreign or ancestral, like Aubrey. Aubrey Cunningham. A name you might comment on as cool if you were the type of person to put some stake in names. Before Aubrey, there had been Hillary. So British, so remarkable, even if the man had been neither. There was a Parker once, too. Sporty. And Tiernan, Mackenzie, Addison, Carson, Tucker, Rand, Logan. Preppy, boarding school names, with a little bit of an edge. Crispin, Tyler, Presley. Men who might have a trust fund, or a shotgun. Reid, Asher, Pierce.

"Aubrey?!" she yells, louder this time.

"Jesus fucking Christ, Stephanie! What?" He yells, quite loudly, from down in his workroom. In an instant, Ivy is awake and begins to scream herself. As Stephanie slams out of the kitchen chair she'd been sitting in (she painted all the kitchen chairs white herself, and has thoughts of replacing the caning by hand), and heads to the stairs and up them, she thinks that surely it was Aubrey's yelling, and not hers, that has woken Ivy; Aubrey's yelling that must be, to Ivy's sensitive and receptive young ears, so indicative of the marital state to which she has been born into, Aubrey's fault that Ivy is now awake, again, at eight, after she's already been asleep. As she thinks of how high the possibility is that Ivy will now be up for the rest of the night, it is only the fact that she is sure he wouldn't comfort her, is sure he wouldn't even notice, that keeps her from crying. She decides instead as she storms upstairs that she's not even going to talk to him right now, not even going to tell him why she was calling him. Maybe that'll show him.

She goes to Ivy and picks her up. She holds her, and rubs her back, and says in the most soothing voice she can manage, "Daddy didn't mean to yell." Though there's something about talking about Aubrey to Ivy that feels, if not exactly wrong, then headed in that direction. She can almost glimpse a version of her future, a future in which she might be old and sour and bitter and wear a housecoat. And in this future she never did lose the weight, so, really, the constant wearing of the housecoat is most practical. She'll refer to Aubrey when she speaks about him to Ivy not as Aubrey, or even as Daddy, but only as "your father." *Your father is going to have to be more considerate about rearranging his visitation days.* She can see it, somewhere on the horizon, less the part about the housecoat than the part about Aubrey's name not being Aubrey, but still, it's there.

"Mommy didn't mean to yell," she adds, maybe just to be fair. Mommy, she thinks, was just trying to ask Daddy if he would like to have some of the somewhat lackluster but Zone-friendly broiled lemon salmon, with one broiled tomato cut in half and sprinkled with Parmesan cheese (one cup of steamed green beans, one large spinach salad and a half cup of red grapes as dessert.) When she and Meredith had embarked on the Zone, a full four days ago, she'd thought it best, recipe-wise, to start with something from the section of the book called "Less Than Gourmet Cooking in The Zone." She came to this decision after the Mexican Holiday Salad from the "Gourmet Cooking in the Zone" section that she had so painstakingly prepared on the first day had turned out not to be such a holiday, in fact not very festive at all. This happens, she's realizing; things turn out quite differently from how you'd assumed they'd be.

"Da Da!" Ivy says, no longer crying, quite recovered now and also looking very bright-eyed and bushy-tailed. A move back in the direction of the crib sets off instant distress, so instead of taking the scenario any further, Stephanie asks, rhetorically, "Do you want to try coming downstairs for a while, and you can have dinner with Mommy?" and thinks as she does that there can't be any reason why a person can't mash up grapes.

As they head down the stairs, Ivy's entire being, all the energy around her, brightens as she says, "Da Da," again. Stephanie doesn't say, *Yes, Da Da,* nor does she say, *Ma Ma,* as she has on recent occasions taken to saying. She doesn't say anything. She wonders, as Ivy repeats "Da Da Da Da Da" again, right as they walk by the door to his workroom, if Aubrey can hear her. She imagines he can, and then she has to remind herself that she had already decided that she wasn't going to cry.

Balancing Ivy on her hip, she reaches into the refrigerator and takes out her six-ounce piece of salmon, her tomato, and leaves Aubrey's in there. She steamed the green beans earlier, so those just need to be reheated in the microwave. She wonders if it will mess up the ratios if she simply eats all the green beans, hers and Aubrey's, and just saves the spinach. But when is she saving it for? And for whom? For Popeye, perhaps? And if so, she wonders, when will he be here?

She checks something in her new book, *Zone Perfect Meals in Minutes*, fastens Ivy into her high chair, and puts her salmon and tomato under the broiler. She focuses in on the cover of the cookbook, and thinks of how much Meredith loves to cook, always has. No matter how much cooking went on in their childhood, no matter how much Mom loved to be in the kitchen, always cooking, Stephanie never really took to it. She reads the smaller print caption on the spine of the book: *150 Fast & Simple Healthy Recipes!* The exclamation point is not actually on the book, she has added it herself. She's always thought it to be of the utmost importance to embark on things, no matter how hard they might be, with a good and positive attitude. And what better way to exemplify a good, positive attitude than with an exclamation point, really? But even with the exclamation point, she thinks also that maybe the Zone Delivery, the service Caryn used, might be a better idea than she had initially deemed it to be. Surely, having all these Zone Perfect (or Zone Friendly or whatever it is they are) meals arrive in coolers and microwave containers each morning would be so much easier. But the Zone Delivery, something about it, it makes her feel a little bit like a failure.

She's home all the time (and all the time in this case is not merely a figure of speech). She should have no problem at all making dinner, even if dinner, now that she is endeavoring to be in the Zone, involves a bit more calculation, is a bit more of a scientific dance than it used to be. It's not as if in addition to Ivy she has a full-time, incredibly demanding job. People like that could have the Zone Delivery without feeling like a failure; people like the investment banker character in that terrifying book, *I Don't Know How She Does It*, the one that is so beloved by the New Mommy Group, even though as far as Stephanie can tell, no one in the New Mommy Group seems to be dashing off to an investment bank, or to any other job for that matter. Stephanie does not know what the New Mommies are thinking of when they hold the book up and exclaim, "This is so me!" When Stephanie thinks of the book, she thinks that the author, Allison Pearson, is married to Anthony Lane, the man who writes the film reviews for the *New Yorker*. Mostly when Stephanie thinks of the book, she thinks of how she'd like to be the wife of Anthony Lane. And lately, that's less because she's always liked his movie reviews, and more because a life lived with Anthony Lane wouldn't be a life lived with Aubrey.

And anyway, she thinks, charging $39.99 a day, which is $1,239.69 a month (yes, she's done the math) would be something she'd need to discuss with Aubrey, in the spirit of communication and honesty that she would like to do her part to perpetuate within their marriage, even though there is the part of her that says, "Face it, sister, it's gone." And even if she were to go the way of saying, screw it, when it came to perpetuating a spirit of honesty and communication within the marriage, as some people in her marriage have done, Aubrey would notice the charge on their credit card statement. Or, actually, these days, would he? Does Aubrey even pay the credit card bills anymore? Or has he lost complete interest in that, too? Fuck. She should check on that.

Once her less-than-intriguing salmon and her tomato are just about broiled, Ivy starts to fuss. It's because she's over-tired, but she won't sleep, possibly because it's dark out. Since she's in the high chair already, Stephanie thinks it's not going to hurt anyone if she gives Ivy just a little mashed banana. Mashed banana, as soothing as it is to Ivy, has in turn become to Stephanie so similar to sleep. She thinks it would be really great it they both slept. She begins to peel a banana and thinks of her own mother, and how their pediatrician told her that fat babies would become fat adults, and how she and Meredith were always on baby diets, and then, look at what that accomplished. She mashes the banana and tries not to worry. She has possibly begun to worry too much, she can see this. She reminds herself, with her back facing the general vicinity of the workroom door, that there are, of course, plenty of things to be happy about.

Even though they are strictly forbidden on the Zone, along with pasta and rice and many things, Stephanie is happy for mashed bananas. Just a spoonful and Ivy is sitting in her high chair, looking a little sleepy even, murmuring, without any real sense of urgency, "Da Da Da Da."

"Yes, Da Da," Stephanie says back to her, and lifts her out of her high chair and holds her close, with her head on her shoulder and gently rubs her back. Almost instinctively she reaches for the kitchen cordless, mounted like the phones of yesteryear, of her childhood, on the wall. She dials Meredith's number in New York even though she'll just leave a message really quickly before she sits down with Ivy to her salmon. To her surprise, it's not Meredith's voice mail that picks up after one ring (she has somehow rigged her voice mail to pick up after only one ring) but Meredith.

"Hey, Meres, what are you doing at home?"

"I know," she answers. "I'm being a dedicated dieter, which I think also means I'm being a bad restaurant critic."

"Yeah, I was thinking you'd be out."

"Well, I figured since it's the first week, *just* for the first week, I'm not going to review every night this week. I thought I'd take two nights off from going out, to get all my ducks in a row, Zone-wise." Even though the only person who could hear her is Stephanie, Meredith lowers her voice and continues, explaining that for the next few weeks, few months, she's not going to do every dinner and maybe not nearly as many lunches. "I think I could really do okay without lunches for a while. Without lunches, twelve meals a week in restaurants could be closer to six. And anyway," she continues, "I've always been hesitant to review restaurants based on their lunches. Lunches, they're so different from dinners, so much less of an event."

Stephanie listens to the explanation, something about it seems practiced, as if it's already been repeated several times. "Do you feel okay about it?" she asks.

"I feel guilty," Meredith tells her. "But I imagine guilt is good for dieting, right?"

"Yes, I imagine it is." Stephanie smiles to herself. "It sounds like you have a good plan, you sound dedicated, good for you."

"I went to the Food Emporium and bought Egg Beaters, and sliced chicken breast, and cans of tuna packed in water, artichokes," Meredith continues quite thoroughly, "and a head of cauliflower and apples. I shopped around the perimeters like it says to in chapter eight."

"You got to chapter eight already?" Stephanie asks, instantly impressed.

"I skipped ahead."

"You should try to read the whole thing. You'll learn a lot." Stephanie says cautiously.

"Right, I will." Meredith says back right away. Meredith, Stephanie knows this, is never a fan of anything that sounds like it might be the start of a lecture, even if it's a lecture that will help her lose the weight she's never been able to lose.

"Anyway," Stephanie says, not lingering on Meredith's tone, but rather breezing ahead, "do you know what I learned that I'm so excited about?"

"No, what?"

"Okay, Caryn says that if you have fourteen pretzels, one ounce of low-fat mozzarella cheese, and a green apple that it's a perfect Zone snack. So here's what I'm going to do: I'm having exactly that, for breakfast, lunch, and snack, and then I'm making one of the Zone recipes for dinner."

"So wait," Meredith says, "let me grab a pen. Fourteen pretzels, one ounce of low-fat mozzarella cheese?"

"Or part-skim, I think that works, too. Is part-skim the same as low-fat?" Stephanie asks.

"No, it's not," Meredith says.

"Okay, well anyway."

"Okay and one green apple?"

"Right."

"Not a red one?"

"I don't know, Meredith."

"Okay, and that's the right proportions and blocks and everything?"

"Yes, Meres."

"For someone Caryn's size or for someone your size, or my size?" Meredith asks, and truth be told, Stephanie, in her excitement over the preapproved-by-Caryn snack, did not actually account for the different body mass indexes, and the different block ratios for the different weights you may find yourself at, at different stages of the diet. She feels a flare of annoyance, the kind she's been feeling more and more often lately. She's not entirely sure if it's because Meredith won't be enthusiastic about the snack combination, or because this diet, like so many things lately, is so much harder than she'd expected it to be.

"I don't really know," she admits, and sighs. "I'm going to look it up when we get off the phone."

"Okay," Meredith says. "We can just adjust it if we need to."

"Maybe we'll get seventeen Goldfish pretzels," Stephanie says, trying, as ever, to look on the bright side.

"Right, but, Steph?"

"Mmm?"

"I'm a little confused. If pretzels are made from white flour? Can we have them?"

"Oh, well," and Stephanie feels again, for a second, for maybe more than a second, like she might cry, but stops herself. If she's not going to cry about Aubrey then she's not going to cry about Goldfish pretzels. Goldfish pretzels, so youthful and reminiscent of the happier parts of childhood, should not be cried over. "I think it's fine, Meres," she says slowly, measuredly, "but listen, if you don't want to do it that way, there's a whole book of meal suggestions, I'm sure you can find something else."

"No, I want to do what you're doing. But, Stephanie?" she asks, pausing for a moment and then beginning to speak much faster. "It's very hard, right? And I know it's only been four days, but I'm really hungry and I am pretty sure I have a headache and I think I feel a little light-headed if I get up too quickly." When Meredith sees what she thinks may be an opening, she tends to run off with it. She gallops.

"It's been four days." Stephanie answers, "and you're supposed to be hungry."

"I thought it said somewhere that your blood sugar is supposed to be so balanced that you're not supposed to feel hungry or headachey or fatigued? I think I feel all those things."

"Meres, let's give it a few more days," *Let's*, she says silently to herself, *stop raining on my Zone parade*. "Let's talk about something else."

"Okay," Meredith agrees. "But, just, even if they are somehow technically allowed, how possible *is* it to have an entire bag of those delicious Goldfish pretzels on hand, and only eat fourteen at a time? Can people really do this? And by people, I do mean people whose spirits are, if not broken, then slightly bent, seeing as they are on a diet and therefore might really need and deserve a bag of pretzels anyway?"

Stephanie doesn't say anything, instead she waits for a moment for the Goldfish pretzels to stop tormenting Meredith on their own. And after a longer pause, Meredith asks, "How's Ivy?"

"Oh, she's good, she's right here. She woke up for some reason. I'm not sure why. So I gave her a little snack and she actually just fell asleep while we were talking."

"Oh, sleep. Good," Meredith says softly.

"Yes, very, very good. Maybe I should go test the waters and see if it'll actually stick if I put her back in her crib."

"Oh, of course, I'll let you go."

Stephanie contemplates the walk to the stairs, through the family room, past the door downstairs to the workroom. She predicts Ivy waking up like clockwork the moment she tries to put her down, or even, just going down into her crib and everything being so quiet. "I have another minute," she says.

"What'd you give Ivy for her snack?" Meredith asks. Stephanie wonders if it's more of a polite question, something to connect them in case this bonding by dieting doesn't work, or if Meredith might be inquiring after Ivy's food because she's sure it's more interesting than her own.

"Bananas."

"You know if we stay on this diet we can't have bananas, like ever again?"

"I think it's fine," Stephanie says even though inwardly she shudders a little bit at a world without bananas, and not just because of Ivy, and not just because of sleep.

Meredith exhales, not loudly, but a little bit more than the regular breathing out, and asks, "How can you look at the world, at your future, and know that, if you're doing what's right, if you're doing what's best for yourself, then there won't ever again be bananas?"

Stephanie wonders what sorts of things Meredith might be equating with bananas right now, what other things she worries might never again be in her life (Josh, a boyfriend, a life beyond her career). She wonders what things she herself would equate with bananas right now (a husband who isn't in an emotional coma, a world that wasn't shrinking in on her, Martha Stewart calling to offer her a job). "I think you're being melodramatic," she says.

"I'm not sure if I am."

"Well, maybe not then, but I think you're having the wrong attitude."

"Maybe," Meredith concedes, albeit briefly, "but what if I'm not?"

"I don't know, Mere," she says because she can't think of anything else to say, "I really don't."

* * *

After they'd gotten off the phone, after Stephanie ate her Zone-friendly dinner alone, with one hand, while Ivy slept on her shoulder because she didn't want to risk waking her up and she also didn't want to put her down, she gets up and starts down the hall. She stops halfway through the family room, and looks at the door to Aubrey's workroom, and she goes to it and opens it. She stands at the top of the stairs, rubbing Ivy's back in soft circles, comforted by the softness of her lavender velour onesie, comforted by the softness of her daughter's little body underneath.

She's aware of the light behind her flooding into the barely lit basement and she wonders if Aubrey is aware of it, too, if he's aware of anything. The light from his computer screen glows out at him, and she can't see what's on it. She wonders if it matters whether it's Internet poker, an Internet pen pal, or even Internet porn, if she really cares what the reason is anymore.

Aubrey's leaning back in his chair and even though he's looking right at the screen, he doesn't seem to really care about what's on it either. Maybe it's gained a lot of weight, too. She'd thought for a while that was it, that it was because she had gained so much weight, that that's when he lost interest in her, when he disengaged. But then, their friends aren't fat, and even the friends that are just his, not theirs, they're not fat. And his job isn't fat, or the world, or Ivy.

If he were having an affair, she thinks he'd be nicer. She thinks he'd be guiltier, and she thinks that would make him charming and salesmany again, which are things she once liked about him, even though now she can't imagine why. She imagines if he were having an affair he'd try to cover up for it by doing nice things for her. He'd buy her little presents, he'd send her roses. She smiles in spite of everything, in spite of the flowers he would send her if he were cheating on her, at the memory of how much she always loved it when he used to send her roses, at how happy she used to be.

She turns and shuts the door. As she walks away from it, she does know she could confront him. She could say so many things, she could demand so many answers. She could brace herself for when he looked up at her, so much like Rob Lowe in *About Last Night*, explaining to Demi Moore, "I don't love you anymore." And as much as she knows she could, she isn't sure she can. For as long as she can remember, when everyone else would describe her as so sweet, so nice, an amazing friend, a wonderful person, a fantastic athlete, a lovely woman, she had

always smiled. But she'd also wondered why no one ever described her as strong. Because that was always what she'd seen
herself as, was always the first thing she thought of when she
thought of herself. She wonders sometimes if it was never true.
But she doesn't think that's it, she thinks it's more that now,
everything has changed.

seven

the strangest things seem suddenly routine

Understanding the implications of the Zone can completely change your life. All you have to do is read this book, follow the simple dietary guidelines it recommends, and put them to work for you in your own life.

Meredith stares at the words on the page, stares longer until her vision blurs. The Zone might be, for her, kind of like New Jersey. She looks away from the page. She'd like to think it could be possible that dieting—successful dieting, whatever that might be— might be best actually *done*, rather than read about. And yet with the Zone, she wonders if she's really ready, if in her early stages of remedial reading maybe she hasn't quite learned enough. A mystery, she thinks, wrapped inside of a riddle. (She is reminded of the way they wrap dates in bacon at Pipa, on the lower level of ABC Carpet & Home; she's always been a tremendous fan.)

But she has determined—she thinks—to face this challenge. She has resolved to embrace the very team-spirited and inherently athletic focus Stephanie has spelled out for them. It shouldn't be that hard. Even though she's never been the "sporty one" (or the nice one, or the pretty one, which may or may not have simply meant the *thin* one) she'd like to think she has at times taken an athlete's approach to things. Anyone who works as hard as she does has an athlete somewhere inside. Anyone who is willing to have upwards of twelve meals a week in restaurants, anyone who has a job in which there is always something to do, always more to be done, can think of herself as athletic in some respect, and surely, can handle the challenges of a diet. This is what she tells herself, this is what she wants to believe.

Ever since her fifteenth year, when her mother first took her to the Diet Center in Chevy Chase—she can still remember the parking lot, the waiting room, the bran muffins and the vitamin tins she received, Mom looking nervous and worried but trying not to show it—she'd never been able to see dieting as anything but certain failure. But if Stephanie is going to do this, in her cheerful, optimistic, and ever-sporting way, if Stephanie is going to succeed at this, then she wants to as well. Meredith has always suspected that Stephanie has been better at running her own life, what with the perfect husband and the perfect baby and the perfect house. Though it isn't Stephanie who is perfectly poised for the *New York Times* to call (thus usurping Douglas Harris, editor in chief of *The NY*, as her employer but also as the placer of the best phone call she ever answered), and then what? A three-book deal? Film rights? Her own television show?

Meredith closes *The Zone,* puts the book aside, and makes an effort to focus her attention on the more immediate future. She reaches for the phone to call and confirm her reservation for the night. She takes a few deep breaths as she listens to the ringing, but trying to calm herself while listening to a phone not being picked up is impossible, she stops. And then they pick up.

"Thank you for calling Ouest. How may we help you?"

"Hi, it's Abby Gilbertson calling. I'd like to confirm my reservation for tonight."

Meredith always confirms, she doesn't like to leave anything to chance; she's certain she's simply far too busy to leave anything to chance. The moment she flips her phone shut, all in one motion, Meredith looks at her watch. She needs to start getting ready. Getting into her disguises is a lot more involved than the run-of-the-mill getting ready for work, or dinner, or some other sort of outing. She will, by the way, not say the word *date.* Not right now.

If she can manage it, Meredith always tries to get ready at home. It requires a lot of stuff, a lot of makeup, outfits, wigs. And while, of course, it is a necessity of her job, to make herself into someone else, to call herself by another name, she feels that holing up in the bathroom at work with wigs and makeup and outfits might seem unserious, too theatrical, and *The NY* is a serious place. And while she has always thought of makeup as important, for any number of reasons, she doesn't want to spend all the time applying it at work.

In addition to her own credit card, which she so rarely uses, she has four other credit cards with four different names: Abby Gilbertson, Emily Shea, Sarah Marin, May Williams. Meredith has found that it's best to repeat; four names, she thinks, are enough. More than four and she might start to lose track, get tripped up, the way that it's so much harder to remember a lie than it is to remember the truth.

Meredith has a vanity, an antique desk with a mirror attached to it and a deceptively large drawer in which she has all the makeup, a collection matched in its vastness and impressiveness only by the beauty products that line the shelves of the medicine cabinet in the bathroom. If asked what she liked best about being a restaurant critic, no matter who asked, Meredith would say it was, of course, the restaurants, getting to go to every last one she ever dreamed of, the inventive food, the theater of it all, the celebration. And then, on top of that, writing about it and sharing it with readers. She won't admit to anyone how much she enjoys the makeup, and the disguises. But she actually really does.

Before she sits down, she heads to her closet, and from the row of hatboxes lining one of the upper shelves, she selects one of her wigs. The long, blonde one with layers that has the hint of retro—possibly it's from the seventies. She thinks that tonight she'll wear the sparkly metallic Stila eye shadow applied with a heavy hand. As she eyes a pair of high heels that she could never wear for an entire day in real life, she thinks she'll wear the Laura Mercier dark plum lipstick.

Meredith pauses at the table right outside the closet, upon which her iPod is nestled securely in its Bose iPod dock. She smiles at what a clever contraption it is, and wonders what they'll think of next. She loves that in the world of electronics, not unlike in the world of restaurants (and come to think of it, makeup, too) next is always soon. She picks up the iPod and scrolls quickly, expertly to the song she wants. She has always been a great believer in the importance of good background music, and she almost always listens to the same song, campy though it may be, when she gets ready. It's from the soundtrack to the play *Hedwig and the Angry Inch* (it was also a movie, which wasn't nearly as good as the play, they never are), and is called, appropriately, "Wig in a Box."

She sits down at the vanity and reaches for her foundation as Hedwig's voice comes melodically through her speakers. *I put on some makeup, turn on the tape deck, and put the wig back on my head.* Hedwig has such a beautiful, alluring voice. As Meredith puts on her own makeup and secures her own wig, she sings along happily to the lyrics, "This is the best way that I've found, to be the best you've ever seen."

And, sure, the song is sung by, and about, a hermaphrodite transvestite lounge singer who doesn't really belong to any world, and therefore won't ever really belong to anyone. And yes, it's from a play (and then a movie) that isn't altogether cheerful. But that's not what Meredith thinks about. Because even if underneath the surface it might not be such a happy song, it's always been her favorite. She likes singing along, especially to the part when Hedwig puts on his wig and exclaims that suddenly he is Miss Farrah Fawcett from TV, and she can almost see his eyelashes batting.

She doesn't sing all the words out loud though; she kind hums over the lines where Hedwig wakes up, and turns into himself.

eight

go ouest

Tom Valenti's Upper West Side bistro, Ouest, is located on Broadway at Eighty-fourth Street, not on Broadway at Eighty-second Street, which is where Meredith has asked the cab to let her out. Oddly enough, she made this same mistake on her last visit, too. The driver has already pulled over, the meter has already been turned off, so Meredith decides not to bother with, "Oh, I'm sorry, I meant Eighty-fourth Street. Could you take me there?" even though, honestly, sometimes she would.

She pays the driver and steps out, stretching her legs (and her very high heels) over a small stream of slush and onto the salted sidewalk of Broadway. She looks up at the looming Barnes & Noble on the corner, the same one that greeted her the last time she got out on this corner by mistake.

Crossing her arms tightly in front of her and angling her head slightly inward and down to best protect her blonde wig from the wind that is whipping down the wide expanse of Broadway, she hurries the two blocks to Ouest. She tries to clear her head. She always tries to clear her head pre-reviewing. As a sorbet might be served between courses to cleanse the palate, Meredith has long thought it best to enter a restaurant with as clear a mental palate as possible. She tries conscientiously not to let her mood, her feelings on other things, the weather, her outside life, affect her reviews. She aims for complete focus. Meredith is always amazed at people who claim to be able to be completely focused, who claim to be capable of clearing their heads.

She pulls open the heavy wood and chrome door, made even heavier by the aforementioned whipping wind, and enters the warm, dark-red tones of Ouest. Her eyes are drawn immediately to the long, regal mahogany bar curving beautifully at its corner. Sitting right at that rounded corner, regal and a bit beautiful himself, is Kevin Smith, not the writer/director/good friend of Matt Damon and Ben Affleck, but the senior vice president (of something) at Merrill Lynch, and by all accounts handsome and charming enough to stand apart from the initially misleading name. Not everyone could, some people, less sure of themselves, might spend the better part of certain evenings feeling like maybe they didn't quite measure up to a writer/director/friend of Matt and Ben.

Standing by the hostess station, looking tall, fashionable, and perhaps slightly concerned—-she often looks slightly concerned—though less so since her first experiment with Botox—is Leslie Darden, fashion editor at *The NY*. Though Fashion and Food (both in capital letters, of course) might generally be considered things that are of interest to two very different types of people, in a city like New York that's not actually true. And, at *The NY*, both Fashion and Food fall under the umbrella of "Living," so Meredith and Leslie's offices are right down the hall from each other. Leslie is always up for a night out, and that's good, because Meredith needs to be sure she has people in her life who are up for a night out. And she likes Leslie; she's hardworking, a trait Meredith has always been a fan of, and she writes well. She makes fashion close to interesting, even for someone like Meredith who is far less interested in fashion than she is in other things.

Meredith smiles over at Kevin, and nods in the direction of the hostess stand. Before heading toward Leslie, she pauses for a moment to take in the room. It's a beautiful space with great energy. Meredith loves discovering new restaurants and sharing them with her readers, but she's also quite partial to writing pieces that check back on a favorite, which is what has brought her, several times over the last few weeks, back to Ouest. Smiling and feeling warmed by the restaurant, she heads to the hostess station. Out of the corner of her eye she can see Kevin, putting a few bills neatly on the bar, taking a last sip of his drink, and walking over to join them.

Meredith isn't sure if the conversational chemistry will work at dinner or not. Generally, she does try to give it some consideration, does try to pick people who will enjoy speaking with each other at dinner, since for the most part, Meredith will not be speaking with them. However, with all the other things that have been on her mind—good fats and protein blocks and eicosanoid levels (yes, really)—whether or not Kevin and Leslie will have anything to talk about has pretty much slipped her mind. She used to worry less about whether her dinner companions would get along, because before they moved out of the city her dinner companions were so often Stephanie and Aubrey. And of course, they get along. They, Meredith thinks, should be the poster couple for getting along, so peas-in-a-pod-like and happy they always are. And they were great dining companions. Even though Stephanie doesn't like to cook (would much rather retile a bathroom by hand), she has always had a great sense for spices, for recognizing them, and Aubrey is always, without question, fun to be around. Meredith had never thought of three as a crowd, but rather as the perfect number for reviewing. With three, you could get two different opinions, without the social aspect taking over.

Meredith and Kevin maneuver through the crowd and the three meet up at the hostess stand together.

Kevin leans over and kisses Meredith hello, and both Kevin and Leslie, as they were reminded this afternoon to do, say, "Hi, Abby." Meredith always makes an afternoon call, just to remind her dining companions not to call her by her name. "It's Abby," she'll caution.

"Hi," Meredith says and smiles. "Kevin," she continues, gesturing toward Leslie, "This is my friend Leslie." Meredith, an admirer of precision, is usually more descriptive in her introductions. Generally she'd say, "Leslie is my friend from work, Leslie writes about fashion, Leslie is my colleague," because Leslie, to be technical, is more a colleague than a friend per se, but to say "friend from work," right here in front of the hostess, could be risky. Say the hostess is also a student at FIT and follows fashion voraciously and actually recognizes Leslie somehow, from, let's say, fashion shows? If the hostess were quick (and for this scenario that would be very quick, an expert really at deductive skill) and interested not only in fashion shows but also in the welfare of her employers, and put two and two together, all could be lost. Really. You can't be too careful in New York.

Leslie smiles and tosses her perfectly coiffed hair and extends a manicured hand, bejeweled with a purple and green cocktail ring, to Kevin. Kevin takes Leslie's hand and smiles and says something, something that Meredith doesn't hear because suddenly she feels uncomfortable. *Is that,* she has to ask herself, *a sparkle in Kevin's eye?*

Leslie, in a voice a bit huskier than Meredith thinks is actually her own, says, "Well, hi, Kevin," and then, "I've heard so many nice things about you." *Except,* Meredith thinks, *that's not true.* Meredith doesn't think she's said any sorts of things about Kevin to Leslie.

Meredith turns her attention to the hostess, and says, "Abby Gilbertson, for three."

"Is your party all here?" asks the hostess. Meredith glances at Kevin and Leslie, just to the right of her, indicating, *Yes, all here.* The hostess smiles, and gathers three menus, taps them together efficiently. "Right this way then," she says, and begins walking, past the stairs leading to the upstairs loft where Meredith sat last time, and into the main dining room.

"Guys?" Meredith says to Kevin and Leslie, whose attention is presently a bit far away from the directive announcement of the hostess.

She is quite sure now that Leslie might be looking a bit sparkly-eyed herself and yes, she's pretty sure, too, that she finds this disturbing. And as bad as she is at clearing her head, she's quite skilled at latching on to something and not letting go. Generally, this does not work out well for her. She tries very hard to focus on her work and vows to remain so focused for the remainder of the evening, as opposed to, say, retreating into a spiral of weirdness.

Once they are seated, before a waiter has arrived to talk to them about cocktails and wine, Leslie smiles widely, all perfectly bleached teeth, and asks, "So, how do you two know each other, again?" Meredith is sure the word *again* doesn't need to be there; she's certain she never told her a first time. She does not want this. She was so busy thinking about being in the Zone, pondering if a person could ever try most of what's on the menu at Ouest, and still in fact be in it (or is that on it?). She didn't think about the possibility that Kevin, single and dashing, and Leslie, single and fashionable and really quite adorable, too, would not only conversationally work out, but would actually *hit it off*. And she hadn't thought at all about how she wouldn't like it.

"It was about eight years ago. Eight years, right, *Abby*?" Kevin asks Meredith, all the emphasis on Abby. Without waiting for her agreement or disagreement, he turns back to Leslie and explains, "In a share house in the Hamptons. It was the one in Southampton, on Mecox Road, I think."

Meredith looks up from her menu and agrees, "Yes, Mecox Road," except when Meredith looks back on her share house experience in the Hamptons, she doesn't need to differentiate between houses and streets and locations. For her there was only one year, one street. It was not, as they say, for her. Meredith's social skills are apparently not anywhere near honed enough for such an exercise in mass cohabitation. But she did meet Kevin in that house, and of course she liked him, everyone did, he was friendly and good-looking and had a great job, even then. Meredith has long thought that she'd like to wind up with a banker or a lawyer or some other form of junior tycoon, like Kevin. This is partly stereotype-based—she likes a strong-willed, corporate ladder–climbing type of guy. Partly it is because she has never subscribed to the belief that opposites attract, and she feels that ultimately she'd be best suited to someone as dedicated to his career as she is to hers, to someone who is striving, pushing himself, going places. And, partly, her reasoning is based on the fact that she is superficial. She is. She's accepted this about herself, she thinks it is, if not okay, at least very understandable in a city like New York.

"Mecox Road," Kevin repeats again, all bright-eyed and reminiscent. Kevin had a better time that summer than Meredith did. Kevin's good time was apparently not at all hindered by his opinion of himself in a bathing suit, his self-esteem not at all affected by having to spend the better part of the summer in one.

"Good times," Meredith says and wonders if it's been quite a while, too long really, that they've been sitting without an invitation for a drink order, without even a visit from the busboy to fill their water glasses. Or if it just seems that way. Though there is a part of her that wants to direct the conversation between Kevin and Leslie, she forces herself to focus on the menu. She likes the menu at Ouest, it's unusual; so many things on it that you wouldn't normally see on a grill menu.

The waiter arrives, water doesn't, which Meredith thinks is

too bad, not only because she's thirsty but because at this point it's been too long and she'll have to mention it in her review. As they're asked if they'd care for a cocktail, Meredith thinks one of the newer Sancerres from the well-planned, and in her opinion excellent, wine list would go very nicely with the skate with savoy cabbage and bacon potato ragout (she thinks as long as she stays, for the most part, away from the bacon potato ragout she *might* be in the Zone). But also, she imagines that not having any wine at all would probably be the best thing.

After a pleasant reading of the specials, the waiter departs with Kevin and Leslie's orders for wine and Meredith's request for a bottle of Pellegrino. Flat water appears next, as does a stainless steel, cylindrical breadbasket filled with crisp baguettes, accompanied by a chickpea mash and olive oil. Meredith takes a small amount of chickpea mash on her bread plate. Barry Sears, PhD, creator of the Zone, is a fan of the chickpea, and even, in moderation, of olive oil. She glares at the baguette that she can not have, and touches it to see if it is warm. It is. She keeps an eye on the menu, another on the atmosphere, the other diners, and part of her mind on the proper ratios of proteins and carbs and fats, and even though she hasn't decided yet what she needs Kevin and Leslie to order, she keeps an ear on their conversation, anyway.

And do you know what she hears? Do you know what she hears as she is trying so very hard to concentrate on her review, and also on controlling her eicosanoids, the heretofore unknown superhormones? She hears Kevin saying to Leslie, "I really like your necklace, it's so brightly colored." Meredith's mind unwittingly kaleidoscopes back to late August, Mecox

Road, eight years ago, before there was even an inkling of Josh, when she'd thought Kevin was her banker/lawyer/junior tycoon. And it might have ended less than gracefully, there might have been an incident in which she returned his gift of a Brita water pitcher to him in the dark of night and maybe he'd been confused as to why because maybe he'd never known she'd thought of him that way.

Leslie smiles and flips her hair, chestnut with all these red highlights, some that are almost pink but so well done that they don't look tacky at all. "Oh, thank you," she says, and then continues, very seriously, "Some people are all about gray and black and navy in colder weather. But I'm really partial to bright colors, to embracing them year round."

Kevin nods as if this were a subject of the utmost importance to him.

"It's because I'm from an island," she says seriously, fingering the turquoise enamel on her necklace.

The waiter arrivers with Kevin and Leslie's wineglasses, and sets them down. Meredith wants to turn to Leslie and say, *You are from* Long *Island,* but instead turns to the waiter and says, "On second thought, I'd like a martini, please. Grey Goose, straight up. Very dirty. Oh, and I think we need just one more minute before we order."

And Kevin gazes at Leslie.

The waiter smilingly retreats and Meredith efficiently calculates in her mind which dishes she has already sampled twice, which she hasn't, which need to be ordered and which no longer need to be in the lineup. She "suggests," to Leslie and Kevin what they "might like" to order, and in the interest of efficiency, requests that Kevin double down on appetizers. She thinks it'll be okay, and she does want to be sure about the gravlax.

Meredith concentrates on the lines of the menu, trying to fathom how on earth to properly measure blocks of protein and fat and good carbs, not bad. Slowly (or maybe it's a bit quicker than slowly) she begins to think it might not be possible to write a good restaurant review while in the Zone. She contemplates a Zone-friendly approach to restaurant reviewing and wonders what indeed would be missing from the world were critics to try, in all seriousness, to review Babbo while avoiding carbs. Or, rather, what would be missing from her world were she to try to do that?

She tries not to think about that, and decides instead that as long as she's here, she shouldn't think too much about ratios and blocks. And it's not like she hasn't done anything dietetic. She did, after all, forgo the Sancerre. She wonders how much such a sacrifice counts for as she takes a first sip from her martini. *Well-executed martini,* she thinks.

"Everything's beautifully presented," Leslie says when their dishes arrive and Kevin nods and smiles at Leslie approvingly. And Meredith, were she inclined to say anything at this juncture, would say that yes, the appetizers came in a more than timely fashion and the quality of the food and the presentation were so exemplary that it more than made up for, in fact canceled out, any initial wait for water. And as she loses herself, loses track of the Zone, she is for a blissful few moments, at one with the mushroom croquettes with goat cheese and pickled ramps. As she samples off Leslie and Kevin's plate, Leslie and Kevin not really noticing, she thinks how the salmon is unremarkable, but then salmon often is. But the asparagus flan that accompanies it is perfectly cooked, the asparagus and its subtle seasonings blended together flawlessly. She notes again how at Ouest, the sauces are rich but the food is never overwhelmed. It's a truly perfect balance and she thinks how hard a balance like that is to find in other places, in the Zone for example. She happily moves on to savor a sturgeon presented as if it were a trout. She ponders its wonderful risotto accompaniment, unique, festive almost, with soybeans.

It's not until she places her fork down after a sampling (perhaps more than a sampling) of the warm apple crisp with vanilla bean ice cream and caramel sauce, pound cake bread pudding with carmelized bananas and coconut ice cream, as Leslie laughs delicately at something surely witty that Kevin has just said, that it hits her. Kevin is the leading man type, by all means. But he's not the leading man type in romantic comedies, who despite his good looks and good job and dazzling personality feels quite inclined to date the somewhat beleaguered but plucky (and perhaps a bit overweight) heroine. He is the type of leading man who likes to date models, or some slightly toned-down variation of such. And she wonders if she always secretly thought, all these years, that maybe he'd come around, that maybe he'd be the romantic comedy type of leading man after all.

Kevin smiles at Leslie dashingly; Meredith takes a small, hopefully fortifying sip of her espresso (it has strength and boldness but no bitterness) and her heart ungraciously sinks. She wants the type of heart that fills up when others find love. But yet hers is the heart that thinks, *I have so few single friends left.*

I have so few people left with whom just to go see a movie. Hers is the heart that thinks, *It took me such a long time to warm up to Leslie at all, must I lose her so quickly?* And her heart, while it's on the subject, it would very much like to pose one more query: If Kevin didn't "think of her that way," even if it was eight years ago and she was a big enough person to deal with that quite gracefully (ungraceful incident involving the unnecessary returning of a Brita water pitcher notwithstanding) shouldn't he, out of common courtesy, not like her friend? Even if Leslie was still at this point, and now might always be, more of a coworker than a friend? Or had the statute of limitations on that quite run out?

* * *

"Thanks so much, Meredith," Kevin says, switching effortlessly from Abby to Meredith as soon as the three are out on the street. The transition is never as easy for her. It's often a while after she's taken off her wig and her makeup and written up her notes from the evening that she's still thinking of herself as someone else. "This was great. And it's always so nice to see you. Anytime you need a dining friend, I'm your man." Meredith is reminded of a Cake song she loves, "Friend Is a Four Letter Word."

"I'll definitely be calling on you soon," she answers, "it was great to see you, too."

"All right, supermodel," Leslie says next. Leslie calls people supermodel, she has a way of saying it that's friendly and fun, a way of saying it that's not condescending, even though she herself looks like very much like a supermodel. "Thanks so much, I'll see you tomorrow."

"Indeed," Meredith says, and can't help thinking that the thing with friends when you're in your (almost) mid-thirties, is that a lot of them by this point have gotten married and had babies, even your best friend, who also happens to be your sister. Especially her. And should you find yourself not married, and not with baby, and for whatever reason not a lot of friends who are single, the thought of making a new friend, one who is single like you, one who might be around on Friday nights when you might want to see a movie really does start to appeal. And she thinks it's not Kevin specifically, not really; it's more that there aren't that many people left to go see a movie with.

Kevin turns to Leslie and says, "You live downtown, right?" And Leslie nods and smiles, of course she smiles. "So do I," he says next. "We should share a cab."

Sometimes Meredith thinks that she might like living downtown. Now is one of those times. Kevin's arm goes up, and a taxi pulls up, and Kevin says something about, here Meredith you take this one, we'll get the next one. And she says something about goodnight.

"Hi," she says, leaning forward in her taxi, "could you go down to Sixty-fifth and cross there?" The driver makes no indication as to having heard her or not, but heads off at a speed much faster than necessary, south on Broadway. She thinks the direction, if nothing else, could be looked at as optimistic.

"Cross Seventy-ninth Street!" the driver says loudly, turning too far around in his seat for her, really for anyone's, liking.

"That's fine," she says and leans her blonde but also fake hair against the back of the seat and closes her eyes for a minute. *That's fine,* she repeats in her mind.

And if she unwittingly set up Leslie and Kevin, that's fine, too. It's been a long time since she thought of Kevin that way. And it's fine, she tries to think, that long before her second martini, she pretty much abandoned any attempt at adhering to the principles of the Zone.

As the taxi makes a hard left onto Seventy-ninth Street, Meredith looks back up Broadway. She can't see them standing on the street anymore, waiting together for their taxi. She thinks that if she could, if she could not only see them, but also hear them, that she might hear Kevin asking Leslie if she'd like to go to dinner one night soon. Or, maybe he's leaning over to her right now, and saying, "Hey, maybe this weekend, do you want to go see a movie?"

nine

the detox diet

Ever since she first saw it, Stephanie has always loved the movie *She's Having a Baby*, the one that stars Kevin Bacon and Elizabeth McGovern as a young suburban couple. In fact, it's right up there, along with *The Cutting Edge* with Moira Kelly and DB Sweeney as one of her all-time favorite films. She'd always thought of DB Sweeney as one of the most underrated actors of his generation. But that's not exactly what she's thinking of right now.

She's thinking of this one scene from *She's Having a Baby*. It's this part where Kevin Bacon, who's at the time terribly tired of the couple's baby-having efforts, the charts and the fertility times and the scheduled sex, meets another woman. He meets this woman by the fountain at the Museum of Natural History in Chicago and when he looks at her, he looks at her like he's going to forget for a while all about Elizabeth McGovern. And then right after that, the very next scene, Kevin Bacon is on the train, heading back to the suburbs and he looks really tired. For the longest time, Stephanie always thought he'd just looked at the woman (who, by the way, happened to be French) standing in front of the fountain and had then turned right around and gotten on his train and gone home to Elizabeth McGovern. It was the longest time she thought that, until someone pointed out to her that, no, he had in fact had an affair. Even though it was all off camera, it still happened. Just because you didn't see it didn't mean it wasn't there. And for a long time, Stephanie had wished she didn't know that.

"Okay," Stephanie says out loud to herself, once Ivy has rested her just-burped self, her precious blonde head, down on her shoulder. She tries to make a mental note again not to talk out loud to herself. She thinks there might be something alarming to the trend that has been, for a while now, developing. And so she thinks to herself, rather than saying out loud, *I am not going to go on UrbanBaby today.* She is sure there is darkness there, in the nameless, faceless lines of pink and green text. And she's sure spending all that time lurking in a chat room, even one about babies, staring so long at a computer, it's so Aubrey-like in its isolation, if you think about it. And at this point, Stephanie would really rather not.

There's the Junior League of Ridgewood, she's considering looking into that. There's the New Mommy Group that she's already part of and just needs to make an effort to like more. She missed the last meeting, she really shouldn't have; if she's learned anything from all her years of team sports it's that you show up. No matter what. You show up and you play. By the rules. She's always thought so, and believing in that has always worked out well.

She puts Ivy down in her crib, and Ivy stays down and Stephanie takes a moment to be happy for that. She wants to have a moment in which she's aware she's happy; lately she thinks they're harder to come by. And also, she wants the Baby Sleeping Gods, whoever they are and she's sure they must exist, to know she really appreciates it, to know she really, *really* does, whenever it is that they make it so that Ivy sleeps. Even if it is mostly during the day.

As she makes her way downstairs, instead of going into their office, where there is darkness in the sunlight that glints so cheerfully across the side of Aubrey's desk, she heads through the family room and into the kitchen.

She has a new system. She has been putting perfectly sliced squares of part-skim mozzarella cheese into Ziploc baggies. She's pretty sure the answer is to have everything planned out and baggied up in advance. She pulls a baggie from the red cardboard box, reaching simultaneously into the cabinet where she keeps the Goldfish pretzels. Baggies, baggies everywhere replete with premeasured blocks of proteins and fats and carbs. Brilliant, flawless. Except of course for the part-skim mozzarella cheese. That's actually a bit complicated because part-skim mozzarella cheese is in fact both a fat block *and* a protein block. And if you think about things like that too much, it can be quite discouraging, discouraging enough so that you'll need to devote a fair amount of time (time you might not feel you have) to reading the testimonials peppered throughout the book, all the many success stories—Kathy L., Lori P., Don R. to name but a few—in order to get back on track.

She counts out pretzels and puts them into piles of fourteen. She thinks she'll sign up for one of those breast cancer walks, or AIDS walks, or MS. The ones where you walk all day, every day, for three days and sleep in tents at night. She'll bring Ivy with her. As she slides the pretzels into their baggies she thinks how in *The Zone* by Barry Sears, PhD, there is no mention of Pepperidge Farm Goldfish pretzels. She wonders if they are possibly a trick learned later in *Mastering the Zone*, or if maybe, unbeknownst to her, Caryn just made it up. She wonders.

She thinks of Kevin Bacon on the train ride back to the suburbs and the way he looked, so exhausted, so tired, so defeated, so different from the way he looked when he looked at the French woman. When he looked at her, he looked so alive. Aubrey doesn't very often look alive anymore.

When the phone rings a moment later, it's all she can do not to say, *Thank you,* out loud, as she picks it up.

"Hello."

"Look at you answering the phone on the first ring," Meredith says in a pleasant and jovial tone of voice, especially so for Meredith. And yet it annoys her, which is so unlike Stephanie and especially so unlike her toward Meredith, even though Meres has the propensity to be—especially lately and more and more frequently—somewhere in the general vicinity of annoying.

"Hi, Meres."

"Okay. So, Steph, I'm just saying, the Zone sucks."

Stephanie takes a deep, measured breath and lets it out. She does this, she's pretty sure, as much for Meredith to hear her as for its purported relaxing qualities. "I don't think the Zone sucks."

"Okay, how much weight have you lost?"

"Meres, the same as yesterday. I'm only weighing myself once a week. You know you're not supposed to weigh yourself more than once a week," Stephanie says, though actually as she says that she wonders, *Does Meredith know that?* Is that information garnered actually from the book or did she get that from Caryn, too? Or maybe did she just make it up herself? For the life of her right now, she has no idea.

"Okay, so four pounds?" Meredith says. And the way she says it, Stephanie can't help but notice that she sort of spits out "four pounds," like it's nothing. *Four pounds*, she says, like it's not a big deal at all, like it isn't a little bit of a triumph. But it is.

"Yes, four pounds," Stephanie says. She says the number with pride and tries not to think of what a small number it is when viewed in the context of how much more she has to lose. It's still a triumph, or even a victory. She believes that.

"Okay, well, good," Meredith says, pausing (could it be reflectively? Or is it far more likely just a pause?) and then she continues, "I'm happy for you, it's just, I've lost none." Stephanie doesn't say anything, she waits to see if Meredith is going to offer up any self-analytical insight, if she has some story to tell or if, rather, "The Zone sucks," is her only story.

Meredith doesn't say anything.

"I mean, Mere, are you actually doing it?" she asks, as gently as she thinks she can. "Are you counting everything up and adding it properly? Are you measuring things? I have this system, maybe it'll help you, see I use baggies—"

"No, see that's just it," Meredith cuts her off, before even waiting to see what the baggies could be for. "I can't bring baggies out to dinner with me," she continues, sounding, Stephanie thinks, just a bit closer to incensed with each word. "But I could avoid things. Maybe if we did Atkins? Then I could just avoid all carbs? The Zone isn't just avoiding all carbs, it's so much more complicated than that."

"Maybe you shouldn't look at it as more complicated, but rather as more flexible?" Stephanie offers, trying not to think about other things, trying really just to think about helping Meredith, about getting Meredith to stick with this, with her, because that will help. It will help both of them. "Really, Meres, when you think about it, The Zone truly is more flexible because it does in fact allow carbs. Just not bad ones and you just have to have them in the right proportion to your fats and your proteins." And as Stephanie says this, she feels like she gets it, like she understands, like she's in control. And that's one more thing than the previous zero things of which she'd felt in control.

"It's too much math," Meredith says back quickly. "You know I hate math. And it's *the Zone*," she continues in a singsong voice, but not such a nice singsong voice. "And then, once you've figured that out, it's not as if that's enough, it's all, okay now let's move on up to the next level, let's try *Mastering the Zone*, let's buy another book, in addition to the recipe book that I never get to use because I never get to eat at home."

"I thought you were eating at home?"

"Stephanie," Meredith continues, a quick and halting emphasis on each syllable, *Steph-a-nie*, "you know how hard it is for me. It's not like I can just sit down each night at home to my

Zone-prepared dinner. It is really hard for me to justify eating at home. Do you know how much work I have to do? Do you how much harder I make it on myself if I stay home?"

"I'm not saying you don't have work to do," Stephanie replies. "I'm just saying it because you were the one who said you weren't going to go out as much."

"I said lunch. I was talking about lunch."

"Okay, right."

"But I don't even know if I should do that, I mean lunch is important, it's as important in some places as dinner," she explains, and then as an important addendum, adds on quickly, "it's just dinner without the cocktails."

Stephanie thinks this might be an opportunity for positive reinforcement. Surely they're everywhere if you just know where to look, and maybe that's what it is lately, maybe lately she's simply forgotten where to look. "Well that's good then. Because I think I read somewhere that drinking can play a big part in making weight loss difficult."

"What's that?" Meredith asks, and Stephanie feels a small, tiny internal triumph, Meredith is actually listening rather than talking. It's a rarity, and like the loss of four pounds, a victory.

"Drinking. All the drinking can make losing weight harder."

"Really, Stephanie?" Meredith says a bit caustically, "I could have sworn it was the eating." Stephanie doesn't say anything.

Stephanie would count to ten, she would count to ten out loud if she felt that would help, but she doesn't really feel it will. She takes a deep breath and counters, "Well, I think that you can't look at it as a race to the finish. You have to look at it as a lifestyle change, a permanent change you're going to make in your life, and I think that's really the case with any diet we would do."

Meredith exhales; it's an exhale that says, *Whatever, Stephanie.* Stephanie knows this as she looks at her baggies so lovingly prepared for the next two days. She knows this as she glances through the archway to the family room and the door beyond it and she feels for a moment such a rush of despair that she can't think of anything to do except stay on the diet. "And also," she says slowly, measuredly, "I don't think you have to get the *Mastering the Zone* book, I think that's just if you want it, just if, you know, you want to take it up a level."

"It's like freaking Dungeons and Dragons with all the levels!" Meredith says next. "Between the Dungeons and Dragons and the math, all you'd have to do is throw in a field hockey match and it could be a Greatest Hits of everything that sucked about high school."

"Speaking of field hockey," Stephanie says, "it does say that exercise is a big part of this program. Of every program." And maybe she says that just a little bit to be mean.

"I just think that if we're going to do this together—"

"Not *if* we are. We are. We're doing it together," Stephanie reminds her.

"Yes, yes, I know, and I swear, really I'm not trying to be a pain."

"No, of course not," Stephanie says and she's joking, and she's not.

"No, Steph, really. I'm not trying to be awful, it's just maybe, couldn't we try to find something that might work for both of us? It's not like you've wasted time on the Zone, it's not like it's all for nothing. You'll just start the next diet four pounds ahead of the game, right?"

"What were you thinking of?" Stephanie asks, taking slow, measured breaths. *Look for the positive*, she tells herself. *Surely, it's everywhere.*

"Well, to tell you the truth, I have felt bad about not embracing it, our diet, because I think it's important to embrace it, the way you embrace things, and so I did some research. I read up on all these different diets. I think I'm very informed now, and I think I found some that might be easier for me to embrace. And things, generally, are easier for you to embrace, right? I don't think it's as hard for you, you're not as hindered as I am by the need to go out to dinner."

"No," she says, "I'm definitely not hindered by that."

Stephanie thinks of the words *easier for you*, how Meredith says them as if there is so much truth in them. And she can't really wrap her head around how she could ever go about explaining to Meredith that *easy* is no longer in her vocabulary, that the fact that someone isn't required by her important employer, for her prestigious and coveted job, to eat out night after night in the best restaurants, doesn't mean life is *easy*. She tries to be sure that the creeping irritation, the one that spends so much time lately creeping, doesn't appear in her voice. She tries to make sure the thought, *Oh my God, Meredith, lately sometimes I just wish you could talk in sentences and not in paragraphs* doesn't find its way into the conversation either, and asks again, "Okay, Meres, which diet were you thinking of?"

"Maybe Atkins? I was thinking maybe we'd do Atkins and I can review steak houses. There are so many steak houses in

New York, old standbys and some great new ones, too. Can you believe I haven't even been to Craftsteak?"

"Craftsteak?"

"You know, it's on Tenth Avenue."

"No, I don't."

"I've actually heard a lot of very good things about it. Do you know you can have mayonnaise on Atkins? Sometimes I think I could live in a world without bananas if mayonnaise were allowed."

And Stephanie, mostly she thinks she's just so tired, mostly she thinks that, but she soldiers on. "I don't know, Meres, I heard that Atkins only works as long as you follow it perfectly and as soon as you mess up the tiniest bit, if there's a drop of sugar in your tuna salad—do you know they actually do that, at the deli they put sugar in the tuna salad—then you gain all the weight you've lost back in about a second."

"I read that actually," Meredith says solemnly, sounding a bit discouraged herself. "And I've often suspected they put sugar in the lobster salad at Sables. But if they don't, imagine, you could be on Atkins and just eat container after container of the lobster salad from Sables. I really do think it is, hands down, the best lobster salad in the world. The best I've ever tasted, that's for certain. And I've tasted quite a lot of lobster salads in my day."

"Alright, even so, I'm not sure I think Atkins is the best way to go."

"You think?"

"I do."

"Well what about maybe the South Beach Diet? People really like that, and they even have all the prepackaged foods now."

"I don't know," Stephanie says, although there is part of her that can picture the South Beach Diet dinners, can picture how easy just popping them in the microwave could be. "I've heard a lot of good things about Weight Watchers?"

"I don't think I have time to go to Weight Watchers meetings."

"I've heard from a lot of people who have been on tons of diets that at the end of the day it's really Weight Watchers that works. It really does the most in terms of getting you to change your bad habits, change your life." And as she says it, Stephanie actually feels some of the hopefulness returning, the hopefulness that Meredith has been sucking right out of her, ever since she picked up the phone, and on the first ring at that.

Meredith has nothing, nothing at all to say about Weight Watchers.

"And you know," Stephanie continues, and her voice is more than hopeful now, maybe it's a little wistful, "I think it sounds really nice about Weight Watchers, there's such a support system. The whole diet, I think it's built around the concept of community. There's a whole community of support."

"I'm not sure I have the time to start going to Weight Watchers. It's just, are you really sure Atkins is off the table?"

"I think so," Stephanie says, and then, "How do I explain this?" Because she does want to explain it, she really does want Meredith to be able, in some small way at least, to understand. "I like the Zone. I'm starting to feel like it's working. I feel empowered. You know, I wanted something to happen and it happened. I made it happen." It feels so good to get it off her chest, to get it out there, and she exhales, and this time the breath is different, it's not one of impatience or of trying to relay that impatience, but rather of relief. Relief, with a little bit of free-dom thrown in for good measure.

"And that's a new thing, how?" Meredith asks.

Stephanie pauses, waits a moment. "Do you have any idea how rare that feeling is in my life?" she asks softly.

"Honestly, Stephanie. I think that's all your life is."

"*What* do you mean by that?"

"Nothing," Meredith answers, and Stephanie doesn't want to think of how far off the mark Meredith's answer would have been if she'd actually answered.

"Let's move on," Meredith says next, and Stephanie thinks that's probably for the best. "What about the half diet? Where you eat half of everything?"

"What?"

"You cut it in half and eat it. Half."

"What stops you from eating the whole thing?"

"I don't know, throw it away."

"That's terrible. People are starving in the world."

"I'm starving."

"Meredith," Stephanie says. "I just don't think I'm starting a new diet right now."

"Okay," Meredith says, and pauses. Silence for just one mo-ment before she adds, "but just one thing?"

"What?"

"I think maybe if we start something new, we should try to do it when we have a weekend to set aside and then we can do either *French Women Don't Get Fat*, or *The Detox Diet*. With both of those diets, I think you start off by eating only boiled vegetables for the first forty-eight hours."

"What?" Stephanie says, paying complete attention again, as something runs through her, so quickly. It's not a chill, it's something worse, more awful. It's in a whole different league than momentarily feeling cold.

"*French Women Don't Get Fat.* It's a huge bestseller. I read there's something in there about how you boil up a pound of leeks, and you eat only boiled leeks for a weekend, just to start. For forty-eight hours. I mean, obviously I'd have to not review at all that weekend, but I thought we could try it."

"No, what's the other diet you said?"

"*The Detox Diet,*" Meredith says and something in Stephanie turns on; it's as if she can feel a light switch scratching her, somewhere inside her stomach, and she can feel it burning there. And Meredith keeps talking, "But I think it might actually be a lot harder than *French Women Don't Get Fat.* I think it's from the seventies and it's all vegetables all the time, which could get extremely tiresome."

"Uh-huh," Stephanie says, and for the life of her, she really doesn't think she'd be able to say anything else.

"To tell you the truth, I think if it came down to it, if it were a matter of trying something different, I'm starting to think that *French Women Don't Get Fat* would probably be the way to go over *The Detox Diet,* you know?"

She knows. She gets up out of her chair, and it's so strange, this feeling, this feeling like she has known all along, and at the same time, she's only known for just this second.

"Yeah," she says, locating the baby monitor on the counter, the green convex picture of her daughter inside it. She walks over to it and picks it up.

"Because I think I could eat only vegetables, or it might be only leeks, for forty-eight hours. Forty-eight hours isn't such a long time. You can do anything for forty-eight hours if you put your mind to it, right?"

"Right." Stephanie thinks of Aubrey. She thinks of how so much of the time lately Aubrey's eyes look like they're two completely different sizes. She'd started to wonder if maybe people's eyes got that way, so different from each other, when they had to lie all the time. She'd started to wonder, more and more frequently, if maybe people's eyes started to look like that when they had to look at people they used to love, but didn't anymore.

"Meredith," she says, grabbing the baby monitor, walking out of the kitchen, and into the family room. When she gets to the door, the one that leads down to the workroom, she tucks the cordless between her ear and her shoulder, "I have to go." She turns the handle on the door.

"Oh, really? Right when we were finally getting to some common ground about diets? It's not because you'd rather do the detox diet, is it? Because if you do, we can talk about that?"

"No," Stephanie says. "I don't want to do the detox diet." She starts down the stairs, the word *detox* almost ringing in her ears.

"Okay, that's good, because real quick, just think of all the French restaurants I could review."

It's as if the word *detox* is a force pulling her, pulling her to the workroom, and it's as if she knows exactly what she's going to find there. At the bottom of the stairs she doesn't stop, she keeps walking, quicker now than when she was still descending.

She walks, baby monitor in one hand, phone in the other, to the corner of the room. She goes to Aubrey's desk and stands in front of it. She puts the baby monitor down. And there's a bottle right there, sitting right next to his mouse, and she feels like she doesn't need to pick it up. She could just leave it there and it'd be the same because she already knows.

"Because there are so many French restaurants in New York, so many of the all-time greats, the classics. Le Bernardin, of course. And yet Le Bernardin doesn't even scratch the surface."

She picks up the bottle, it's half-empty, and as she does, she notices two other empty ones directly behind it, next to the Middlebury College Class of '91 ceramic mug in which he keeps all his pens.

"And there are so many exceptional newcomers, too."

Aubrey Cunningham, it says his name right on it, along with *Vicodin*, along with *Take as needed for pain.*

"And I think with the diet there's some way that you can really eat what you want, and go anywhere. So if that's the case, the possibilities could be endless."

"Meredith, I have to go," she says.

"Stephanie! Have you even been listening to me? Where'd you go? Did Aubrey just get home or something?

Stephanie thinks of Aubrey's ACL surgery, timed perfectly so that it was long enough after they moved into the house, and long enough before Ivy was born. And she can't remember if that's when he became awful, if that's when it was, because she can't really remember a time when he wasn't. Awful.

"If I had to say, I'd say you haven't been listening at all."

She opens the mini-fridge and stares at the bottles and bottles lined up inside. Was he nervous to throw them away? Was he afraid she'd see them and know? Why didn't he just take them with him and throw them out on the way to the train station, at the station, on the train, somewhere in the city?

"Are you mad, Stephanie?"

"Meredith, there's no way I can make you understand," she says next and she wonders if that's what Aubrey will say to her soon. If that's what she'll say to Ivy one day. She wonders if there will ever be a time when she'll be able to know how far all of this will actually reach, how many things it will actually affect, has already affected, while she's stayed upstairs in the kitchen all this time trying to pretend he wasn't having an affair. She wants to know when that time will be, when she'll be able to understand this, understand any of it. She has no idea, she just knows it's not now.

"Now who's being melodramatic?" Meredith asks with a little laugh and when that little laugh, that little poorly timed attempt at injecting humor is met with nothing, not even a little laugh of Stephanie's own, she says next, a bit exasperated, "I could say the exact same thing to you, Steph. I could say you don't understand. You don't understand how hard it is to diet and to do my job."

Stephanie shuts the door of the mini-fridge, she notices the plug on the ground next to it. It's not plugged in. There isn't even any outlet nearby. It's just lying there. "Of course I understand how hard it is," she says, "I've always understood." She sits down at Aubrey's desk. She puts a hand on the top drawer handle.

"One, you don't understand how hard it is. Think how hard

you think it is, and then multiply that by a hundred thousand. And two, you haven't always understood, you just haven't."

She pulls on the handle. It's locked.

"Meredith, I can't do this. I can't do this right now. I just need a break. I just need to take a break, I need to catch my breath."

"I feel exactly the same way. My God, I was beginning to think we'd never see eye to eye on anything again, but thank God, we do. I need a break, too. Maybe two weeks, and then we could start back up? Maybe we could even try the detox diet then?"

"Meredith," Stephanie says softly, seriously, "I don't want to take a break from dieting. I think I need to take a break from this, from us, just for a minute."

"What?"

"I just really need to take a break from this, from us."

Stephanie knows that Meredith, on some level, is trying to figure this out. And she can't help her, and she knows Meredith, she knows she's racking her brain right now to say something, something that will make sense out of all this, or even just something snappy. On some level, some part of her that isn't surrounded by bottles upon bottles of Vicodin, she is surprised that all Meredith comes up with is a slightly spiteful, "Fine." And then after that, there is a pause in which Stephanie, on that same lost level, wishes she could explain it to her, wishes there could be a way in which she doesn't seem so awful. But she's sure there isn't any way. Or at least she's sure she can't figure out a way right now, and Meredith keeps talking.

"I really thought that this would help us, would maybe make it so that we weren't so far apart anymore, but it's not doing that at all. Fine, Stephanie, let's do that, let's take a break like we're some couple who's dating and who maybe isn't sure about where things are going, if they're going anywhere, and we could just end everything forever but let's first, let's just take a break. Sounds great to me, Steph."

Stephanie doesn't come to her rescue, doesn't try to help her, or make it better the way she almost always does, historically, automatically, with everything. She notices a hangnail and tries to forget about it; hangnails are so much better left alone, as hard as they are to leave that way. Pulling at them, which is always the first instinct, never makes it better, always makes it worse, and hangnails, these little tiny things that you think mean nothing, can hurt so much.

Stephanie stares at the bottle in her hand, stares at the name on it. *Aubrey Cunningham. Take as needed for pain. Aubrey Cunningham.* She stares at it again and everything else is so far from her mind, except for the fact that the name Aubrey Cunningham is the name of her husband. She thinks this is the first time in her life she has no idea how to handle everything that is hers. She has no idea what to do.

She's holding the phone, there's dead air. She thinks she can remember Meredith saying, "You know what then, don't call me," and she thinks she remembers not saying anything, because she has no idea how exactly you say, My six-month-old baby is sleeping, for once, upstairs and I'm standing in the basement with her monitor, surrounded by her father's Vicodin bottles, and I don't really care if French Women Do or Do Not Get Fat because I am not French, even though right now I wish I were because then I'd be in France.

If she were closer to the wall, she might go over to it to turn off the light. It would be better, she thinks, if the light were turned off. She looks into the baby monitor. She looks at all the bottles. She wonders how many others there might be, in how many other places. She's not sure if she'll look. She's not sure about anything. She closes her eyes.

part two

you say you want a revolution?

ten

as lonely as you wanted
to be

In addition to the iPod and the Bose iPod dock, Meredith also has a Bang & Olufsen BeoCenter 2 CD player that she sets on a timer so it functions as an alarm clock. She greatly prefers waking up to a preselected CD. Really, it's so much better than waking up to beeping (unpleasant) or even to the radio (could be pleasant, but pretty much, it's a gamble). For a while, she did like waking up to the radio but in the end there were too many risks. For example, setting an alarm radio to NPR could seem like it was a good, smart, informative choice, but in reality, the world can be such a terrible place these days, news-wise, war-wise, Middle East conflict–wise, that after a morning of NPR she would so often feel defeated, spending her day es-pousing the merits of the one-hundred-dollar-an-ounce caviar at Petrossian while there are a billion people on the planet who exist on less than a dollar a day. It makes a planned contempla-

tion of Del Posto and how much Mario Batali has done for dining in New York seem remarkably less relevant. WPLJ is of
course no longer an option because while Meredith likes a Top
40 station as much as the next person, and will still listen to it
in the afternoons every now and then, otherwise how would
she ever know about songs like Shakira's "Hips Don't Lie," she
cannot stand the morning DJs. Lite FM plays far too much
Barry White in the mornings, and there is not one country
music station in New York City. Meredith thinks it could boggle the mind if you let it.

The timer clicks, the BeoCenter 2 turns on, and the first note
of music fills the room. It's Patrick Park singing "Something
Pretty." It's track five on his CD, *Loneliness Knows My Name*.
She concentrates on the song, it's the only thing she can think of
to do. *I know ugliness, now show me something pretty.* Only, as
Patrick Park sings, all thick and gritty and gravely, "Show me
something pretty," Meredith sings instead, "Show me something skinny." And it doesn't even seem like a big mistake; to
her, pretty and skinny have always seemed so much like the
same thing. *Now show me something skinny.*

Patrick Park continues to fill the room, and she listens for the
next line to make sure she's got it right. *As for loneliness, she
greets me every morning.* True story, that's really the next line,
and it might be a bit too much loneliness so early in the morning. But really what does she expect when she listens to the
songs of a man who titles his CD *Loneliness Knows My Name*?

I think I might need to look into a new CD, Meredith thinks,
sliding out from under the covers. *Maybe,* she thinks, *something
more upbeat, maybe some Jack Johnson.* She thinks also that at

this point, she's had just about enough of being lonely. But after that, she's not sure what to think next. She's not really sure what a person is supposed to do when she's tired of being lonely. She'd just never considered it before. She imagines there could be solutions—joining a club, volunteering or giving something back to the community, taking up a sport. But she also imagines that the search for any solution has already been made infinitely harder due to the fact that the most important person in her life, the one who actually made it so that she never felt alone, now needs a break. And she'd very much like to say, it's not as if Stephanie wasn't kind of snippy with her throughout her entire pregnancy. And it's not as if Stephanie hasn't been quite the recluse ever since Ivy's been born. And has Meredith ever said anything hostile and wrong, anything like, *I need a break*? No, she hasn't.

Out of bed, Meredith embarks on the short trip to her kitchen, and reaches quickly into her freezer for the foil package of Starbucks coffee. As the coffee drips through the coffee-making part of her Krups XP1500 Coffee and Espresso Combination machine, Meredith considers simply starting over. Rather than going with the run-of-the-mill pretty-much-how-most-every-day-starts coffee, she contemplates the myriad merits of making herself a cup of cappuccino instead. With whole milk. Definitely with whole milk, because if you're going to take the time to make the cappuccino, to monitor it, to wait for it, whole milk should really be included in the reward. Does no one else think skim milk tastes exactly like water? Does no one else find skim milk to be, if you really stop to think about it, just a little bit upsetting? But the coffee is already made. And come to think of it, all that's in the fridge anyway is some Zone-friendly skim milk.

She carries the coffee back into her bedroom and sits down at her desk. She greatly prefers to sit by herself at her desk, as opposed to by herself at the round wrought-iron table for four, placed in the living room, right outside the pass-through part of the pass-through kitchen. She doesn't recall it being intentional, but the way the table has been placed, it's right there, so that if you were so inclined, you could pass plates and dishes and plat-ters of food through the pass-through (hence the name), and then, people—people gathered happily around the table, or even just standing right by it—could take these passed plates and set them, happily of course, on the table. Unless no one was there. But then, if you were so inclined, you *could* throw things through the pass-through and with a little bit of aim, even just the small amount that Meredith has, you could probably get it to land on the table.

Her desk is in her bedroom, right next to the window; in order to look out, all she has to do is turn her head slightly to the right. And that works well, as she likes very much to look out the window, to see the city from the twelfth floor, to see everything, and at the same time nothing, of what's going on out there. Today she sees the buildings, as she sometimes does, as boxes. Boxes filled with other boxes, with more boxes. Looking at it like that makes Meredith feel claustrophobic, more than a little itchy in her skin.

She'd like to think of something else; she'd like to think about something more productive. So she wonders if there's a diet in the world, a successful dieter anywhere who can have whole milk—just in her coffee, nothing like an entire brazen glass of whole milk or anything crazy like that—and not feel like a failure, a bad person, someone who can't do anything right, someone who's getting to the point lately where she's thinking so much more about loneliness than she used to.

She's sure if Stephanie were here, even just here on the phone, she'd tell her not to think so much. She'd say, "Try not to think about it, Meres," and maybe she'd add on, "Really, that's as good advice as any." But Stephanie isn't here, and suddenly she remembers that on the Atkins diet, you can have heavy cream in your coffee, because even though milk does have a very high carbohydrate count, for some magical reason, heavy cream doesn't have any carbs at all.

When the phone rings a moment later, she's actually quite grateful for the interruption. Before it can ring a second time, Meredith reaches out quickly to grab the phone. The flick of her wrist, the almost instinctual speed; she is like a frog, a lizard, something with a really big tongue that it uses to snatch up no-see-ums, mosquitoes, and flies. Meredith's phone, any phone within her reach, is a no-see-um, a mosquito, and a fly.

"Hello?"

"Hi, Meredith, it's Leslie."

"Oh, hi, Leslie," she says. She didn't really want it to be Leslie, there was someone else she wanted.

"Hey. So, what are you up to on this Saturday morning?"

"I'm just trying to think of a new place to put my kitchen table."

"What?"

"Nothing."

"Oh, okay then," Leslie answers, and Meredith wonders for a perhaps ill-thought-out moment if maybe she should enlist Leslie, if she should just say, "Oh, I'm just here trying to decide which diet to go on since my sister got me thinking about it so much and then, just like that, abandoned me. So, Leslie, would you like to go on a diet with me?"

She pictures Leslie, and it's impossible to think of Leslie as someone who would ever have to diet. She has always thought of Leslie as someone who is just like that, just skinny. Leslie's tall and lean physique is the type that is metabolic, hereditary. No amount of dieting, exercising, or starving could make a person look like Leslie. So she doesn't say anything.

"Well, I was calling for two reasons," Leslie begins. "First, I wanted to thank you so much for introducing me to Kevin. What a fantastic guy, and leave it you to make a setup so subtle and pressure-free."

But it wasn't a set up, Meredith thinks, quite seriously. *I just needed two people to go to dinner with me.*

"It was nothing," she says. "It was just dinner." Even though if anyone should know there is no such thing as "just dinner," it would be Meredith.

"But still, he's really great, you know."

"I know," Meredith says and she's reminded of an ad she saw once a long time ago, for jeans. She can't remember the brand, but she can remember the campaign. It said, "No one can tell that you have a great personality from across the room." Leslie is the type of woman who men fall in love with from across rooms.

"I'm glad you two hit it off," she adds after a pause. She is not glad.

"I think he's very romantic," Leslie continues. "So many guys in this city, they play games. But Kevin's just not like that at all. We went out last night, and he called just now to see if I wanted to get brunch tomorrow, and then we were talking, he's such a good phone-talker, and so many of them aren't, and we thought we would love it if you joined us, since we wouldn't be brunching at all if it weren't for you."

We would love it if you joined us, Meredith repeats to herself. *We. Love. Us.* And she thinks of brunch with them and can think of nothing she'd rather do less. "Thanks so much for the offer," she says. "But I can't. I've got something I need to do tomorrow."

"Oh, my pleasure, Meredith, really. Doing anything good instead?"

"There's this book I really need to buy."

"Another time then," Leslie says happily and Meredith waits for a moment to see if Leslie is going to tell her she looks like a supermodel, or perhaps Carol Alt, but she doesn't.

"Definitely," Meredith answers back, trying to sound cheerful. "Tell Kevin I say hi." And then, even though she imagines that at this point they don't need her advice, the need to give it is bigger than she is. "Red Cat in Chelsea has a really nice Sunday brunch."

"Thanks so much, Meredith. I'll see you Monday at work."

"See you then," she replies, thinking as she does that Twelfth Street Café down near Kevin's apartment provides one of the more, in her opinion, charming brunch experiences in New York. She's a fan, too, of Pure's brunch on Irving Place, and while there, it's always fun to stop into Casa Mono for a sampling of tapas and one of the best sangrias in town.

eleven

what you don't know
can't hurt you, or not

"Aubrey?" He doesn't answer.

She's standing in their bedroom, right outside the bathroom. He's in the bathroom, he's shaving or he's doing whatever it is he does to his hair, which isn't much. Aubrey likes to live by some dictate, she thinks it was JFK who said it, that a man should be able to shower and dress in under fifteen minutes. She's sure that when JFK said it, there was more eloquence. She's sure that there are other dictates Aubrey might want to try living by. She's sure that he can hear her. And what is he getting ready for, it's Saturday?

"Aubrey?" She notices a spot on the molding where the paint is peeling off. She'll have to fix that.

"Steph, yeah?" he says, and he says it rather normally. He steps out of the bathroom with his towel wrapped around his waist. There's a tiny spot of blood on his face. He keeps touching the spot and she thinks he should get a tissue. But except for that he looks fine. He looks normal, more normal than she thinks she's seen him looking in a while, and she feels lighter, just for a second, and she can imagine everything is fine. She can imagine that last night was just an illusion, a hallucination brought on by too much stress and the inability to deal with that stress by eating, due to the fact of being on a diet. Or maybe he just takes all his pills at night, and she's always too tired, too busy, too preoccupied with Ivy to actually notice what he looks like at this time of day.

"Aubrey, we have to talk."

His eyebrows raise and he makes this clucking noise he likes to make with his mouth. She's filled with rage for an instant, that this is what Aubrey, lately, thinks suffices for an answer. But it seems even rage can be snuffed out so quickly by exhaustion. Exhaustion can knock down almost anything in its path. Ivy's been up for two hours already. It's seven fifteen in the morning and for the purposes of this important conversation, Stephanie has parked her in front of *Baby Van Gogh*. She tries to limit her TV, but what with her husband being a drug addict and her not having slept in a day, she thinks it's okay.

Aubrey walks past her to the dresser and pulls open the top drawer, fishing around and taking out socks and boxers. He doesn't take out just one pair of boxers and one pair of socks, as you would have expected, or at least as Stephanie would have expected, but rather several pairs of each. Three pairs of boxers and three pairs of socks.

"What is this?" she asks, and her voice sounds shrill. When

did she become shrill? And why is he so catatonic, even when he looks normal? And why is it that out of all the things she thought she desired in the world, now that she seems to have them, what she desires most is to throw things?

"Why all the socks, Aubrey?" And when he still doesn't answer, she wonders if maybe it's a drug thing. She does her best to banish such a thought from her mind, as such a thought can't really help this conversation, if a conversation it can in fact be called. He walks past her again, lilting to one side. Aubrey's walk, even long before his ACL surgery, has always been the kind that's just slightly off-kilter. She had always thought of it as lilting, not limping, until now.

He pulls his suitcase out of the closet and carries it back to the bed. He puts it right on the bed, dirty suitcase on unmade sheets. She hates that. He knows she hates that. But she won't say anything about it because she needs to say something about other things, about hundreds and hundreds of pills. She needs to pick her battles. She wonders if he knew this. He is now piling shirts, button-down shirts, into the suitcase.

"Are you just not going to answer me?"

"What?"

"Why are you packing?"

"Chicago?"

"Chicago?"

"Yes, Stephanie. Chicago. The Internet conference that the entire marketing team is attending and as their fearless leader, I will attend with them?" *Right,* she thinks, *right,* even though she doesn't remember anything about an Internet conference in Chicago. *Aubrey's job,* she thinks, *the place he goes every day.*

Every day, in the city. And she wonders, can you be a very good marketer of sports when you are on drugs?

"Well, Aubrey, I think maybe you shouldn't go."

He turns to look at her, half-confused, half-mean, the way he looks a lot of the time when he isn't looking blank, and then looks away. He drops his towel and reaches for his boxers and as he heads back into the closet, taking out a pair of pants and stepping into them, he says, without turning to look at her again, "Stephanie, would you mind then telling me why? And would you mind then telling me what your problem is this morning?"

She wonders if other husbands, other men, would say other things. Things so much nicer, things so much more along the lines of, *Is everything okay? Is our daughter okay? And you, sweetheart, are you okay? Is there something, some sort of help that you need?* Would Aubrey say something like that if he were not a hoarder, and most likely a habitual taker, of prescription painkillers? How long has he been in the basement? *Months now,* she thinks, *longer.*

"I was in the workroom last night," she says. He looks up at her, right at her. "And I found all the bottles, all the pills. And maybe there's a good reason, maybe you want to tell it to me?" She pauses, she waits. "And if not, well I don't know, but I think either way, I think we should talk." Aubrey exhales and doesn't say anything for a minute and Stephanie waits, waits for him to say it's nothing, waits for him to say that everything will actually be fine.

"I can't deal with this right now," he says quickly, bending down to put on his shoes.

"Aubrey, listen," she says.

"No, Stephanie," he says, loud enough and sharp enough so that she's sure the sound will reach Ivy downstairs, instantly undoing all the soothing and educational doings of *Baby Van Gogh*. Or Mozart. "You listen. It's a basement, not a workroom. And I really can't deal with this right now. I'm late. I've got a huge few days coming up right now. Can we just talk about this when I get back?" he asks, except it's not really a question. So she doesn't answer him. For a moment when she first saw the socks, and the suitcase, she thought that he was leaving, really leaving. Granted, he was leaving with only three pairs of underwear, but he was leaving all the same. And for the instant that she thought that, it did feel awful, just not quite as awful as she would have guessed.

"Alright," he says, as if together they have reached some sort of mutual, beneficial-to-everyone agreement. He hauls his suitcase off the bed, wheels it across the hardwood floors. "Thanks, Stephanie, we can talk about this in three days."

She doesn't say anything. She waits five minutes, standing in their room. She thinks if she went downstairs right now that getting into her SUV and backing it over Aubrey, since he is already filled with prescription painkillers, would seem like a very viable option. She waits for the feeling to pass, and even after she's heard his car pull away, it's still lingering. And then it's gone. And then she goes downstairs to get Ivy.

Once Ivy is safely secured in her high chair, making a game attempt at placing her entire plastic yellow dish in her mouth, Stephanie asks her favorite rhetorical question, "Do you want some mashed bananas?" and she wonders if maybe she could mash some bananas for Aubrey and then, when he gets back from Chicago, she could say, "Here, Aubrey, here, have some of this." And maybe the potassium, because bananas are so high in potassium, could make it so that he had a little more energy, had a little more spring in his step, could give him that little bit of pep he seems to so desperately need. And then, the way you realize things in dreams, when you're pretty sure everything might not be really happening, and eventually you'll wake up, she realizes that these thoughts of giving Aubrey mashed bananas aren't new. She's thought them all before, when she didn't know what was wrong with him, when she had no idea why he was this way. Now she knows. And she knows that bananas won't help.

"Aubrey, honey, here, have a banana. It has some wonderful energy-giving qualities, and let's talk about the fact that there are upwards of forty empty bottles of prescription pain medicines in your unplugged mini-fridge, let's talk about the fact that in all likelihood what's been going on here is that night after night, weekend after weekend, you've been taking every opportunity you can get to go down there, take Vicodin, and stare at the computer?" just doesn't have the right ring to it.

The phone rings, and Ivy says, "Da," and Stephanie knows at once that it's Aubrey on the phone, that he hasn't even gotten to the train station yet and he's calling to say he's turned around, and he's on his way back. He's calling to say that yes, he's got a problem, as she has probably already surmised from the vast multitude of prescription bottles that he was hoarding down there in the workroom, or now we're calling it a basement, in what had to have been a gigantic, enormous (really, Stephanie, it was enormous that's what it was) cry for help. He's calling to say, I want your help. He's calling to say, with your help, we'll get through this, we absolutely will.

"Hello?" she says.

"Stephanie, hi. It's Caryn. Do you know Melissa Quinn? I think you've met? She actually lives right down the street from you, on the other side of Linwood? She and I are going to power-walk over to Starbucks? It's such a nice morning. Do you want to come with?"

Stephanie looks at Ivy, drooling sweetly in her high chair. She looks around at her beautiful kitchen, opening up into the family room. And she can't think of anything to say. "Okay," she says, "okay."

* * *

Once they've all power-walked and are sitting in the window at Starbucks, once they've moved one of the large, inviting chairs to make room for the three strollers, and once everyone is in possession of a large amount of caffeine in a white cardboard cup, Caryn turns to Stephanie and asks what must be a completely normal question. It's the kind of question a person might ask another person whom they have recognized as normal, like them, as one-half of a perfectly normal, you could even say golden, couple.

"What are you guys up to this weekend?"

And the correct answer, the truthful answer, would of course be, "Oh, me, you know not a lot, I'll just be swimming alone in a sea of despair."

"Oh, you know," Stephanie says, "not a lot, Aubrey's at an Internet conference of some sort in Chicago."

"They have conferences on the weekends?" Melissa asks.

"Yes, this one's on the weekend," Stephanie says as the pit in her stomach, the one that's been there for a while now, gets a bit darker, more solid than it already was. She hadn't thought of that. How many things has she not thought of? "I think they're golfing tomorrow or something," she continues, "and then on Monday and Tuesday they have meetings." That could be it.

"What does your husband do again?" Melissa asks, and Stephanie would like to find a way to be able to say, it's not a great day, really it's not a great time.

"He works in sports marketing," she says, and she wants to just leave it at that. Really, she does.

"Of course," Melissa says, nodding happily, as if the whole world isn't falling apart. "He's very sporty looking. I hope you don't mind me saying this, but your husband is just so cute and sporty."

"No, I don't mind you saying that," Stephanie says.

"That he is," Caryn adds in, and Stephanie smiles, sure he is. Or at least he used to be, cute and outdoorsy and sporty, before he was someone who merely dressed himself in Patagonia and EMS to then spend the rest of the day in his workroom (or are we calling it a basement now?) taking pills and doing God knows what else. *God knows what else,* she thinks, and wonders if it's possible that there could be more.

"You guys are originally from the South, right?" Melissa asks, and the word *relentless* pops into Stephanie's head.

"Uh, no," Stephanie says, "Aubrey's from Connecticut and I grew up in D.C."

"D.C.'s a great city," Caryn offers, and this is just a conversation, this is just what people do, when they sit at Starbucks with their strollers.

"It's nice," Stephanie says.

"Are your parents still there?" Melissa inquires.

"My mom lives there," Stephanie says. "My dad lives in France." As soon as the words are out of her mouth almost automatically, she thinks, *Except that's not true, except that's a lie.* She thinks of how many lies there must be, wonders if anything she thought was real yesterday will actually turn out to be true.

"That's so cool," Caryn says, "I didn't know that."

Stephanie smiles. Yesterday she thought her husband was having an affair because she never lost the baby weight, yesterday she would have liked that to be a lie. Today she doesn't think it would be so bad if that were true. She pushes absent-mindedly at the stroller, sitting side by side with Caryn and Melissa, who are both doing the same thing. They all look alike. They look like suburban moms and how long has she been a suburban mom, and how long has she wanted to be?

"Do you get to France to visit a lot?" Melissa asks.

"No," Stephanie says, "you know, not so much." She stares out the window at the people strolling by on the street, the people not in here, not inside Starbucks.

Caryn's daughter, Ashley, wakes up right then, and Stephanie thinks that's good, that's a blessing because she doesn't want to talk about Aubrey anymore. And she doesn't want to talk about France. For the life of her, she can't imagine why she brought that up. Except that maybe it makes it easier to understand, easier to wrap your head around how much you have been lied to as of late, if you've been doing some lying yourself. Caryn reaches over and pulls Ashley out of the stroller and takes off her jacket. Stephanie watches, expecting the baby, once she has emerged, to be decked. She often is. She's a baby frequently seen in smocked dresses, even just for a day around the house, a stroll, or a trip to sit in the front right corner of Starbucks. Today though, Ashley is resplendent in a long-sleeved white T-shirt that says *NEW!* written in white on top of a green field. The green field is one of those shapes so often associated with comic books. A cloud that has jagged pointed edges, and if it were a comic book you might see in it *BAM!* or *POW!* but here, *NEW!*

"Cute shirt," Stephanie observes.

"Thanks," Caryn says, her voice an octave or two higher than it normally is, her gaze focused completely, adoringly on Ashley. She reaches out a hand, spreads her fingers wide, and places her outstretched palm on Ashley's chest, right over the *NEW!* and leaves it there. Ashley never takes her eyes from her mother's. She makes a few quick jerking movements, and says quickly, "Gah."

"She *is* a cutie," Melissa chimes in.

Stephanie wonders which came first, the drugs, or the rest of it, if there is a rest of it. Maybe it's just the drugs, though somewhere in some other reality, perhaps the one she's tried so hard not to be a part of, she can hear someone saying to her, *It's never just the drugs, Stephanie.*

"Stephanie?"

"What's that?" Stephanie says, confused for a moment, blinking, disoriented, taking a moment to make sure that it wasn't Caryn or Melissa saying to her, "It's never just the drugs,

Stephanie." She's pretty sure it wasn't because after all it's not as if she's told Caryn about the drugs. Of course she hasn't told Caryn. If she's not going to tell Meredith, if she's gone to such great lengths (she can't even think about it) not to tell Meredith, she's certainly not going to tell Caryn.

"I said, how's it going on the Zone?"

"The Zone?" she repeats. Caryn smiles and nods. Stephanie looks for a moment at Ivy. She focuses in on her sleeping face, her little self wrapped inside a blanket, inside her stroller, and it does help, just to see her there, just to know that with everything else, she does exist. And if Caryn and Melissa weren't right there, she thinks she'd thank her.

"Steph?" Caryn says again, and there's a mixture there that's so easy to point out, an almost equal division of impatience and concern. "Are you okay?"

"Oh, sorry. I'm just so tired," she answers, willing herself to stop thinking, willing herself to take her own best advice, to not think so much about everything. Because, really, and she's always thought so, it's as good advice as any. Melissa and Caryn nod in agreement. And she thinks that's nice of them, and she thinks, really they're nice, they're okay. "You know, I don't think I'm doing so well with the Zone." Only she was, she actually really was, but then everything happened. Even though it wasn't as if anything actually happened, it was more that what had been happening for a long time (how long?) was finally revealed.

"Did you try the Zone Perfect Delivery?" Caryn asks. Stephanie looks to both of them again, and she thinks if she were a different type of person she could tell them. Maybe not the whole story, because she's not sure she even knows it herself, but she could tell part of it, something.

"I'm having a little trouble with perfect right now," she says instead and they think she's just referring to the Zone, to the delivery service, but in a way she thinks it's the biggest admission she's ever made.

"It can get hard, figuring out all the ratios, which is why I'm a fan of the delivery service," Caryn says. Stephanie nods.

"Do you know the Zone made my hair fall out?" Melissa offers.

"I thought that was the South Beach Diet?" Caryn asks her, quite seriously.

Melissa looks back at her blankly for a moment. "You know, maybe it was. It can get kind of hard to keep track."

"It can," Caryn concedes.

"Maybe it was the South Beach Diet. Either way, losing the baby weight is just really hard," Melissa says.

And for a moment, a moment that maybe she'll look back on as blissful, Stephanie forgets everything for a second and adds in, "I mean look at Grace, she never really looked as good after she had her baby."

"Grace from *Will & Grace* you mean?" Caryn asks.

"Uh-huh," Stephanie says.

"Yes," Melissa says, "I know *exactly* what you mean." And they all stare out the window, and Stephanie thinks that maybe, when this is all over, she and Melissa might be friends.

"Anyway," Melissa says after a while, "do you know what I'm doing now, and I *love* it?"

"What?" Caryn asks. Stephanie is listening.

"French Women Don't Get Fat."

"I've heard great things," Caryn says, nodding her approval.

"Hmm," Stephanie says, "maybe I'll try it." As she says it, she thinks that maybe this, the baby weight, as hard as it has been to fix, maybe it'll be the easy thing. Maybe out of all the things that need fixing, this is the only one she can.

*   *   *

As soon as they leave Starbucks, as soon as they each go their separate ways, to spend the rest of their weekends with their husbands or whatever it is they're going to do, Stephanie heads right over to Bookends and picks up a copy of *French Women Don't Get Fat* from the large kiosk right by the cash register. It's a pretty book, pink with a nice illustration of a woman on the cover, a woman who isn't fat. She pays for the book and they put it in a bag for her. She pushes Ivy's stroller with one hand, and holds on to the book with the other. She has this feeling. This feeling like, with both hands, she's holding on for dear life.

twelve

db sweeney

Meredith pulls on a sweatshirt. She pairs it with a pair of black microfiber/fleece combo pants that she ordered from the Athleta catalogue and has, ever since, been quite in love with. She laces up her Nikes, the same ones from before, the ones you could run in, were you so inclined. Athletic clothes. As she roots around for her keys, she thinks she should, especially with the weight loss goals and all, endeavor to be more athletic. An endeavor perhaps larger than an outfit. Not triathalon training or anything, she doesn't think she'd have to go that far. Though it certainly wouldn't fall inside the areas of her expertise, she imagines that what with the swimming and the running and the biking, and quite a lot of it, that training for a triathalon would take a fair amount of time. And, really, who has that kind of time? So, somewhere between an outfit and a triathalon.

To Barnes & Noble, she thinks as she heads out the door, *The Atkins Diet Revolution.*

"Hi," she says softly as she walks by the doorman. They don't actually open the doors here. If they did, she'd have more to say, she could say, "Thank you," of course, for opening the door. The doormen here, they more sit behind a desk. She's not sure which doorman it is today, and it's not because she's oblivious, it's more that she's just never had a strong relationship with the doormen, porters, handymen, lobby staff who rotate through her building. She isn't the type to require a lot of help in the apartment. She can change a lightbulb or unclog a drain as well as the next person, and the staff seems to change a lot, that happens in the big buildings. It all seems so anonymous.

The air is cool as she walks out onto Third Avenue, and she remembers that it's now March. It's actually very nice out, considering it's March. Nice weather in New York doesn't happen nearly as often as you'd think it would, especially if you get your ideas about New York weather from watching all the movies set in New York, so many of them taking place in the midst of some really beautiful weather. It's not like that, not nearly often enough. Remembering her recent thoughts on athleticism, she decides to walk across the park, over to the West Side, to the Barnes & Noble right by Ouest. She wonders now if maybe there was a reason she kept getting out on that corner by mistake. And anyway, she does like the Upper West Side.

It's true, she does long to call neighborhoods in New York other than the Upper East Side her own—she's had her moments with many of them—but with the Upper West Side, it's different; it's more now than just longing, it's crossed the line from longing to lust. Years ago, she never would have predicted it. Years ago, in fact, when she felt romantically inclined toward Gramercy, toward lower Fifth Avenue and University Place, she wasn't particularly interested in the Upper West Side. She didn't think there were any good restaurants there, even though that wasn't actually true as Picholine had been there forever, as had Café des Artistes, and even Café Luxembourg.

But yet, she thinks, as she heads west, entering the park, and veering off the path, *look at the restaurants there now.* Ouest, of course, and Aix, Telepan, and 'Cesca, Per Se, and an outpost of Rosa Mexicano. She could do an entire series, a survey if you will, on Upper West Side restaurants. She should move there.

She fishes her iPod out of her bag. Have mini iPod, will travel. She pauses for a moment, considering if she should select a certain artist, album, or mix. She usually does, but there's something in the air, the air that feels so much like springtime (and for someone who doesn't exactly love winter that feels a little bit like freedom). As she heads through Central Park, in a burst of spontaneity, she selects *Shuffle.* That John Denver is currently playing does of course make her question the whole "leaving the music selection to chance" decision, but she doesn't let herself regrab the iPod and rearrange it. Instead, she pulls her sunglasses out of her bag and puts them on as John Denver sings, *"I'll walk in the rain by your side."*

She approaches the large intersection at Seventy-ninth Street and Broadway, the one with the Apthorp building (which she loves) on one corner and a Gothic stone church on the other. Right as she's crossing, suddenly her attention is caught. A small tent has been set up right in front of the church, in the small space that's there, just to the side of the subway entrance. This tent, it's the kind that doesn't have sides or walls, just the top. It's red and white striped and has red triangular flags hanging down from the edges, the types of flags that always put Meredith in mind of just-opened manicure shops. And also, this tent, it seems to be magnetic, the way it's pulling at her. Meredith has to pause for a moment and very seriously contemplate if the metal poles that are holding up the red and white striped material, if actually they are made of magnets and it is she who is made of metal in the manner of the Tin Man. She's not really the type to say, *Oh, look at the tent,* she's always been the type to just walk past, and she's always been okay with that. And yet here she is, feeling so pulled. If she were in a science fiction novel, the words "right into the center of its vortex" would surely make an appearance. And so she goes there, to the tent.

There are four long tables set up inside the tent, along each of the four sides. The tables have blue plastic tablecloths over them. There are different banners, and cages with dogs in them, and there is quite a lot of barking. Along one side there is a banner larger than all the others: *NYC Loves Dogs Adoption Day.*

And then she sees him.

There, directly in front of her, under a banner that says *DCNY Rescue,* at the table that is by far the quietest of the four, she sees him, this tiny sausage-shaped creature, peering out from between the bars of a metal makeshift pen. He really does seem to be staring right at her. She's quite sure of it. And the way he stares, it is so purposeful. There is such focus, but with a touch, just around the edges, of concern. She makes a beeline across the tent, directly to him. His pen has been placed on the table so she only has to bend down halfway to be exactly on his level.

"Hello," she says softly, and behind him, she can see his little tail wag. The wag is not exuberant; it's cautious, just once to the right and once to the left. Zip zip, and then it's still. He is rather short of leg, but he seems so long on personality, and on wisdom. Meredith looks into his chocolate-brown eyes, so soulful, she thinks, so dark. Dogs for her are not like restaurants or New York neighborhoods or what's on her iPod and what song, exactly, will play next; dogs aren't something she knows a lot about. But she thinks she remembers hearing once that staring right into a dog's eyes could be considered, by the dog, to be an act of aggression. As this little dog's eyes sparkle back at her, she thinks whoever said that must have been wrong. She doesn't think she's ever had an easier time staring into anyone's eyes. And she doesn't think she's met anyone yet who has made such an effortless, flawless, unhindered go at staring back into hers.

His eyes, they really do sparkle, don't they? As she takes a step back, the sausage-shaped dog, he gets up on his hind legs for a moment, a thoroughly charming moment, and from there he moves his two front paws forward in a swoop. She thinks, were it not for the makeshift pen between them, she could have just received five, a low five, but five all the same. She's heard that some dogs, if you take the time to pay the right kind of attention to them, will smile at you, and she thinks this one just has.

She regards him as he settles back down onto four paws with an exuberant toss of his head. He looks back up at her brightly, intently, and when she sees his expression, she is immediately put back in mind of the word *purpose*. She thinks he surely does have an important purpose and that he is aware of that, and for a moment she forgets everything else.

Oh, she thinks, as he raises his paw again. She wonders if she's ever truly been in love prior to this moment. Because never before in her thirty-three years has she ever looked into a pair of eyes, has she ever looked at anything, and felt like such a goner.

"Hello." Meredith hears this and she gets very nervous, because for a second she thinks she might have just heard the dog say hello, but as she looks up, she sees that two women have materialized behind the table as if from nowhere. One is very tall and slender, born with Leslie-like genes, though without the fashion sense. The other is shorter, plumper. Meredith wishes she hadn't just used the adjective *plump*. It would be so much better if she hadn't thought that. She thinks to herself, just call her the shorter one, the one with frizzy hair, the one wearing overalls without any irony at all.

They step out from behind the table and come at Meredith from their two different directions, and Meredith has the distinct sensation that they are gliding toward her. She takes a step back.

"Hello," they each say, and it is almost in unison but not quite, the sound is not a chorus but an echo, and Meredith notices that each of the two women, dressed so similarly, are both wearing white buttons that say in red and blue letters, *DCNY*. She doesn't know what DCNY stands for; she wonders if this tent is political. She hadn't thought so, and she hopes it isn't.

"Hi," she says cautiously. "Can I ask what DCNY stands for?"

"Yes, of course, it stands for Dachshund Club of New York."

"Oh," she says and a lightbulb goes on over her head, *Yes, of course he's a dachshund, I should have known.* Yet, as she takes another look at him (look at those ears, those eyes) the lightbulb sputters. Should she have known, really? It's not as if it's *so* obvious. She isn't sure he is in fact the type of dog a person would look at and say, *Oh, dachshund!* "So, is he a dachshund?"

The women exchange glances. The taller woman inhales in a way that could be called dramatic, and looks Meredith squarely in the eye.

"He's part wirehaired dachshund. Mini wirehaired dachshund. We *think*."

For a moment, Meredith lingers on all the emphasis placed on *think,* but not for long. Before she realizes she has even moved, she is back, directly outside the makeshift pen, looking into those deep, ever-expressive eyes and inquiring, "Are you a mini-mini wirehaired dachshund?" in a voice she doesn't recognize. It is such a higher voice than her own, it is so much sweeter; it's the voice of a much nicer person than Meredith. *Oh,* she thinks, *his eyes.*

The shorter one has something to say. "We think he has quite a lot of terrier in him, too. It's important that you know that. Because he's got some of the temperament of a terrier." Meredith nods; she's aware she is twirling on her hair.

"Norwich terrier, we'd say," adds the taller one, who seems to prefer to speak in the plural, and then as if she somehow knows that Meredith has thus far been referring to them in her mind as the taller one and the shorter one, she extends her hand and adds, quite officially, in a way that almost doesn't sound as if it was said too late, "I'm Ellen, and this is Barb."

"Hi, Ellen, Barb, nice to meet you."

The shorter one (that's Barb) she has something to say again. "Interested?" she asks softly, coyly, almost as if it's a calculated attempt at subtlety and finesse, "In adopting him?" She hadn't thought of actually being interested in him, so much as just being inexplicably drawn to him. But therein lies the very boiled-down essence of interest, doesn't it? The sauce of interest, perfectly reduced.

"It's a really nice thing to do; you'll be saving a life," Ellen adds, as if it were even needed, as if along with subtlety and finesse, threats of impending dachshund-terrier doom were crucial to sealing the deal. Meredith pauses for a moment, takes stock of the situation, and thinks, really thinks, of this little tiny creature. He's actually not *so* little. You probably wouldn't carry him in a bag. She's not even sure the dachshund part is mini, to tell you the truth, but who is she to argue? Yet looking at him, there's something about his body, his face, his concerned expression that makes a person not normally inclined to using such words as *little*, as *tiny*, suddenly feel quite unable *not* to say them. *Little tiny baby dog.* She thinks how she could be saving his life, and how, like the taller one, Ellen, said, that's a really nice thing to do. She thinks maybe when it comes down to it, she doesn't do that many nice things. Maybe she could start. Maybe she could reinvent herself.

"Um," she begins, "what exactly happened to him? Why is he here?" No matter how caught up in infatuation, in dog love,

she may be at this moment, a person so programmed to planning everything out, days, months, years in advance, gets a bit
overwhelmed in the face of such spontaneity. Hers is the mind
that right about now gets a picture in it of a mad, rampaging
mini dachshund, a rabid Norwich terrier.

"We believe," Ellen explains, "that his people became estranged and could no longer care for him."

"I see," Meredith says, and she does, and even in the midst of
all this, she can't help lingering, the way she sometimes lingers on
a certain word. *Estranged.* That's what she is, too. She and
Stephanie were already estranged, even before Stephanie said it,
even before she deemed the time to be nigh for them to take a
break. They were already estranged, and they just didn't know it.

"The people who had him?" Meredith asks, just to be sure
she heard right, wondering if it happened slowly, if it snuck up
on them without their even realizing it. "They're estranged?"

"Uh, yes, but it's not as if they've been in contact. The dog
has actually been with us for a while, so there isn't an option of
his returning to his former home. If you're interested, you
wouldn't have to worry about that, that his previous people
would want him back." And she hadn't actually been worried
about that, though she can't imagine how anyone, regardless of
whether or not they were estranged, could give up this dog. It
happens, you have to roll with it, don't give up your dog because of it. *What is wrong with people?* Meredith wonders. It's
a question she's had to ask much more often lately.

She looks again into his eyes; they are still fixed on her. The
way he's looking at her, it's not frantic, it's not wild and crazy
or like that dog on TV constantly freaking out over Snausages

or some such packaged doggie snack. He's not saying, *Oh my God, person, get me the hell out of here now!* He's so much calmer than that, so much wiser than that, he's just sort of looking at her. She's pretty close to certain that the way he's looking at her right now, it's very wise, it's very sagelike, it's not as if he's looking for assurance of rescue, it's so much more as if he's in receipt of that already. It's as if he is saying with his beautiful brown soulful eyes, *It's all okay, it's all going to be fine. Really.*

"We think there might be some Norwich terrier—that's a terrier," Barb adds on.

"Yes, you mentioned that," Meredith says.

"That or, you know, it could be a Scotty dog—that's a Scottish terrier, if you're not familiar with the term *Scotty dog.*"

"Uh-huh." She nods. She is familiar with the term *Scotty dog* as she imagines most people are, but she won't point that out; she doesn't want to be discourteous, because these people have, she realizes as an unfamiliar warmth spreads through her chest, something she wants.

"And we think there may be some corgi. Welsh Pembroke corgi," Ellen adds. She then looks toward Barb, and the two women nod at each other with what looks so much like expectancy in their eyes. Meredith thinks she sees Barb mouth, *might as well,* to Ellen, but she can't be sure.

"There could be some Chihuahua, but that's really just hearsay." *Hearsay? Heard what? Said who?* Meredith thinks as she somehow manages to snap back to some sort of reality, to tear herself away from those *eyes.*

"Okay, so let me get this straight, he's a wirehaired dachshund—"

"Mini," Barb says. Meredith decides Barb is on thin ice. How quickly people seem to find a way to get there.

"Right," Meredith agrees as nicely as she can, "A *mini* wirehaired dachshund–Norwich perhaps Scottish terrier, but definitely some sort of terrier–corgi–Chihuahua mix?"

"Welsh Pembroke corgi," says Barb.

"Right," says Meredith.

"Yes," says Ellen, and there's a pause, a pause of some significance, and Meredith can't help wondering, *Could there actually be more?* How far back do people actually go with mixed breed rescue dog lineage? She wouldn't have thought very far at all. But then she wouldn't have thought this was a conversation she'd ever be involved in, so maybe who's to say anything about expectations and where they do or do not lead? "But it's—it's a matter of some debate."

Clearly.

"We think you could be safe in saying a mini wirehaired dachshund–Norwich terrier mix," Ellen clarifies. "We think you'd be safe saying that."

We think you'd be safe, is all that Meredith hears. *We think you'd be safe,* that is all Meredith thinks when she looks at him, into those eyes. And so they don't really know what he is, exactly. If you think about it, a lot of people don't know who they are, exactly.

"Okay," she says, "I'd like to be with him," and then corrects, "Uh, I mean, I'd like to adopt him."

"That's wonderful," both women say in unison, and smile, and then, "The adoption fee is three hundred dollars."

"Oh, adoption fee?"

"Yes, it helps support the organization," they say, their smiles wide.

"Oh, right, okay. I just don't think I have that much cash on me. Do I have my checkbook?" she says to no one in particular, to her bag it would seem, as she begins to root around within it. When her search unearths no checkbook, she looks up at the mini wirehaired dachshund–Norwich terrier mix, and a dreadful thought occurs to her. What if when she leaves to the go to the cash machine, someone else comes and sees him? What happens then? Because even if they say they'll hold him, they might not. Because you know you can't always count on things being held, on things being there when you come back for them. You just can't.

She looks from him to the Chase machine in the lobby of the Apthorp right there on the opposite corner. She looks away from the Chase machine, back at him, and it's a feeling she may or may not be familiar with, she really can't tell, but she thinks there is no way she can leave him. And you know how loneliness knows Patrick Park's name? She wonders if maybe despair knows hers.

"Can I take him with me? Across the street to the bank machine? And then I'll come back with the cash?"

"We take debit cards," Ellen tells her brightly.

"Oh, do you?!" Meredith exclaims, "Oh, do you, wow! Oh, great, oh that's really, really great," she says, and there it is again, that voice, the one that's so much nicer, the one she's now heard twice. She happily hands over her debit card, and she thinks of the Chase commercials, how there's one where a young woman, just arrived in the city, gets a new job and a checking account and soon after, a bulldog. She thinks how recently she's seen posters for Chase ATMs with a man walking a Jack Russell terrier, and this dog, her dog, is part terrier, that's important to remember, and she thinks she always knew there was a reason she was quite content (especially for someone who doesn't spend a lot of time in a state that could fall under the general umbrella of content) banking at Chase.

Ellen runs her card through their old-fashioned credit card contraption, the kind that rubs some carbon paper over the card in a quick swipe. Click, click. She listens to it going back and forth instantly over her credit card and as they hand her the three-paged carbon slip, she signs her name, pausing for a moment before she does, to make sure a cursive version of someone else's name doesn't appear out of the pen accidentally. That happens sometimes. The despair—she's sure that's what it was—isn't part of her anymore. It flows out of her body, exiting gracefully through her fingertips, the tips of her toes; she thinks for a second that she can feel it, sparking like electricity, leaving once and for all, out of the top of her tingling head.

"We're so glad you came along," Barb says and Meredith nods, agreeing wholeheartedly.

"We have felt he was one of the most underrated dogs at our shelter," Ellen adds, and Meredith has to keep herself from saying that perhaps that could be because they didn't exactly give him the hard sell and rather really only harped on the fact that he was a terrier, saying *terrier* in the way you might say *maraud-*

ing demon of death. That could have contributed to his being, as they say, underrated. And then she thinks of Stephanie.

"What do you think you'll call him?"

And she doesn't really hear because her mind is back in Washington, D.C., back in high school, and Stephanie is monopolizing the VCR to watch *The Cutting Edge* a third time and then a fourth. And it was this thing with Stephanie, and it will still come up more than you would think; it has been so many times that she's heard Stephanie declare that DB Sweeney is the most underrated actor of his generation.

"I'm sorry, what?"

"What do you think you'll call him?" Barb asks a second time.

"Oh, right, yes. I know what I'm going to call him. I'm going to call him DB Sweeney."

They smile at her a bit blankly; they nod. They put a leash on DB Sweeney. Barb reaches in and picks him up, and hands him to Meredith, and she smiles. They give her a five-pound bag of Iams kibble and tell her that Iams is the best by far and that she shouldn't consider changing brands but if she must indeed consider such a thing, she must only mix in 10 percent of the new offending and poorly chosen food at a time. They provide her with a purple and black stuffed shoe that squeaks and appears to be covered in carpet lint. It has their scent on it she is told, he likes it, so he should have it with him while he adjusts, and Meredith's voice changes again and she becomes the nicer Meredith and she looks at the dog, *her* dog, at DB Sweeney and she asks him, "Do you like your shoe? Do you?" She thanks each of the women again, twice, gathers her things in one hand and DB's leash in another, and together, they turn to go.

*   *   *

In her lobby, the doorman and the porter both depart from their usually vague nodding, there is actual getting up from their stations even without the presence of bags to be helped with or packages to sign for. They welcome DB Sweeney, who wags his tail at them happily, bestowing a sufficient amount of adorableness.

"He's a new little fella, huh?" asks the close-to-burly man with close-cropped gray hair who sits behind the desk and is technically, Meredith thinks, the doorman.

"He is," Meredith says, smiling. "His name is DB Sweeney," she offers, stealing a glance at his name tag. *Steve,* she reads and thinks surely he must be new, surely it's not that he's been here a long time and she's never known his name. Everyone smiles, DB Sweeney wags his tail and looks wise at the same time. There's only a very slight moment of awkwardness—after they have discussed DB Sweeney, where he came from, how he is a mini wirehaired dachshund–Norwich terrier mix—in which there isn't anything to say. Meredith smiles again, and as soon as she tightens her grip on his leash, DB Sweeney seems to know and marches, swaggers almost, *left right left right left right left right* up to the elevator bank.

The first thing that DB Sweeney does when they walk into the apartment is turn around and look at Meredith, right into her eyes, for what feels like a long time. It's not the kind of long time that you wish would end soon, it's the kind where you feel it would be okay if it kept going on for a while.

"This is home," Meredith says and she tries to infuse the word with warmth and safety.

He turns his head back to face forward and stands just in front of her, still by the door, surveying his surroundings. Slowly, alternately sniffing the ground, the air above him and around him, he begins to investigate. He walks through the kitchen, throughout the living room, stopping outside closet doors that Meredith opens for him. He investigates the bedroom, the vanity, the bathroom. He returns to the living room and sits for a while in front of the armoire. Meredith, who has been following him around the apartment, both in awe of his summary and checking to make sure there is no danger that could befall him, anywhere, wonders if he knows the armoire is important because that's where the Bose iPod dock is, and where the speakers are. She thinks she should make a playlist for him, for when he's alone, and she doesn't want him to be alone.

After a while longer, after walking the length of the couch, along the top if it, DB Sweeney settles down on the corner section. He places his paws elegantly, gingerly in front of him and sighs. She hopes that it is not a sigh of resignation, but rather one of accomplishment, one of "I surveyed my surroundings and now I will rest within them." She hopes so. Meredith walks the few steps over to the couch, and stands in front of the corner section. In the very back of her mind, she remembers that she didn't quite make it to Barnes & Noble, that she didn't get the Atkins book, that she didn't take the first step she was going to take on her own. She's pretty sure it doesn't matter.

She kneels down, right in front of DB Sweeney. For the first time since Stephanie said, "Don't call me" (or maybe, even, it's been a bit longer than that), Meredith doesn't feel so alone. DB Sweeney looks up at her with his sharp, inquisitive, chocolate-brown eyes. He puts one paw out and then another, and repeats the motion a few times so he is slowly but surely dragging himself on his belly. He stops when he is right in front of her. He reaches his nose up and so gingerly, so tentatively, he licks Meredith's face. And then, with increasing sureness, he continues to lick. Buoyed, he soon has his front paws on each of Meredith shoulders. He's on his hind legs, still licking, wagging his tail so quickly as he proceeds.

For the first time in a really long time, Meredith starts to cry.

thirteen

women who lock themselves away and only eat leeks don't get fat

Stephanie wraps a towel around herself and walks quickly back into her bedroom. She glances at the baby monitor: all quiet on the Ivy front. And then her eyes fall again on the cover of the book. She'd brought it upstairs with her last night and had placed it, perhaps a bit reverentially, on the dresser. She places her hand flat against the dust jacket and swipes at it, even though there's no possible way there could be any dust. She looks at the cover, at the slender French stick figure marching across it, a lithe illustration to guide her way, to shine a light upon her darkness. *French Women Don't Get Fat.*

She puts the book down and changes quickly into some comfortable Sunday clothes. She pulls on loose black loungy bottoms and an old Lehigh sweatshirt. She can't remember where she picked up this sweatshirt that has long been her favorite; she doesn't know anyone who went to Lehigh and it has no sentimental value. She looks at herself in the mirror, also quickly, at what she still thinks of as Sunday clothes, loungy clothes, even though now, more and more often, such an ensemble will make an appearance Monday through Friday, to say nothing of Saturday. She pulls her still-wet hair back into a loose ponytail and hurries downstairs to boil her leeks.

To tell you the truth, she didn't read the whole book.

There was a lot in the introduction about food preparation. A lot of things about food preparation tend to be off-putting to Stephanie, especially now. And then there was this part about how you aren't supposed to read or even watch TV or look at the computer (even something other than UrbanBaby) while you are eating. Stephanie reads the newspaper while she is eating. It's the only time she can find in the entire day to do so. When would she read the newspaper? And *then* there was this whole thing about how there was no glory in quick weight loss. Really, she was certain there was. It was right about then that she'd started to lose hope.

But then—then!—as soon as she had disconsolately skipped ahead just a few pages, she got to the beautiful section about the "Magical Leek Weekend." As had in fact been mentioned to her before, what you're supposed to do is boil up two pounds of leeks and eat only leeks and drink the leek juice for forty-eight hours. It "recasts" you and magically gets you to a place where you can eat delicious foods for pleasure. In the glow of the light from the end of the tunnel, Stephanie did wonder if maybe the "Magical Leek Weekend" might also make her, in the manner of French women everywhere, chic. Seeing as it was magical and all. In addition to not getting fat, she didn't imagine French women often became slovenly and unkempt either, didn't imagine French women spent a lot of time in a faded Lehigh sweatshirt, whose origins are a mystery, and leggings.

Once she's gotten the two pounds of leeks clean, and it takes a really long time to get two pounds of leeks clean, Stephanie boils them up, thinking all the while that there is indeed glory in quick weight loss and that such glory will be hers at the end of a mere forty-eight hours.

* * *

She doesn't know if it's all in her mind, but at the end of a mere two hours, she has a pounding headache. It is all she can do not to eat Ivy's various homemade baby foods and mashes, to take them right from her little baby hands, as she feeds her lunch.

By three o'clock, as Ivy is at last napping again, it is all Stephanie can do to lie listless in the family room, sipping leek broth, mesmerized by the vivid blues and reds and greens of *Baby Van Gogh*.

By nine-thirty she sits in the kitchen, filled with hostility. She makes herself an English muffin, and eats it. Thinking that the English muffin would have been better had she taken the time to spread something on it, she eats several large spoonfuls of the Le Pain Quotidien (French!) hazelnut spread that Meredith brought with her on her last visit. Next, she stands by the window and looks out as she eats some peanut butter right from the jar, enveloped by this new and yet somehow familiar sense of failure. She looks at a streetlamp and imagines they still live in the city, and there are lights twinkling everywhere. She rinses her plate and her two spoons before putting them in the dish-washer and turns to head upstairs.

The phone rings. She thinks maybe it's Meredith and thinks that she's the person she most wants to talk to in the world right now, but she can't. She thinks that like other people who live in this house, even if that word, *live*, is loosely defined, she just can't deal with this right now. But she doesn't know what else to do.

"Hello."

"Hey."

"Hey, Aubrey," she says, and she softens for a moment be-cause she forgets everything. How could she forget anything? How, after the months of the way he has been? And then she re-members, and she hardens. She thinks she has to, it has to go that way, there can't be any other way.

"I'm sorry," he says.

"Are you in Chicago?"

"No, I'm in the city. I got a room at the Athletic Club. I just needed to think. I just, I knew that you knew. I went down there and everything was out, and I saw it and saw it for what you must have seen and I had to get out of there, and I couldn't, I can't really talk to you about this. And I'm sorry. I'm so sorry, Stephanie."

"Aubrey," she says. *Oh, Aubrey,* she thinks and the things she feels—sympathy for him, an urge to protect him, sorrow—aren't what she wants to feel. She wants only to feel angry at him, to feel lied to, and let down, to feel abandoned and be-trayed. And she doesn't know what it might mean, what it might say about her, that she wants those things. "How long has this been going on?" she asks.

"A while," he answers vaguely.

"Since you had knee surgery?"

"Uh. Uh-huh."

"That's longer than Ivy's been alive," she says, and she says it softly because that makes it so much worse to her, and she wonders if it makes it so much worse to him, if anything does. "Why did you start?"

"Steph, I don't want to do this."

"I know."

"First, it *was* for the pain. And then it just, it just started as a way to take the edge off, you know?"

"I don't, Aubrey. I really don't."

"And then it just got to the point where everything was an edge. And then it got to the point where I just couldn't imagine my life without it. I'm going to stop. I'm not going to do it anymore."

She wishes for a manual, and she wishes for an instruction book. She pictures a paint-by-numbers book, with directions inside that are easy to follow. She wonders if something like that could help her.

"I think I should come home," he says after a while. And she thinks of Ivy. She thinks maybe she shouldn't be in the house with him. She wonders if maybe she should be in the house without him, if maybe he needs to stay in the city for a while, but that's a whole can of worms, isn't it? And it's a very visible can of worms, the kind that a lot of people in Ridgewood could see and she thinks that if she had a manual, in it, it would say, *Aubrey needs a therapist,* and she thinks she's thought that already before.

"I think you need to see someone."

"What?"

"Like a group or a therapist."

"God, Stephanie. I don't know."

"What?" she asks him. "What don't you know?"

"I never thought I'd be in therapy."

"Well, I guess we never thought a lot of things."

"I think I should come home."

"Will you see someone? I can find someone for you. I can help."

He doesn't say anything, and then he says, "Okay."

"Okay," she says to him, to too many things, even as she suspects that she shouldn't. *Okay* might not be what is suggested in the handy manual she would so like for there to be, if there were actually a book you could buy, *What to Do When Your Husband Is a Drug Addict.* Come to think of it though, maybe there is. She looks on the nightstand, at the most likely never-to-be-opened-again copy of *French Women Don't Get Fat,* and thinks there's a book for almost everything else.

"Okay, Aubrey," she says. "Okay."

fourteen

fun, interactive
activities

Meredith makes a right onto Fourth Street and heads down the block toward Knife + Fork where she'll be having the reasonably priced and quite inventive prix fixe menu. As she approaches, she's trying to remember if there were in fact a lot of carbs in the prix fixe menu the last time she visited. She doesn't think there were; she remembers being impressed with the quality of the meats and she remembers thinking good things about the vegetables. But the carbs, of course, they could have been there (as they have a way of being) and she could have just not paid attention to them. Because there was a time, a time that now seems so far away, when carbs weren't wrong, when their very existence didn't have to be fled from. There was a time. That time is not now.

In the two weeks since DB Sweeney's arrival, Meredith has come into possession of *Dr. Atkins' New Diet Revolution* (she ordered it online, next day delivery, sometimes it's just so much easier that way). She has not eaten more than twenty grams of carbs per day, and in case you've never actually jumped on the bandwagon that is Atkins, ten grams of carbs is about a cup of raw vegetables or a slice of tomato (which isn't allowed anyway, we'll explain that later). And she has to say for the record, it wasn't actually as hard as she thought it would be. She's prepared a variety of sausages and shared them with DB Sweeney. She's ordered bacon, egg, and cheese sandwiches at the deli on Lexington Avenue, right by the subway, the kind she had not ever considered eating before, even though she hadn't been dieting. They were just not something she felt a person should eat. But eat them she did after sliding the bacon, egg, and cheese from the roll, and giving the roll to DB Sweeney.

It was very unfortunate when after a week of Atkins, DB Sweeney threw up repeatedly and developed a bad case of diarrhea, possibly due to the Canadian bacon she'd taken to frying, or possibly due to the pork rinds (yes, really, pork rinds, which are an Atkins-approved snack), and she'd had to take him to the vet, who was nothing at all like the vet played by Chris O'Donnell on *Grey's Anatomy*, not in the slightest. The vet said DB Sweeney should perhaps lessen his intake of human food and had given him prescription Fantomycide, which was, he said, the equivalent of doggie Pepcid or doggie Zantac, if you will. He'd given it to her in a bottle that said DB Isley and she'd had to resist a strange and rather strong urge to tell him that DB Sweeney's last name was Sweeney.

It was upon contemplating that it was she who had driven her mini wirehaired dachshund–Norwich terrier mix to projectile vomiting and more than a little ill-timed diarrhea that her enthusiasm for the Atkins diet began to wane. And yet, she soldiers on. (But she no longer shares her Atkins food with DB Sweeney.)

She has rearranged her reviewing schedule. She's been drinking her coffee with heavy cream. She has found herself quite buoyed by the fact that a restaurant reviewer in New York could find steak houses to review until her cholesterol-addled heart was content, until the cows, quite literally, came home. And even though Knife + Fork is not a steak house, she feels she can persevere, can stay the course, even though last time she was here she'd been so impressed with the care that had been taken with the bread, how the charming waitress had gone to the trouble of explaining that all the baking was done right on the premises.

She has had a low, throbbing headache for the last two weeks straight. She has felt extremely fatigued, much more so than usual. She has felt a new, heightened sense of irritability for all matters not directly related to DB Sweeney or the acquisition of necessities for him (there are so many things to buy!). She has had a foul and sour taste in her mouth which she suspects might translate into the "meat breath" that was referenced in the book, along with a helpful suggestion to partake of some of the parsley surely served as the garnish on the potato (that could not be eaten) that came on the same plate as her porterhouse, rib eye, or butterflied filet. The parsley didn't help. She has lost five and a half pounds.

And five and a half pounds is not nothing.

Her cell phone starts to ring. She stops midstride, almost teetering off her calf-colored knee-high high-heeled boots, the ones she bought knowing she would never wear in real life. Among the many merits of spending so much of your time in disguise, pretending to be someone else, is being able to buy things you'd never actually wear, because even if you wouldn't, there's a chance that someone wearing a wig and carrying a credit card that says either Abby, May, Emily, or Sarah would. She grabs the phone quickly (it's about to ring twice!) and glances at the display. *Private number.* She hates that. It could be the restaurant about her reservation, so to be on the safe side, she scans her memory quickly to recall which name she used for her reservation tonight, which credit card she slipped into the front section of her wallet before she left her apartment and a slightly forlorn looking DB Sweeney.

"This is May," she says, with sureness, with confidence.

"This is bullshit!" comes the speedy and somewhat venomous reply.

She can picture him, there behind his gigantic glass desk, the East River shimmering through the floor-to-ceiling windows behind him, his expensive suit, a custom-made shirt with his initials stitched under the pocket, the deliberate cuff links, the product-heavy hair worn too long, the beginnings of a double chin, the beady eyes. *Doogie,* she thinks, almost reflexively. Doogie is also known as Douglas Harris, editor in chief of *The NY,* but Meredith had determined at some point previous that calling him, mostly only in her mind, Doogie, sometimes makes his offensive and expletive-laden existence a bit easier to take/exist with/work for. She starts to tuck her hair behind her ears and then remembers she's wearing a wig, the shoulder-length, very light blonde one, and hopes she hasn't knocked it off-kilter. She puts her hand on her hip, mostly to keep it away from her hair, and also, a little bit to steady herself. She clears her throat quickly. "Hi, Douglas."

"I've got copy on my desk. Your next two reviews. The Palm? Meredith? What is innovative or new or interesting or happening or hip or alive or now about the Palm?" he says it all very quickly, as if it is one word, one sought-after media concept, *Hiporaliveornow.* "Except for the fact that you can walk there from the office, what are you doing at the Palm, and why for the love of fucking I don't know what are you writing a review of it?"

Meredith clears her throat, "Douglas, you'll see that I've sent two reviews and the one after that is—"

"Fucking Sparks! Are you fucking kidding me? Did you get a fucking time machine and go back to 1990? Meredith, we don't pay you to write reviews about restaurants people don't want to read reviews about. We pay you to be innovative, to be industrious, to go to new places. And I'm reading these reviews? Did you fucking eat anything other than the steak? Because the descriptions of that are the only parts that sound remotely fucking like you. They suck."

"I can understand that you're upset."

"I'm not upset," he says, rather calmly.

Okay. "I'm doing a survey of steak houses in New York," she says, speaking calmly and assuredly, partly in order to convey to Douglas and to herself that calmness is always an option, and partly to irritate him. "I'm starting with the old standbys, the Palm, Peter Luger's, etc., and I'm going to work my way up to the newer ones, to Dylan Prime—"

"Dylan Prime opened in fucking two thousand! Where the fuck were you in two thousand?"

"*And* all the way up to Craftsteak and to STK, which just opened. I thought I'd even do a sidebar of all the barbecue in the city, too."

"I think you should think again. I think you should get over Frank Bruni's survey of fast-food restaurants in the *Times* and stop wishing you'd done that and stop with the fucking surveys."

"I don't look at Frank Bruni's fast-food survey as something I need to get over."

"Oh, I do. But great job with your Ouest review, by the way."

"Thanks," she says as the world spirals around in the bizarre reality that is a conversation with her surely bipolar boss.

"But I digress. Start writing reviews of new restaurants, of ridiculous fucking restaurants, of places where readers who are hip and consumer-driven and have disposable income want to see and be seen, and give that to me and give that to me ASAP."

"Brasserie was on my list," she says, thinking it might mean something, might say something about hipness meeting steak. She's always thought that if you looked at it in the right way, at the very modernist bathrooms for starters, that Brasserie could be considered hip.

"I'm not even going to justify that with a response."

She'd like to tell him that it should be about the food. That it shouldn't be about the swankness of the place, the see-and-be-seen qualities of a restaurant. And she believes that; her reviews have always been more about the food than about the fabulousness, which is a word Douglas actually uses. But she can't really say that right now, because she hasn't actually eaten quite enough of the food. And even though he is for the most part an idiot, Douglas does have a point.

She stands on Fourth Street, the exact same person she was two weeks ago, in the exact same dress size, living the exact same life only in a different wig, only now she has turned in sub-par work, only now she has disappointed her boss. She wonders at how much of a price did those five and a half pounds actually come. She tries not to think horrible thoughts of how maybe Douglas has just saved her from embarrassing herself and her magazine by submitting a poorly researched review of an old standby steak house even if it is a New York classic. She tries not to stress out over how much more work she'll have to do in order to make up for all the time she has recently spent eating only protein.

"I have plenty of notes at home. I can e-mail you another re-view tomorrow."

"Why e-mail? Do you know you haven't been in the office at all for the last two weeks? What's the deal with that?" And she thinks that along with everything else, now might not be the best time to share with Douglas the news of the joyous arrival of DB Sweeney.

"I've been working from home," she says, stating perhaps the obvious, but it is, she thinks, something that might need to be stated. She has an office at the *The* NY offices, a very nice one actually, but in no way does she really have to be there. Con-tractually, she doesn't ever have to go to the office as long as she gets her reviews in on time, and yes, properly. Columnists, restaurant critics especially, who spend almost every night doing research aren't often expected to be in the office. Meredith was in many ways an exception to the rule, spending as much time as she did at her office.

Douglas doesn't say anything. She imagines that is because Douglas knows she is completely within her contractual rights to always work from home, and maybe he's wondering why, if that has always been the case, she's spent such a large part of the last few years at her desk.

She pauses for a moment and wonders about that, about the why of always being at the office. She thinks it might be because except for the purple velvet sectional couch, except for the electronics, she's never really liked her apartment. Until it was the place where DB Sweeney lived.

"Douglas, listen," she begins again, because he's still not saying anything. She pictures him, Montblanc pen in hand, doodling *fuck fuck fuck* all over his black leather Coach desk blotter. "I've got to go right now, I'm standing outside Knife + Fork, in the East Village," she pauses, lingers right after *East Village*, she hopes the East Village doesn't say "steak house" to Douglas, who has Manhattan neighborhoods labeled and judged and preconceived almost as much as she does. "I'm late for a reservation, so I've got to hang up now."

"What's this Knife + Fork?" he asks, ignoring any mention on her part of the conversation's need to end.

"It's a wonderful jewel of a restaurant on East Fourth Street. Lovely atmosphere, friendly service, fantastic prix fixe. They bake all their own bread," she says, knowing as she does that she sounds a bit like the lead-in to a rave review, and that is her intention. She thinks she mentions the bread (with which they really do a wonderful job, presenting it on a crafted piece of butcher block, with the highest quality olive oil and a smattering of sea salt) as a silent penance for trying to write all those reviews without eating any carbs. And she thinks she'll have to eat carbs again. She wonders if she really thought it through, if it occurred to her that dieting while being a restaurant critic would require perhaps quite a bit of integrity-compromising.

"It sounds interesting enough," he says dismissively, and she reminds herself she likes her job, really she does. She loves her job and she can't imagine not having it, at least not until the *New York Times* calls to tell her they are in fact very desirous of her talents, until she receives the call with an offer for a three-book deal on food, on restaurants, on cooking, until they sell the film rights and she becomes the star of her very own television show.

"Tonight's my third visit. I can have a review for you by midday."

"Good. E-mailed or in person?"

DB Sweeney, she thinks. "E-mailed," she says.

She turns back in the direction of the restaurant, envisions the imminent flipping shut of her phone—ending the call with Douglas, ending these thoughts of diet failure that again seem to be rearing their ugly snakelike heads—one quick motion that will bestow so much happiness even if it is so fleeting. Fleeting happiness, she wonders sometimes if it's better than none at all. She's starting to think so.

"Yeah," he says, and she waits, and so does he, for a beat, "I need a reservation at wd~50 for Tuesday."

"Not a problem," she says, and he says a quick goodbye and

disconnects. She flips her phone shut, noting that it did not bring quite as much satisfaction as she was hoping for; sometimes the things you look forward to don't. She carefully adjusts her wig and sees her friend Jill standing outside the restaurant, waiting, and she hopes she hasn't been waiting long. She hopes Jill remembers that tonight Meredith's name is May. Usually she finds Jill a bit annoying because of a childish fascination she's always had with cartoons. *The Lion King* often looms large in her conversations, the release of *Curious George: The Movie* was, for Jill, a very big deal. But tonight Meredith doesn't find that as annoying as she finds it convenient. She wants to ask Jill which channels on cable are best for locating cartoons and puppets at night. She's sure that's the best thing for DB Sweeney to be watching, to keep him company when she isn't there.

As she greets Jill and they enter the restaurant together, as they order their wine and their prix fixe dinners, even as she eats, even as she's making mental notes (and one or two slyly written in her notepad) she has an eye on the future, she can see her folder on her desk, the one with the notes from her last two visits here. She can see folders from other places, too, places where she ate carbs and where she did her job well. And she thinks if she puts her mind to it, she'll have a good review, an honest one, a real one, about Knife + Fork and if she spends some time after that, she's sure she could even write a few carbheavy spares. And she finds herself hoping that it won't take that long, looking through all the folders, scouring all the notes, because she'd like to be finished with it, she'd like very much to read this book she just bought, called *Beyond Fetch: Fun, Interactive Activities for You and Your Dog.*

fifteen

thunderstorm consolation

As a thunderstorm rages outside, a wheezing sound emanates from DB Sweeney as his partly wirehaired fur flies off him by the handful. Meredith holds him under his front two legs, trying to restrain him from his earlier endeavor of trying to climb, quite literally, right up the wall.

In *Beyond Fetch: Fun, Interactive Activities for You and Your Dog* there are a total of one hundred and nineteen activities, seven vacation tips, and sixteen craft projects. And out of all of that, out of that entire tome of doggy bonding, entertainment, and enrichment, there does not seem to be a section on what to do with your little friend when he is literally climbing the walls because the weather outside has turned inclimate. And inclimate, in his little doggy psyche seems to be the exact same thing as extremely frightful.

That gives Meredith an idea. "Oh, the weather outside is

frightful," she sings in what she hopes is a happy voice, "but the fire inside's delightful." Nothing.

Just to be clear, she does think *Beyond Fetch: Fun, Interactive Activties for You and Your Dog* is an excellent resource. She and DB Sweeney have tremendously enjoyed some of its suggestions, especially the ones from the section "The Best Mind Games," which is all about indoor activities such as "Treasure Hunt," and the slightly-to-very-embarrassing "Love Seat Game." They keep DB Sweeney quite amused, engaged, and entertained, without even having to wander around the neighborhood. As it turns out, DB Sweeney seems to have quite an interest in fighting every large dog he sees, right down to the death. Sometimes going for long walks with DB Sweeney is not so much peaceful and bonding as it is extremely stressful. Meredith imagines many dog owners, before they were dog owners, must have looked forward to the long walks alongside their dogs. That could make her one step ahead of the game, she figures, since she never longed to be a dog owner. But couldn't it be that it's possible to long for something without even knowing what it is? Just in the same way she's sometimes sure it might be possible to miss someone you haven't met yet?

To be fair, there are five items included in *Beyond Fetch* that fall under the heading of "The Best Ways to Relax," complete with doggie massage instructions. And it's not as if those instructions didn't have some merit, quite a lot really, it's just that DB Sweeney, at present driven to despair, so immensely preoccupied with the thunderstorm, would have none of it, none of anything it seemed, least of all a misguided attempt of Meredith's at doggie massage.

She moves on, sings a few lines of James Blunt's "You're Beautiful." She's not sure why that song—it's really a fair amount more melancholy than it is soothing and uplifting, but then, DB Sweeney is quite beautiful. "You're beautiful! You're beautiful," she repeats with what she hopes is less melancholy than James Blunt usually infuses into his lyrics. "I saw your face in a crowded place." Still nothing.

DB Sweeney wriggles free of what might not have been to him such a soothing grasp. He gets up on his hind legs, and makes this horrible gagging sound. It's not that he's choking on anything, it is just a sound he makes, mostly on the aforementioned stressful walks when he passes the borzoi who lives on Sixty-seventh Street of whom he has become increasingly unfond.

Maybe it would help if she played James Blunt for him on her iPod, through the Bose speakers. Or better yet, she thinks she'll play him his new CD, *Dog Gone Songs: Music to Soothe the Animal Spirit*. She ordered it from Target.com to play for DB Sweeney, just in case he had any issues with separation anxiety when she went out at night. Not that she'd really thought he would, because other than the desire to fight every dog larger than him (and when you are the approximate size of a mini dachshund, the number of dogs who are a great deal bigger than you is myriad and vast) he has always been a brilliant sage. He has never had a house-training accident, has never destroyed property, has always just stared at her wisely and assuredly, and made her feel safe. Except when he encounters something on the pavement that he finds to be especially dirty. DB Sweeney loves dirty things, and whenever he comes across them, he feels the need to pivot himself sideways and shimmy down to the pavement. This movement is apparently what he has determined as the absolute best way to smear as large a surface area of his body into whatever sidewalk disgustingness it is that he has found. Even brilliant sages have their weaknesses.

DB Sweeney stops his gagging noise and settles back down onto four legs and looks at Meredith like he would very much like her to do something, like he would like her to make him safe. And she knows, as she has known at times before, but never in this way, so completely, that it is time for her to step up.

She scrolls quickly through the iPod and selects the album *Dog Gone Songs: Music to Soothe the Animal Spirit* and puts it on, turning the volume up, but not too loud because there is quite a lot of oboe (or could be it's bassoon) and she's long thought that an oboe, or even a bassoon, played too loud can indeed sound quite threatening. She grabs her phone quickly and dials Dévi. They pick up on the first ring.

"This is Emily Shea," she says quickly. "I'm sorry but I'm going to have to cancel my reservation for tonight." They locate her reservation and thank her for calling. Next she reaches for her BlackBerry and sends off a quick joint e-mail to her two planned dinner companions for the night: she's so sorry but something has come up and she hopes they'll be up for a rain check in the near future to sample Indian food in the Flatiron District. E-mail, she thinks, is so much easier, so much better sometimes. With e-mail, so much more can be left unsaid; you can cancel plans without people having any idea that compared to your dog they don't matter nearly as much.

She opens up her copy of 97 *Ways to Make Your Dog Smile*, she stretches out on the floor with it, in the hopes that DB Sweeney might want to take a look at it, too. There are some good ideas in it, and some stunning pictures of very fetching dogs, too.

"Look, DB Sweeney," she says, holding the book out to him. He has no interest. "No, look. Look, really," she tries again. She's no stranger to the school of If You Don't Get the Reaction You Seek Initially, Why Not Try the Same Tactic Again. She's taken a few classes there. And she doesn't see why he wouldn't like this book with all its helpful suggestions and charming pictures of adorable dogs. She likes the book; she found it, by the way, on the Internet, too. And on that, do you have any idea how many things there are on the Internet for your dog? It is a vast multitude of offerings that could truly boggle the mind. Even if your dog has already decided that he will not dress. (Well, to be truthful, Meredith decided that for DB Sweeney, but she's pretty sure that on that topic, as on many others, they are of like minds.) There is so much stuff out there in the world to buy for your dog, from books to CDs to beds to dishes to bowls to treats to travel bags, a cornucopia of plush toys. She has purchased a few more than several plush toys for DB Sweeney, including a bear in a bee costume which she thinks is an exact replica of the busy bee the Weimariner had in the movie *Best in Show* and she gets a kick out of that, though of course she sees no similarity between the Parker Posey character in that film and her own character.

DB Sweeney loves his plush toys, he carries them around, from living room, to bedroom, to pass-through kitchen, to small square area right in front of the door, one by one, with such love and care and tenderness that Meredith is sure he thinks of them as his babies. She gathers them all up and presents them to him soothingly.

"Look, DB Sweeney, look at your babies," Meredith coos, gently pushing a yellow duck, Daniel Duck to be specific, in his direction. He doesn't acknowledge it at all. It looks as if his eyes are making a game attempt at rolling back in his head. She hopes he doesn't start with the gagging sound again. It's so unsettling, really. Upsetting could even be the right word.

"What about Vernon Vermin?" she asks, presenting what might actually be a beaver but somewhere along the way she decided looked very much like a woodchuck. "And who's this? Is this Busy Bee?"

She moves slowly, cautiously, dragging herself on her stomach to where DB Sweeney is situated, half on the carpet, half off. She didn't think it possible to feel so concerned, so loving, so responsible, so at a loss. She puts one hand on him, on one shoulder, he lets her. She puts her other hand out. He lets her. In one motion, one that is almost graceful, she slides him toward her, over carpet. Once she has him, she steadies herself with one hand, and in motions slightly less than graceful she gets herself and DB Sweeney up off the floor. She walks with him over to the computer and sits down at it. She goes to Google.com and types in *dog relax thunderstorm*. And, as you might now imagine, a tremendous number of results come up. Among them: several sites offering doggie foul-weather gear; one-on-one dog training; interestingly, a link to Target to buy *Dog Gone Songs: Music to Soothe the Animal Spirit*; one for something called G-

Doga; and one for a day care and grooming place called Biscuits & Bath.

Presented with this list, confronted with the links and descriptions, the Google ads and Amazon links running up and down the sides, so many things go through Meredith's mind. They always do.

* Surely there must be more books she should be buying. Surely.
* Maybe, even though they'd already decided against it, maybe DB Sweeney should consider dressing, because if a Google search involving the word *dog* is any indication, there would be so many things for him to wear.
* Maybe she should look into getting DB Sweeney a private trainer?
* But then, if she's going to consider doing that then shouldn't she consider getting a trainer for herself? She wonders if a Level I trainer at the Equinox would cost more or less than the "Positive Reinforcement Only" trainer listed here.
* What is G-Doga and do people really do this?
* And Biscuits & Bath, oh she has already thought about Biscuits & Bath. Sometimes lately when she lies in bed at night, when she can't sleep, she wonders if, except for his apparent hatred of larger (read most) dogs, running as deep as his love for all dirty things, she wonders if she should take DB Sweeney to one of the group obedience classes at the Biscuits & Bath or will it just interfere too much with her work schedule?

* Oh, and also, sometimes, when she lies in bed at night and she can't sleep, she wonders if she'll never find what she's looking for, her lawyer, her banker, her junior tycoon, and if it says bad things that the last time she went on an actual date (not counting Josh, she doesn't want to count Josh) she wore one of her wigs.

She clicks at last on the link for G-Doga and discovers that it's a yoga class for dogs, held weekly at the 92nd Street Y. The subtitle says, *Doggie and Me Yoga.* The animated words *Zen, Relaxation, Stress Release, Thunderstorm Consolation, Peace,* and *Freedom* jump out at her from a lavender wallpaper. She clicks; the class meets on Wednesday nights. Granted that is a work night, but there's something about it, and she says to herself, *Just add on a lunch.* Frank Bruni has lunch. Just recently he wrote about a lunch he had at L'Atelier de Joël Robuchon at the Four Seasons Hotel. She wonders if Frank Bruni is ever on a diet.

"Look, DB Sweeney," she says, pointing at the lavender screen as a transparent image of a somewhat perplexed-looking Clumber spaniel with his tail in the air emerges slowly into solid view. "What's this? Do you think you might like it? Do you think you might want to embrace your inner Zen doggie?"

There is a flash of lightning, followed by a clap of thunder. DB Sweeney leaps onto the desk, sending piles of paper onto the floor.

"No, no," Meredith says as calmly, as reassuringly as possible. Reassurance, she thinks, is what she should be going for. "You mustn't climb on the desk." She reaches for him but he is wily in his hysteria and evades her. Using the keyboard of her laptop as a springboard, he leaps off the desk, and charges, like a bullet, for the living room. She closes her laptop and slowly follows him back into the living room, where she sits down next to him on the corner section of the purple velvet couch.

She looks at DB Sweeney, who seems to have relaxed slightly. He's also making a very concerted effort at wrapping his body completely around her waist. Every few moments, his body shudders. She keeps her hand pressed gently against his side and notices how the spaces between each shake of his body are almost exact, perfectly timed, as if they're programmed, determined long before this thunderstorm. She wonders how many thousands of years of instincts inform so many things about DB Sweeney, how many generations of dachshund, terrier, and corgi came before him and for some reason felt it was imperative to be wary of the thunderstorm. She wonders how many things she should be wary of that she doesn't even know about.

"Nothing bad is ever going to happen to you during a thunderstorm," she promises him, and he looks up at her, with his big, brown, soulful eyes. The way he looks at her, it seems to say, *You think so? Because I'm not so sure I believe you on that one.* In fact, it says that pretty clearly. She pets him, a long steady pet from the top of his head, over his wiry back, down to his tail, and tries again, "You will never be hurt by a thunderstorm." And right then, DB Sweeney puts his head down on his paws and lets out a world-weary sigh, and Meredith thinks it is a sigh that is weary not only of this world but of many, because he knows so much. She looks at him and looks out the window and thinks that what she tells him is true, he will never be harmed by a thunderstorm, no matter what his instincts, no matter what all his history may tell him. And it's not an overwhelming sadness, but it is sadness she feels as she looks at the top of his head because she's thinking of all his history, and she's thinking of all the things he might never do.

He might never catch a squirrel. He might never just get to run right out his kitchen door, graceful and free across the backyard, because she doesn't have a back yard, or even a kitchen door. DB Sweeney will never get to sire a litter because the DCNY had him neutered, and she wonders if he cares about that. She wonders if he cares that he may not have a great love of his life. It doesn't occur to her, as she thinks this, that perhaps the great love of his life is her. She gets a little caught thinking about the things he won't have, the things he may never have, and she tries to think of all the ways she'll make it up to him. She sighs herself and thinks that he may never be the type of mini wirehaired dachshund–Norwich terrier mix, who will run on the beach every evening at sunset, who will hunt small vermin in the middle of a forest in his leisure time. But he will get to go to the 92nd Street Y, and he will get to practice G-Doga: Doggie and Me Yoga.

sixteen

the waiting is the hardest part

There is no diet. There are a hundred diets. There could even be, if you took the time to look into it, more than that. But there's also Aubrey. And Ivy. Aubrey needs her right now. Stephanie thinks that he might need her now more than he's ever needed anyone or anything, that in some really dismal way this might be the pivotal moment of Aubrey's life. In the midst of that, it just doesn't seem like the time to try to lose weight. It really doesn't. And she had hoped that would be enough, that knowledge. She hoped that it would make it so that when she looked at herself, she didn't see a stranger, so that she stopped being so aware of all the extra that was never there before. It didn't.

For nine months, she would go out into the world and she was pregnant. Pregnant! People would smile at her and beam at her, and they would want to touch her, and sometimes they even did. And maybe that was just because they wanted to be a small part of everything that was beautiful and magical and special about her. And then she had this miracle, she had this baby, and when she went back out into the world, she was just fat. Stephanie wonders if there are so many people who don't go on diets, not actually because there is no good diet, but because they, too, have too many other things going on that they can't deal with. And that makes it somehow a little bit better, because that makes it so that she is not the only person, and she likes that. She's never really wanted to be the only person, she's never been such a fan of being alone.

And Aubrey isn't alone. She wants to tell him that even though she hates him a little bit, and maybe a little bit more each time that he tells her he's got everyting under control, because she doesn't believe him. And she feels a lot lately that her whole life is waiting, waiting for everything Aubrey tells her not to be true.

Aubrey, right now, is at his therapist. And it seems weird and strange and as if the universe isn't right at all (and actually it's not) that Aubrey is at a therapist. If anyone would not have seemed the therapy type, it would have been Aubrey. Aubrey, smart and handsome and before the knee surgery, always pursuing something sporting. Genial and friendly and warm. She never would have thought, had she ever thought about it before, that he would have been in therapy. Of course she never would have thought him to be a drug addict either. And it could be true, what she's started to think lately, that she isn't very good at seeing things.

Aubrey's therapist, he's actually more than a therapist, if there are gradations, if "more" is the right word here. He's a psychiatrist, which is an M.D., too, so he can prescribe drugs, though Stephanie imagines more drugs are not what Aubrey needs. Unless somehow that would help him. She has no idea how to help him. The therapist's name is Dr. Daniel Petty and his office is on Seventy-ninth Street, close to Amsterdam Avenue, and that's not altogether close to Aubrey's offices in Midtown but it's closer to his office than, say, a therapist in Ridgewood. She'd found Dr. Daniel Petty through their insurance, through the website, and it had been quite easy, to search. She was given different choices under *Specialty*, all these little boxes she could check off: *substance abuse/medications management*; *marriage/family*; *grief/bereavement*. She checked them all.

And the very fact that Aubrey had agreed to it, to Dr. Daniel Petty, the fact that he'd gone through with it, made Stephanie very sure that he didn't have anything under control at all. Because really, why would he? It made her decide to not go on a diet anymore, and it made her decide, without even realizing it, to just start waiting for more bad things to happen. He'll be back really soon, and she doesn't know what to do with herself while she waits, and Ivy's already upstairs and there's nothing else to do. She can't even think when the last time it was that she watched TV that did not consist of a *Baby Einstein* video, even though she loves TV almost as much as the movies. She misses TV, but when you're so out of TV for as long as she's been, she doesn't know if there could really be any way to catch up. Too much has happened. It's easier just not to try, much in the same way that after missing the first season, she just didn't feel she could take up *24*.

"Hey."

She turns around quickly; she didn't even hear his car pull up, didn't even hear him come in.

"How'd it go?" she asks him.

"It went okay?" he asks it back.

"Just okay?"

"I've got it under control," he says, walking behind the couch, standing there.

"You liked him though, you think he'll help?"

"Yeah, it was fine."

She nods.

"And you know what I was thinking on the ride home?" he asks her. There are so many things he could say right now. She wonders if any of them will help.

"What's that?"

"I was thinking of how many Tom Petty songs could actually be about therapy." She stares back at him; she blinks at him. That can't be the only thing he was thinking.

"Really, Aubrey? That's what you were thinking?"

" 'Breakdown,' for starters. 'Breakdown, go ahead and give it to me'?" She doesn't say anything. " 'Runnin' Down a Dream'? Or what about 'I Need to Know'?" He flicks his wrists, his hands in loose fists. She is appalled to see that he is pantomiming drumming. "I don't know how lo-ong, I can hold o-on."

"Aubrey."

" 'Even the Losers'?"

"Aubrey, stop it."

"No, come on, you try one, it's fun?"

She still doesn't say anything, and they just stay there, Stephanie turned halfway around on the couch, twisting her neck, Aubrey standing behind her, and they just look at each other until Aubrey picks up the remote control from the table beside the couch. He reaches out, points it at the TV, and then he leaves the room. As soon as she hears his footsteps on the stairs, the stairs to the upstairs, as soon as she's sure he's out of earshot, she says the name of her own Tom Petty song, softly.

" 'The Waiting Is the Hardest Part.' "

She turns to face the TV, even though it's been so long, there it still is, right there in front of her. On. There's a woman in a white suit, dancing. A voice-over, a woman's voice, is saying, "There's more than one woman who has tried and failed more times than she can count." *Really*, Stephanie thinks, *I could have sworn, I really could have, that it was only me*. She listens and she hears, "There is more than one woman who feels like the fattest person in the room." And she thinks again, *Really, because lately I always thought that was me*. Cher is singing in the background—what song is it? She's not good at that, at hearing lyrics or a tune and knowing what song it is. But she listens anyway, she needs a place to rest her mind. She thinks maybe that's what it is, people who get all caught up in songs and lyrics; maybe they're just looking, looking a little harder than everyone else, for a place to rest their minds. *This is a song for the lonely*, so says Cher. Stephanie thinks of her sister. Meredith has always cared so much about her music, has always known every lyric to every song. *This is a song for the lonely*. She thinks, if she remembers correctly, Meredith always really liked Cher.

part three

watch this

seventeen

i'm here because of db sweeney

Meredith stares at her computer screen, at the Weight Watchers website. She's arrived here because, as you can imagine, everything went to hell with the Atkins diet once she felt it a professional imperative to partake freely of carbs. She's also here because she read in *Departures* magazine that Mario Batali is on Weight Watchers. She's always had tremendous respect for Mario Batali, has always been a great admirer of his work. And because of that, and because she feels that she is perhaps a bit short of people to look up to, she figures she'll give Weight Watchers a try.

And so she's here, on WeightWatchers.com, where she has recently signed on to follow the diet online, and where she is making what she feels is a concerted effort to figure out this thing they call *Points*. As far as she can tell, every food has a points value, and it's just a matter of figuring out each value, and adding properly. And is it only her? Is she the only one who realizes the extreme closeness of the relationship between dieting and math? And is it at all possible that such could bode ill for the ultimate dieting successes of anyone who is really bad at math?

A pop-up window has popped up on her screen to remind her that those who attend Weight Watchers meetings—actual meetings with other dieting people—are three times more likely to lose the weight and keep it off than those who go it alone. It even invites her to type in her zip code to find a meeting nearby. And while at times she does feel it is a possibility that she could know herself better, she feels extremely confident in the knowledge that the actuality of her attending a weekly Weight Watchers meeting, even if it was nearby, even if it was in her apartment, if all the fellow watchers of the weight came over and gathered around her purple couch, perched gamely on the ledge of her pass-through kitchen, the likelihood of her attending such a meeting is not very likely at all.

And doing it online, it's easy. All she had to do was give her credit card number, enter her current weight in, and select a goal weight. The credit card part was easiest. The typing of her weight, the number, *her* number, was significantly less uplifting. It never seems to make a difference, no matter how much she doesn't want to be associated with a number, that number never seems to go away. The typing in of her goal weight, it did nothing to lift her spirits. Even though she made it higher than she imagined would be ideal (whatever *ideal* might look like, feel like, actually be), it was still so far, so many numbers away.

"Come, DB Sweeney," she says, walking to her closet, removing his leash and shaking it at him, in the way she has deter-mined has the highest likelihood of resulting in DB Sweeney's being desirous of a walk, as opposed to say, running into his leopard bed (she ordered it on the Internet at WallyBed.com) and pushing his paw in the air at her in what looks strikingly like the universal hand motion for *Go away.*

"We're going to our G-Doga Doggie and Me class! Yes, yes we are!"

In the lobby of their building, they stop together to say hi to Jerome, the weeknight doorman, and he tips his hat at DB Sweeney in salute, as DB Sweeney marches by jauntily, all charm, charisma, and confidence. Meredith smiles and says, "Hi, Jerome," and there's eye contact and goodwill. That's not to say that previously there was bad will, there never was, it was just sort of a blank.

* * *

Meredith and DB Sweeney head up to the second floor of the 92nd Street Y. They pass through a door at the end of a hall, and walk into a large room. There aren't lines painted on the floor, or bleachers, or basketball nets. But even so, the room puts her instantly in mind of a high school gym. She pushes the thought from her mind, as surely it can't be a good one.

There are eight yoga mats of assorted colors—blue, purple, green—spread out into a large circle in the center of the room. Meredith scans the eight mats in a clockwise direction. There are seven dogs. With each dog there is a person; and in the case of one dog, two people. However, it's actually quite hard to pay any attention to the people when there are seven dogs, each sitting on a yoga mat. The definition of "sitting" is used loosely here and ranges from actual sitting, to straining on the leash, to, in the case of a rather energetic Boston terrier, doing something that looks like dancing. Meredith has heard (actually with more frequency lately since she herself became the proud owner of a dog) how people, couples, sometimes meet each other at the dog run, how in some parts of the city, it's a bit of a pickup place. Right now, she can't imagine that, can't see how you could notice any of the people, how any of them could make even the slightest impression in the presence of so many dogs.

There is a large apricot poodle, straining on her leash, causing Meredith to steal a quick glance at DB Sweeney. She doesn't mean to alarm him and she hopes the combination of large dog/straining/perhaps overly excitable behavior won't result in DB Sweeney turning to his on-hind-leg stance/gagging noise behavior. She imagines such a stance would not be Zen and that a Zen, peaceful dog is probably the best thing to be here. Next to the poodle, there's a small Pomeranian, also apricot; then a Westie; another large dog looking a bit like a cross between a wolfhound and a sheepdog; a black pug sitting remarkably peacefully on his mat, his tongue lolling gently out the side of his mouth. *A Zen dog if ever there was one*, Meredith thinks, and figures he must be an old-timer. And last (but you can just tell, not least) there's the aforementioned Boston terrier, doing a side step, her bulging eyes rolling around in her head, her mouth wide open, displaying what appears to be only one tooth.

At the head of the circle is an empty mat. *That must be for the G-Doga master,* Meredith thinks, and she pauses for a moment, she feels like she has to, on the absurdity of that phrase, *the G-Doga master.* And yet it seems to be the only one that fits. She and DB Sweeney don't have a yoga mat. She feels this is perhaps cause for concern, until the woman holding the large (possibly preparing to be marauding) apricot poodle seems to read her mind and says, "There are mats in the blue bin, right there behind you, by the door."

"Oh, thanks," Meredith says to her, and she can notice her now, in her yoga ensemble: loose flowy pants with slits up the back and a tight-fitting tank top. As she heads to the bin and selects from all the bright blue and orange mats, one that is light purple with white circles on it, Meredith thinks she would like a pair of those pants. As she joins the circle, she thinks maybe it would be nice to sit next to the helpful apricot poodle woman, but yet she worries a bit about the propensity said apricot poodle may have to stress DB Sweeney really far out. So instead, she situates herself between the overly enthusiastic Boston terrier, who is now preoccupied with administering long, soulful licks to her yoga mat, and the peaceful-seeming black pug.

The door opens and in walks a beautiful (and also very peaceful-seeming) Bernese mountain dog. He is like a bear, and Meredith admires the sheen, the luster of each color in his coat, the sparkle in his eyes. He is so sagelike and wise that Meredith somehow momentarily forgets that he is so large and that large sometimes (okay, often) freaks DB Sweeney out. The Bernese mountain dog walks slowly, saunters really, to the empty mat at the head of the circle. DB Sweeney watches him, but he doesn't become agitated, actually he just watches him, and nothing happens. And then something does.

He must have walked in right after the Bernese mountain

dog. He's just finished taking off his shoes, and he walks in his bare feet and faded, wrinkled khakis rolled up once at the bottom, up to the front of the circle, to the mat where the Bernese mountain dog is sitting, regally staring down the Pomeranian, who has commenced barking (yapping might be the better word choice) and is spinning himself in circles.

"Rocco. Peace," says the man who just walked in, pressing his hands briefly together in a prayer position in front of his chest as he takes his place on the mat behind the mountain dog. The Pomeranian is silent and looks up at the man with wide eyes. *The G-Doga master*, Meredith thinks, and this time the phrase doesn't seem absurd at all.

He's wearing a dark green T-shirt with white lettering on it, but the white lettering is so faded, it's hard to make out what it once said. She stares a bit longer and thinks that maybe at one point, at some point long before this class, that maybe what it said was *Green*. He has very dark, curly hair, a mop of curly hair really, but it's shiny, like his dog's coat. It looks good on him. He has very pretty, quite piercing green eyes, and she thinks she gets why people say green eyes can be very striking, because they really can be. He has nice skin, it's very smooth and splotchless. He's very lean and muscular, sinewy almost, and he's not a large man, not by any means, and she wonders if maybe she's taller than he is. He looks younger than she thinks she looks, but maybe that could just be his casual attire, the beaded necklace worn close around his neck. And Meredith would like to point out here, and she would hope that you knew this anyway, that she's really not the sort to study a man standing in front of her in this way.

"How's everyone doing tonight?" he asks, and he has a deep voice, it carries very well, it projects. Throughout the room there are murmurs of "good" and "hi" and "how are you." There are a few barks, and assorted squirming noises, rustling and panting from the four-legged classmates.

"Great then," he says, deeply. "Okay." And Meredith regards him again, this sinewy man with all the curly hair and the beads and the bare feet. Outside of this room, she would have walked right past him. If she were the type to still go to bars, she doesn't think she ever would have noticed him in one, would not have considered him one of the people who couldn't tell she had a good (though at times somewhat judgmental) personality from across the room. She's not across the room from him right now, she's just a pug away from him, but she wonders if he can tell anything about her personality, her character, from where he is. Because she feels right now, as she looks at him, in a room filled with what must be yoga-loving dogs, very closely to the way she felt when she first saw DB Sweeney. She feels a bit like a goner, like it's all over for her, all through. She feels that if she were the type of person to use hokey expressions at leisure and at will, she might say something, something along the lines of, *Put a fork in me, I'm done.*

But she's not the type of person to think that way. And, he is an instructor of a yoga class for dogs at the 92nd Street Y. And, surely he's younger than she is anyway, and shorter than she is, to say nothing at all of all-around smaller in physique. *Pull yourself together,* she tells herself, inadvertently tightening her grip on DB Sweeney's leash. DB Sweeney looks up at her, in that way of his that is very wise.

"Okay," he says again, scanning the room. "I see some new faces tonight, that's great. So, you guys with the pug are new?" He says pointing next to her to the mellow pug. The pug is the one dog who has two people.

"And this little guy," he says, stepping forward a little bit, closer to her and DB Sweeney, stooping down for a closer look, "he's a . . ." He lets it linger there, a question. DB Sweeney looks up at her and then at him, back to her again. She smiles at him before answering.

"He's a mini wirehaired dachshund–Norwich terrier mix," she says in a voice that sounds a little different than the one she usually hears.

"He's got some corgi in him, too, I think," he says, ruffling the crest of fur on the top of DB Sweeney's head, and looking up at Meredith from his vantage point on the floor.

"Yes," she says, widening her eyes and nodding enthusiastically. "How did you know?"

"You can see the way he looks up at you; it's in the eyes," he says, taking his first and second fingers together and pointing them at his eyes and then pointing at her eyes and smiling, and she thinks the room feels so warm. "It just really says corgi to me." He gives a quick shrug of his shoulders and gets up and heads back to the head of the circle, and Meredith waits. She waits to hear the sounds of wires snapping against each other, to see some kind of sparks, any indication that this particular room at the 92nd Street Y was about to be consumed by an electrical fire. She notices that next to her, the Boston terrier has a pile of plush toys arranged in front of her, babies just like DB Sweeney has, the ones he so carefully and tenderly carries from room to room. The little Boston picks up one of her babies (a natural-colored elephant with pink tusks) and begins smacking it down, side to side with quick, furious jerks of her head.

"Jessica," the G-Doga master, whose name she doesn't even know yet, says to the Boston terrier, "peace." And Jessica puts her baby down in front of her.

"All right," he says, now back in front of his mat. "New Guys, why don't you take a second to introduce yourselves to the room. Just tell us your name, your dog's name, and what it is that brings you here," he says. His voice is calm, relaxed; placid like a lake.

He points first at the couple with the pug, one finger this time, an effortless, fluid flick of his wrist that seems to Meredith so graceful. The couple, a pretty redhead and a tall guy with close-cropped dark hair, smile at each other. The redhead laughs; it's a laugh just between them, a private joke, everyone has them. The redhead takes a breath and starts talking, "Hi. I'm Hope, and this is Ben," she says and then looks down and gestures at the pug, "and this is Max." Max seems to be asleep. "We practice yoga together, Ben and I do, and we love it and we heard about this yoga class for dogs and so we wanted to share it with Max. And also, we wanted to make sure he felt at peace because we just moved into a new apartment."

Meredith notices the way the tall guy smiles at the redhead when she's done talking. And the way she smiles right back at him. She wonders if it was always so easy for them, if they were just born that happy and in love, if there was never any loneliness or struggle or isolation or fear. She's sure there never was.

The G-Doga master points at her and DB Sweeney next,

"You guys?" he prompts. She hesitates for a split second, she has to, because she has to think about her anonymity. Someone here could be a chef, or a restaurant owner. Maybe she should use a different name? She has to say something. And so she does, really quickly. "Hi. I'm Meredith, and I'm here because of DB Sweeney," she says and nods her head vigorously a few times, and leaves it at that. She thinks maybe the G-Doga master could be looking at her a bit quizzically, but he doesn't say anything and no one else does either, and she just nods her head again and even though she really hates waiting, she waits for the moment to pass.

"Great then," he says, and puts a hand on his chest. "I'm Gary, and welcome to G-Doga, and welcome back everyone else."

Gary? she thinks. *Gary?* For as many names as she has loved and thought were very cool names indeed, and for just as many names as she has thought to be boring, mundane, dull, Gary has been one of the few names, along with Barry, that she actually dislikes. She thinks that a yoga teacher, a G-Doga master at that (wait, is the *G* for *Gary,* do you think?) should have a more spiritual name, a name more in sync with his yogic mission in life. A yoga teacher should be called Eagle, she thinks, or Yan. Sebastian perhaps, or Paisley. Not Gary. Though Gary could be short for Gareth, maybe? Gareth is an excellent name.

"Okay," he says next, "last thing for the new folks. If you haven't checked out the book *Doga* by Jennifer Brilliant and William Berloni, I highly recommend it. I, for one, find it inspiring, and it's great if you're interested in continuing your doga practice at home, something I strongly encourage." He claps his hands together twice, slowly, loosely, fluidly, and the Bernese mountain dog stands up regally. "And last, last thing," Gary says with a chuckle, gesturing to his dog. "this is Ellery." And Ellery, it seems, nods at the class. Maybe, or maybe she's just imagining things.

Gary places his hands in front of him now, back in prayer position, and she notices that all the other people are standing on their mats, behind their dogs in the same way Gary is standing behind Ellery. Or not. The woman with Jessica, the Boston terrier, is standing on her mat at least, and Jessica is dancing in a circle around her, tossing her head exuberantly, her feet moving in a quick side-stepping motion. The woman with the Westie is saying softly, "Carlie, no," as Carlie smears her face sideways across the wood floor much in the same way DB Sweeney does when he comes across something especially vile on the sidewalk.

"Let's start with three *oms*," Gary says and then, yes, says, "*Om.*" It's very deep and resonating. Around the circle some of the dogs are quite focused, and others are quite not; all the people answer Gary's long, reverberating, completely unselfconscious *om* with their own. As *oms* fill the room, Meredith joins in, too, though she is a little embarrassed, a bit self-conscious as she looks around to see if anyone is looking at her. Her *om* is not free. Hers is a self-conscious *om*, and she can't say for sure, but she imagines such a thing, a self-conscious *om*, is frowned upon at best.

But before she can fully ponder the oxymoronic qualities of an embarrassed, stifled *om*, Ellery, the Bernese mountain dog, reaches his nose skyward, or ceilingward as it were, and lets out a long, low, quite soulful howl. It's a wonderful sound, and then

Gary begins another *om*, and the others chime in, Meredith included, with a far less self-conscious *om* than her first one. All the dogs, the ones that were focused and also the ones that were not, sit on their mats, and each one, the apricot poodle, Jessica the Boston terrier, Rocco the Pomeranian, Carlie, the face-smearing Westie, the giant sheepdog mix, the Zen pug, and yes, even DB Sweeney, each one reaches a nose skyward and lets out his or her own take on a howl. Meredith hears DB Sweeney's howl and it's a little high, and it sounds to her so much like *wooooo*. She wants to get down on the mat with him, and hug him. She wants to tell him that he is absolutely fantastic and amazing and wonderful all at once. She is so taken, looking around at all the gently howling dogs. There is something reserved about them—they're all wild things in this moment, and yet they're also not. She's struck by the desire to hug every single one of the dogs, to hold on to each one, tell every single one of them how special and important they are. For reasons most practical, she resists the urge. Rather, she puts all of her enthusiasm into her last *om*, as it seems everyone else is doing, too. And the dogs continue to howl.

Next, Ellery, who clearly seems to have this down, presses his two front feet into the floor and scoots down, his hindquarters reaching upwards.

"Downward facing dog!" Gary says happily. He looks out at the assembled circle and repeats, "Downward facing dog." He nods and then in a more imploring tone, "Guys? Want to give it a try?" To Gary's credit, or perhaps it is to Ellery's credit, the apricot poodle crouches down and gets into a position somewhat resembling the one Ellery is in, though she keeps her head up.

"Kind of an upward facing dog, great job, Cassie," Gary praises. Jessica the Boston terrier gets down on her belly and begins crouching toward him as if she were stalking her prey. Gary nods seriously at her. The sheepdog mix sits down, the pug is sitting on his haunches contentedly, and the Westie is heading determinedly for the door.

"Okay, people," Gary says clapping, the Westie stopping midstride to see what the clapping is about, "let's join in here with a sun salutation. Person of DB Sweeney? You're gonna want to take off your shoes."

"My shoes?" Meredith says, even though she heard him. Suddenly she feels nervous. It's not really about the shoes, it's more about the fact that it does seem that the people will be participating in the yoga, and she's never done yoga.

"You got it," he says with a grin, it's a very lovely grin. DB Sweeney is standing on his mat. He's not doing doga per se, but in the scheme of things, he might be closer than some of the other dogs.

"Um, Gary," she says to his back, as he has now turned around and is heading back to his own mat. He turns around again and she motions him toward her. She would like to think the motion is subtle. He walks a few steps toward her, a look of casual concern on his face. She angles her head down, lowers her voice, "It's just that I haven't ever done yoga. I thought, you know, just DB Sweeney was going to do the yoga."

"Not a problem," he says, smiling. His smile is so warm. "Just hang out. Watch everyone else and join in when you feel comfortable. Yoga is about going at your own pace and doing what feels right to you."

"Uh, okay," she says, looking down at her sneakers and thinking to herself, *You will unlace them.* "Any pointers?"

"Sure thing, two: try to say *practicing* yoga rather than *doing* yoga. It's an ongoing thing, it's a practice not an action." She nods her head, taking it in. "And if you look at them closely enough, you'll notice dogs are always practicing their yoga. And have fun," he finishes with another grin. "I guess that's three things."

"Thanks," she says, and bends down to unlace her sneakers. She makes an effort not to think too much about how many other people's bare feet have been on her borrowed yoga mat, too.

"Let's all come to the front of our mats," he says next from the front of his own mat. She takes her place right behind DB Sweeney and watches and listens as everyone begins their sun salutation.

"Look up, reach up, inhale. Bring your hands through your chest center and look down. Fold down, and set your hands to the floor and then lift halfway up here." As everyone, in unison, looks up to the sky and reaches their hands above them, and then swan dives down, all extremely flexibly she notices, she sees how each of the dogs gets so excited—so really puppyish is how she would describe it, even though she's never had a puppy. Their tails all wag quickly and they excitedly circle their mats, even DB Sweeney, except he is tail-wagging and circling over on the next mat with the happy couple and he is circling along with the now quite zealous black pug.

DB Sweeney, she thinks, *really?* And she thinks DB Sweeney does not know from happy couples and it must be very novel to him, as novel as doga. Except of course for the fact that Gary did say that dogs are always practicing yoga.

"Now you should come into your high push-up position. And you should be able to see your ankles here. Can you see your ankles here?"

Even though she is not in the push-up position, Meredith tries not to think about if she can or cannot see her ankles.

"Gently lift your chin and take a deep breath in and then hover, and now, to your low push-up."

Meredith is starting to feel a bit dumb listening to the yoga practice and not doing it. Or practicing it. But yet the dogs are so excited, and so cute, and so charming, and so fetching really, every last one, that she feels a bit less dumb than she would in other circumstances.

"Upward facing dog," Gary says next, and everyone arches forward, "and downward facing dog," and everyone is now in an inverted triangle pose, and breathing, and then Meredith thinks she can do that, and she gets herself into the position and it's really not hard. She stays and she breathes and DB Sweeney hustles right back over to her, and together they listen to Gary's velvet voice as he says over and over, "Inhale. Exhale." She winks at DB Sweeney, who has situated himself right underneath her, and she can feel everyone breathing in and out with her. She gets the strangest feeling, one that she doesn't think she's had before. She doesn't have a name for it, but she suspects it might suffice to call it being part of something. She smiles, an upside down smile, at the thought of really being part of something.

And so with Gary's next direction, "Walk or jump forward,"

she decides to follow right along, though admittedly she makes the decision to walk, rather than jump forward. She wonders if maybe G-Doga class is really just people *practicing* yoga with their dogs around them. Except of course for the thing that he said about dogs always practicing yoga, which could be a bit of a brain scramble if you let it. But even so, even if they just do these sun salutations, she thinks that would be okay.

She peeks up from her forward bend to see the placid-voiced, curly haired Gary slipping out the door. Alas. A moment later there's a clicking sound and music begins piping into the room, coming through speakers hidden somewhere. Meredith tries to remember her focus, remember her breathing, and stay in sync, and then everyone's standing again at the front of their mats, and so is she, and so is Gary.

As she hears the soft *cha-cha* of a snare drum, a tinkling, and a twang, an unmistakable country melody, Meredith loses focus on her breathing and tries to figure out if she knows the song, the endless game of Name That Tune she forever plays whenever she hears music. *The summer air it was heavy and sweet, you and I on a crowded street . . .*

Ha, Meredith thinks, *Deanna Carter,* and the song is "We Danced Anyway." She feels a small triumph, the kind she often gets when she recognizes a song, or properly identifies a mysterious ingredient, an elusive spice, but along with that, there's also a sharper feeling, she's also a bit surprised. Because while Deanna Carter is one of her favorite country music singers, she thinks she's only ever heard her on the Bose, the Bang & Olufsen, or the iPod. Deanna Carter, she doesn't think, isn't someone you come across very often in New York. Being a fan of country music in New York City is a solitary experience. And she has never once thought that in New York City there might exist a country music–loving doga instructor; and not only that, but one who is really very cute (albeit saddled with a rather unfortunate name). But then, what is it that people always say about New York? That you can find anything you want here? She thinks about that for a moment, and then something amazing happens.

The dogs, all of them, start parading. They fan out along the perimeter of the circle of yoga mats, all following Ellery in a remarkably straight line. Their tales swish and their eyes gleam and not one of them, not even Jessica, the rowdy Boston terrier, or Carlie, the face-smearing Westie, get out of the line. There at the end of the line, following closely behind the apricot poodle, is DB Sweeney. He is all the way across the room, graceful and independent and free, doing what looks like some swaying of his own, and looking remarkably rhythmic. In that instant, he looks back over his haunches at her quickly, and she has the sure sense he looks to check on her. She smiles at him, to let him know it's fine, that she's fine. And there's something about the way he looks at her and holds her gaze for a moment longer that makes her think that was his plan all along.

Meredith looks quickly around and notices that all the people, they're all now sitting back down on their mats in various degrees of cross-leggedness and swaying. And they're all, each one of them, clapping. Meredith has no idea how they got there, or when. As DB Sweeney marches along, as the music plays, it's clear, quite clear really, that the only thing to do is to get on the floor, the only thing to do is clap, and sway, and sing along. She starts singing softly and surprises herself as she hears her own voice getting louder, boldly singing the chorus along with everyone else. "And the band played songs that we had never heard, but we danced anyway."

*   *   *

Later, after the parading has come to a finish, after Gary has once again led the people and dogs together in a rousing closing sequence of om/howl, the dogs all, almost magically, settle into what Gary calls "final relaxation." Meredith lies on her back with her eyes closed thinking that G-Doga is not half-bad at all, thinking as she listens to Gary repeating "Inhale" and "Exhale" that his voice reminds her very much of an Elvis Costello song.

When the class has come to a close and the other people are rolling up their mats and nodding goodbyes and attaching leashes to the collars of their dogis, and Meredith is doing the same, Gary walks over to her.

"You did great today," he says. She looks to see if the other new people, the people with the nice pug, are still here, if he could have been talking to them, too. But they're already gone.

"Thanks," she says, and she's about to leave it at that, but doesn't. "I enjoyed it a lot more than I thought I would." He smiles, his eyes shine so much in the way that DB Sweeney's sometimes do. "I mean," she continues, "not that I thought I wouldn't enjoy it, it was just, it was great." She would like to add on that she is a very smart person, always has been, is in fact leaps and bounds smarter than she sounds right now. But she doesn't. "I love that Deanna Carter song, by the way. Great choice."

"Thanks," he says. "And DB Sweeney did wonderfully. It's amazing how tuned in these guys are as soon as they arrive."

"It is," she says, nodding. She should have more to say, but yet, no.

"And you did beautifully with your first sun salutations."

Beautifully, she thinks and says, "Thanks, thanks a lot."

"Have you ever considered coming to yoga on your own?" he asks.

"Uh, not really, I don't think."

"You should," he tells her. "I teach a class on Sunday afternoons at this great studio on Eighteenth Street. Right by Third."

"Really," she says, still forgetting that she knows so many more words.

"Well, then," he says and again, he smiles at her. The smile shows more teeth this time but yet it is not one that gives any indication as to whether he thinks her smile is nice, too, or as to whether or not he has the ability to tell things about her personality from across a room. "Sunday at three thirty, it'd be nice to see you." He takes a card out of his pocket, hands it to her.

She glances down at it, on one side there's an address, a cell phone number, and an e-mail. His last name is Hugh, which doesn't really help the Gary, at least she doesn't think so. She flips the card over and there's the name and address of a yoga studio on Eighteenth Street.

"Thanks," she says. "I'll definitely try." She gets out her wallet and puts the card inside it. She thinks she really will try to make it to his yoga class. She actually doesn't see a downside. She thinks she'll try.

"Cool," he says and turns to walk over to Ellery, who is peacefully waiting on his yoga mat.

She looks down at DB Sweeney, who seems to be smiling up at her. She smiles right back at him, gets a good grip on his leash, and together, they start to head home.

eighteen

join us

It was not the next day. Let it not be said that Stephanie Cunningham, née Isley, ran off like a lemming to a Weight Watchers meeting just because she heard Cher singing a (rather poignant) song on TV. But does anyone say that anymore? Does anyone actually say, with a straight face, without irony, *née Isley*? Stephanie thinks probably not. Probably, if she were going for inclusion of her maiden name, in this day and age, it would have to be Stephanie Isley Cunningham. And it should have been something she did from the start, from when they'd first gotten married, perhaps even with a hyphen. But she hadn't. She'd just completely jettisoned Isley. And it wasn't even a backlash against her father, the name of her father, who may or may not live in France (which is a story for another day), because Isley was actually her mother's maiden name. (And that's a story for the day after that.) She'd just become Stephanie Cunningham.

She'd been, at the time, quite excited to be. She imagines that to start using Isley again now, even combined with Cunningham, either with or without a hyphen, might send certain messages, messages that, even with everything, she doesn't think she should send.

It was a full three weeks later that she decided to go to the Weight Watchers meeting. Three weeks in which Aubrey seemed to be doing his best not to be a lying, disappointing pill popper, three weeks in which she had slowly started to think that she should consider going back on a diet, mostly because there was always something in them that she found hopeful. That none of them had worked so far seemed beside the point. It wasn't so much the diet as it was the distant promise, the small chance out there, somewhere, a pinpoint on the horizon, that it would work. And she could use that right now, even if it was just a promise, even it was just a distant one. And she could also use to feel less like a beluga whale. She saw a beluga whale once, in fifth grade, it was visiting the National Aquarium, and she drew a drawing of it that she doesn't have anymore but wishes she still did. It was a beautiful drawing and a beautiful beluga whale, though less so now that she feels she so closely resembles it.

She leaves Ivy with Jenna, the nanny, the sitter, depending on your choice of phrase, and drives to the Ridgewood Elks Lodge on North Maple Avenue, the site of the Thursday at 5:30 Weight Watchers meeting. The concept of Stephanie leaving Ivy alone with Jenna is new. Very new. She left her once last week, too. It went okay, and so she's decided to try it again. She doesn't plan to do it constantly, not as a routine or anything—definitely not that. But just on occasion, just every now and then.

She walks into the large main room of the Elks Lodge and it reminds her of a gym, and that makes her think of Aubrey. She wonders how many things will always remind her of him, no matter what happens. There are folded chairs lined up in rows. At the front of the room there is an easel with paper on it, like for Pictionary, she thinks, though most likely not as entertaining. There are women, women of all shapes and sizes, filing into the rows and taking their seats. There are more women forming a line in front of two makeshift tables set up along the far wall. She thinks she's supposed to get in the line. She does, and as she slowly makes her way forward, there are so many things to buy. An electronic scale. A cookbook. A cookbook just about pizza. Pizza? Who would have thought? There are different brightly colored packages of snack bars called Two Points Bars, and other smaller ones called Mini Bars. A soup ladle. A *Complete Food Companion*. Stephanie picks up boxes and puts them back down as she goes. She backtracks, picking up the things she thinks have the highest likelihood of helping—the electronic scale, the Mini Bars, the *Complete Food Companion*—and carrying them with her.

By the time she reaches the front of the line, almost everyone is in one of the folding chairs, the lines and lines of folding chairs. She feels late. A woman has taken her place in front of the Pictionary easel and is writing across a page with black marker. *You Bite It, You Write It,* she writes, and underlines it with a thick, long line. Underneath the line, in all caps, big block letters stretching across the length of the page, she prints,

ACCOUNTABILITY. Stephanie looks at the words written there, mostly at the last one. She takes off her shoes. She takes off her jacket, too, and sets it on the floor next to her shoes. She wonders what else she could take off, if the removal of socks, even lightweight spring wardrobe socks, would make a difference. Earrings? She thinks probably not, but she does take her sunglasses from the top of her head and places them neatly on top of her jacket. She reaches the front of the line, and a woman with a name tag, *Maureen,* smiles at her, and indicates with a sweeping gesture a small square scale set on the floor, right in front of the table. She steps on the scale, a scale without any display or numbers—really it's more of a platform. Maureen has a computer and on it must be Stephanie's weight, flashing in digital numbers for all the world to see, or at least for Maureen to see.

Maureen takes Stephanie's other, less soul-destroying information, name and credit card, and types it all in. She hands Stephanie a booklet, it's called a *Membership Booklet* and up at the top, there, written in ink, is her weight. It's about four pounds higher than it was at home this morning. That could just be her clothes, or that could just be that it's the end of the day instead of the beginning. She means that literally, not figuratively, even in light of everything that's going on.

And four pounds, in the scheme of things, relative to the pounds that need to be lost, doesn't really mean a lot. She studies her *Membership Booklet* a moment longer and she thinks the same thing she thinks whenever she gets on the scale, whenever she looks in the mirror, whenever she thinks about a lot of things these days: *Will it ever get back to where it was before?*

And even though she's here and that's something, and even though Aubrey goes to see a therapist every week and says he doesn't take pills and that's something, too, she'd have to say that a lot of the time lately, she's started to think the answer might be, *Maybe not.*

"Okay, Stephanie Cunningham," Maureen says, reading from the screen. "First of all, welcome," and the way she says it, it's so friendly and warm that Stephanie does feel welcome, "and second of all, what we need to do is set a goal weight for you."

"A goal weight?"

Maureen smiles reassuringly and nods. She lowers her voice conspiratorially, "Here's a trick: set your goal weight a little higher than you'd like it to be, and then you can just lose the last four or five pounds once you're on Maintenance."

That doesn't make a lot of sense to Stephanie and she imagines she's far away from maintenance. She thinks of her scale, at home, at the beginning of the day as opposed to the end, and she takes Maureen's advice and sets her goal weight four pounds higher than she would, ideally, like it to be.

"No wait," she says right as Maureen is about to type it in, and she changes it to five pounds higher than she'd like it to be.

Maureen keys it all in and prints out a sticker, pastes it into Stephanie's *Membership Booklet*, and gives it to her along with a *Welcome Book*, a slide rule called a *Pointsfinder*, and a small booklet called a *QuikTrak* daily planner. The *Welcome Book* has rainbow colors across the bottom and says *Join* in large white letters with *Welcome*, in smaller blue block letters, printed over it. There is a picture of eleven hands, all joining together in the center and resting on top of each other, like the game played in childhood, or a team rallying together before a game. Stephanie stares for a bit longer at that image, letting herself remember all the good memories it brings to mind.

Maureen points with her pen to the *QuikTrak* book. "Now, the most important thing," she intones, "is to write everything down. They'll be talking about it more in the meeting today, and your group leader will be able to answer any questions you might have, but just be sure to figure out what everything is worth and to keep track of it all."

"Be sure to figure out what everything is worth and keep track of it all," Stephanie says back to her, out loud, without actually intending to.

Maureen smiles warmly at her, and Stephanie notices that Maureen is wearing a necklace on which there is a large, round, gold pendant. It stands out against her white T-shirt, and Stephanie sees that across the pendant the word *Faith* is written in black letters. It looks familiar, and she thinks she's seen a variation on Caryn, a silver one, though maybe hers said *Hope,* and not *Faith.* She can't remember. She hadn't exactly admired it on Caryn, hadn't really felt like she could be a fan of inspirational word as fashion statement, but in this context it seems okay; in this context she doesn't dislike it nearly as much.

"Okay," Stephanie says, "And, thanks."

"Have a great first week!" Maureen answers and smiles broadly, encouragingly, a smile that says, very clearly, without mistake, *You can do it!*

Stephanie gathers her white plastic Weight Watchers–logo bag with all her purchases, her jacket, her shoes, and her sunglasses and takes a seat toward the back in an empty folding chair. The woman seated in the next chair doesn't look like she needs to lose that much weight, and Stephanie wonders if she's been coming to meetings and counting her points for a long time, or if she just loses weight really easily, counts points really quickly.

Someone has just received a gold star, a sticker, for making her first goal. Five pounds. The leader explains that everyone gets a gold star with their first five pounds, because even though it may not sound like the biggest number, it counts for a lot. Stephanie watches the woman for whom now everyone is clapping smile as she pastes her gold star onto the back of her *Membership Book*.

Stephanie looks down at her *QuikTrak* diary, sees that there is a page for each day of the week, lines for each food's description, and columns for points used and subtracted. She notices the boxes to be checked off for water, fruits, and vegetables. On the last page of the book, there is a section, across the top it says, *This Week I Commit To*, and underneath there are lines and lines of empty space to fill in.

The leader goes to her Pictionary easel and reads, out loud, "You bite it, you write it." She smiles and adds, "You nibble it, you scribble it. You snack it, you track it." Everyone claps. The leader goes on to stress the importance of taking responsibility, of acknowledging everything and not sweeping things under the rug.

"In the end," she says, "if you do that you'll only be hurting yourself." Stephanie wonders if she should be taking notes. She looks around; nobody else is. And then, slowly, one by one, hands are raised, and people are called upon.

A woman sitting close to the front, in a gray tracksuit raises her hand. "I wrote everything down this week. Everything. If I had a bite of a cracker, I gave it a half a point, or a quarter of a point if it was a small bite. I was really conscious of everything, of every nibble, every snack, much more so than I had been before. And I lost two point eight pounds." Everyone claps, and the leader gives the woman a gold star.

"I lost point eight this week," someone else says, to which there is a small smattering of applause. "I was disappointed, but since I went out to eat four times and drank three of those times, I guess it's okay."

"It *is* okay," says the leader. "And what's most important is that you're being honest with yourself about your actions. What's most important is that you're being honest." She nods wisely, right after the second time she says *honest* and hands out a gold star.

"And," someone else says, "point eight pounds is almost one pound. If I could lose a pound going out to dinner four nights, I'd be really happy."

"Going out to dinner is really hard," another woman says, and Stephanie tries hard not to hear that, or at least not to think too much about it, and that's easy enough because someone else has raised her hand and the leader has called on her.

"I took a water pill and lost four pounds." She doesn't get a star.

"You know how we talked last week about the Laughing Cow cheese and tomato on the multigrain English muffin?" asks another one from the front row. The talkers are always up in the front. "I added alfalfa sprouts to it, and it really added some substance. It's an excellent two-point lunch."

"I gained," someone else confesses, "and I was very frustrated because I felt like I was doing everything right. But now I see a lot of it could be that I wasn't being as honest with myself as I could be."

The leader nods at her sympathetically and says very seriously, "It's very hard. But it really, truly, is never too late to stop believing the little lies we tell ourselves. Like how that cookie doesn't really count when it does, or that eating an entire tub of fat-free Cool Whip isn't any points. You just have to learn to recognize the lies."

"It's never too late to start being honest, to start telling the truth!" Maureen of the Scale calls up from her post at the back of the room.

Stephanie looks around the room at everyone. She's sure that this meeting, that Weight Watchers, must mean different things to different people, but in this very instant, to her it's like group therapy and AA and dieting all rolled into one. To her, for a moment, it's like a special Elk Lodge gathering for people who might have lied, who maybe fell short of being honest with themselves and with a few other people, too.

She looks at her *QuikTrak* book and thinks how she will write down every single thing. She feels very strongly that "Kumbaya, My Love" is going to start playing through some hidden speaker at any moment. She feels very strongly that she will lose the weight, that she will follow this plan, that Weight Watchers could in fact be the answer to the question she has been, for almost nine months now, asking. And she feels something else, too. She hasn't felt this way in forever. She looks around the room again, at all the people who have to do what she has to do, at all these people. She feels like she's home.

nineteen

try easy

Sundays are different now. Sundays used to be drinking coffee at her desk, as opposed to the table by the kitchen. Sundays used to be reading everyone else's magazine, everyone else's restaurant reviews and as much of the *New York Times* Sunday edition as she could muster before she (a) felt brain dead, (b) felt that any second the onslaught of world events would send her over the edge, or (c) got the needling, unpleasant feeling that she was endeavoring to read every article in the Sunday edition because Josh had told her once that she could spend more time reading the newspaper. Whichever came first. Sundays used to be for planning out the meals she would have, and for sometimes taking the train to Ridgewood to see Stephanie. And Meredith thinks that whoever said, "The more things change, the more things stay the same," should reconsider.

Sundays are now for walking DB Sweeney around the neighborhood and to the park, though not quite yet to the dog run because even though, as Gary said, dogs are always practicing doga, Meredith has concerns that DB Sweeney might not be Zen enough for the dog run. Sundays are still for planning out her meals, but now not only the ones in restaurants, but also the ones she'll eat at home, the ones in which she will endeavor to know the exact point values. And in some cases that will be easy because many of those meals will come in frozen cardboard boxes containing little black plastic trays filled (though filled may be too enthusiastic a word) with tiny portions of fettuccine Alfredo, and macaroni and cheese, and three-cheese lasagna. And all three of them, to Meredith, taste the same. And yet, Meredith doesn't mind this as much as she thought she would because these Weight Watchers dinners and snacks and dessert treats that now line her shelves, allow her for the first time in recent memory, the few months now that she's been "on a diet," to eat processed flour without breaking rules.

She has, so you know, lost two pounds in the past two weeks. She has sacrificed for these two pounds and wonders still if she gave the butter-poached lobster at Perry Street a fair shake, since she mostly pushed it around her plate, unable to fathom how many points all the butter used in the butter-poaching part could actually be. Her review did include close to a paragraph on the candlelight—she thinks Perry Street has got candlelight down, along with excellent service—and perhaps too lengthy a debate on how she feels about eating with the West Side Highway *right there*. When she thinks of that review, she's not completely sure if the two pounds are really any victory at all. And she's also not sure, as she stares at all the cardboard boxes on her shelf, that it isn't a very bad sign indeed that cheese, in the case of these one-point cheese crackers of which she is fond, is spelled not with the traditional and proper *-eese*, but rather with an *-eeZ*. She imagines it has to be.

She turns away from her cupboard to look at the clock on her kitchen wall. It's already 2:45, time to get going. Sundays are now also for yoga. She heads into her room to change into the Be Present yoga pants, the intriguing ones with the slits up the back, worn by the woman with the apricot poodle (she ordered them online and had them FedExed). As she steps into them, flowy and soft and quick drying (or so it said, she hasn't yet gotten them wet), she wonders if people wear makeup to yoga class, when it's just for people and not for dogs. She'd worn makeup to the G-Doga class, but then she hadn't actually planned on exercise, had not planned on saluting the sun, though she imagines this time she will. She decides on a little bit of makeup, waterproof mascara and lip gloss at least. That sounds good.

She walks over to DB Sweeney, who looks up at her a bit forlornly, the way he does when she leaves. She tries not to feel guilty that she is in fact going to see the G-Doga master without the dogi, but it doesn't work. She still feels guilty. She reminds herself that it's been weeks since she's been to the office, weeks that she's been e-mailing her reviews in. She tries not to think that she's been phoning them in, too. But really, she's been with DB Sweeney so much more than other people, people who have offices to go to (well, who actually *go* to the offices they have to go to) get to be with their dogs, and so the yoga class isn't so bad. Really, it isn't.

"Okay, sweetie, sweetie dahling," she says to him. She has taken to speaking to DB Sweeney in an accent she can't quite identify but thinks might be Swedish. She does not know why. "Be a good mini mini! Mommy will be back *sooon*. So soon, so soon!" She says this all with quite a lot of enthusiasm, even though she read in *MetroDog: The Essential Guide to Raising Your Dog in the City* that you're not supposed to do that, that you're just supposed to leave your dog as if you're leaving someone for the afternoon, someone you've been with for five years. It's not Meredith's fault that she can't follow those directions, she's never been with anyone for five years. She has no idea how she'd leave them.

"Bye, DB Sweeney," she says again, this time with as much composure as she can muster. She takes out Gary's card and flips it over to double-check the address of the studio and she thinks, *studio. Stu-di-o*. There's something so artistic about the word; she feels there's something about it, too, that sounds very slimming. DB Sweeney shifts his position, lies on his stomach with his back legs out behind him. Meredith recognizes the position from the *Doga* book that she picked up. "Oh, hip opening pose!" she says to DB Sweeney without any irony at all. "Well done!" And then she heads out the door.

*   *   *

Meredith checks in with a woman wearing a tank top and two braids, more Laura Ingalls than Pippi Longstocking.

"Would you like to get a package?" she inquires, indicating with a swish of her wrist, more Vanna White than Laura Ingalls, a lucite stand with shiny cardboard rate cards displayed. Meredith takes a quick look, but even as pro-yoga (and pro-yoga instructor) as she's feeling at present, she resists the urge to buy a ten-class package, though it would be, in the end, more economical. She has a theory that as soon as you buy a nonrefundable package of any sort, bad things will happen. She acknowledges the propensity her back has had to go out in the past, which ultimately results in a lot of staying in. And while staying home all the time with DB Sweeney certainly holds its appeal, it would make it *even harder* for her to be a diligent and dedicated restaurant critic. It's not the first time lately that she has, albeit briefly, considered the merits of packing it up and becoming a television critic instead. She wouldn't have to try so hard to diet were she, let's say, the television critic at the *New York Times*. And she does think she's been trying hard, even though it might not seem like that to anyone else.

"No thanks," she says. "I'll just get the one class. But can I buy a bottle of water from you?"

"Absolutely," comes the cheerful reply.

Meredith leaves her socks and sneakers in a cubby up front, rededicates herself to her not getting all wound up over the foot fungus that could be lurking everywhere (hiding out and waiting, just waiting for the right moment to pounce), and heads into the actual classroom to unroll her mat. She thinks she'll pick a spot in the back, that for a few reasons it'll just be better that way.

"Hey, Meredith, you made it," Gary greets her as she walks in the door.

"Yeah, hey," she says, and wishes there had been more.

She takes her mat to a spot in the back right corner, trying as she does to ignore the slightly heated feeling in her cheeks. She notices the person next to her is sitting slumped over her knees with her head on the floor, her arms lying loosely beside her. Meredith decides that now is a fine time to assume that exact same position, and flops herself down just so. It is, admittedly, not the best position for further conversation with Gary, but perhaps that is not so bad, as further conversation with Gary is making her a bit hot under the collar, and that's saying something as she's wearing a long-sleeved T-shirt over a spandex top, neither of which have any collar to speak of. She inhales and exhales. She thinks that could help. She waits, and it's such a strange phenomenon for her, and stranger still that lying here on a borrowed rubber mat, *waiting* isn't driving her slowly to despair. Not even a little bit.

"Alright, guys. Welcome. Great to see you all here on this almost springlike afternoon," Gary says to the room. His voice still sounds to her like an Elvis Costello song, and she hears the people around her rustling. She turns her head to the side, and the others appear to be setting themselves up at the front of their mats, standing straight and at attention, their palms in prayer position. *Om time,* she thinks and hurries to her feet.

She catches Gary's eye on the way up, and just as his voice is the same as it was in G-Doga class, his eyes are still so green, but she notices something else, too. His eyes look so kind, and she thinks that's not something very often seen in people's eyes. Eyes can often be sparkly, and sometimes even they're nice, but kind is so much harder to come by. As Gary's first *om* fills the room, deep and resonating, she makes a mental note to remember that, or to at least try. Everyone joins in and says *om*, too, and it's not as fun as it was with the dogs, but it's still very energizing and focusing.

Soon the class has moved into sun salutations, and Meredith is actually following easily along. It's hot and it's sweaty and she's somewhat winded easily enough, but she can follow from her vantage point in the back of the room. As Gary gives instructions, as the sun salutations continue and they move on to other poses, things she understands and can (kind of) do, poses called warrior one and warrior two, nothing seems impossible. There's something about this, she realizes, that seems very athletic indeed. If that's correct and she's quite sure it is, then it's the first time in her entire life that she's been involved in something athletic without wanting nothing more in the world than to be able to pack everything up and go home. As she gets sweatier, and even as she has to concentrate more and more in order to be able to breathe, she thinks she's actually enjoying herself.

As they move through more poses, stopping in each one to inhale and exhale, as she's trying not to think (because Gary said not to) but thinking anyway, because if you've ever tried not to think, it's really hard, she sees Gary out of the corner of her eye, slipping out the door. And the music begins to pipe in. She thinks it's okay that she can't do the more advanced poses that the group is moving on to now, because the music is piping in, and she does so love the music. They go as a group, or the group goes and she tries her best to keep up, all the while not giving herself too hard a time (but tempted to). She listens to The Bellamy Brothers' "Let Your Love Flow," followed by Ben Harper and Jack Johnson singing "My Own Two Hands." And she thinks, if nothing else, she should ask Gary if she could see his playlist.

"Okay, guys," he says after a while, "let's try dancer." She thinks instantly that she probably can't do dancer, and then, even though he's addressing the class, it's as if Gary is speaking only to her. "If you're new, if you've never tried dancer before, just follow along as best you can. Remember to stay connected to your breath and the rest will come."

The rest will come, Meredith thinks, and as Anne Murray sings, "Could I have this dance for the rest of my life," she listens to Gary's instructions. She bends her right leg back and at the same time puts her left arm up straight in the air. She concentrates, she focuses. She grabs her right ankle with her right hand and begins to stretch in each direction, and she feels graceful and free, even though she's only stretching a little bit, not fully and swanlike like some of the people around, who she shouldn't be looking at, she should only be concentrating on herself.

"Come forward a bit more if you can," Gary says, and again it's like he's only talking to her, as if she's the only person, the only graceful dancer in the room.

"Confidence," he says deeply, "strength and stability." And she gets a little thinky right here, even though thinky is not what you're supposed to get in the midst of a yoga class, but she thinks, *Confidence, strength, and stability,* and she repeats it to herself. She'd been worried that yoga would never be for her, because she's always been a bit too type A, about a bit too many things, but *confidence, strength, stability*? No kidding? It's like a type A mantra in a way, isn't it? And who said yoga wasn't for the type A? Who said it, because they were wrong! And then she gets so enthusiastic about that thought, about the thought that yoga *is* for her, that maybe yoga could be the answer, that she falls right out of her dancer (well, truth be told it wasn't quite a dancer) and onto her mat.

She looks right over to Gary, but he doesn't single her out. He looks out at the room, at the yogis in various stages of dancer, some are fully extended, some are stumbling, too. One or two people are in the position from before with their heads on the floor and their arms behind them, and so Meredith gets into that position, too, and she listens to the music (Dave Matthews Band, "The Space Between") and to Gary's voice.

"Don't try too hard," he says. "Try easy."

Meredith takes her head off the floor and sits back on her heels and looks right at him. He looks right at her, and he says it again, "Try easy," and as he does he reminds her once again of DB Sweeney, because she suspects he might be a brilliant sage, too.

She stands up again. She grabs her left ankle with her left hand this time, and she kicks her foot back into her hand and stretches her other arm forward, and she looks at her reflection, and her dancer, she thinks, is beautiful. *Try easy,* she thinks, and she lets herself think, because not thinking, well that's just really hard. What she thinks is, *This might be a really important moment.*

And even though you're supposed to relax and give in to svi-vasana, the pose at the end of the class where everyone lies on the floor corpselike, pretty much Meredith can't wait for it to be over so that she can go to him. She wants to hug him, she wants to hold on to him, she wants to tell him that what he said before, it just might have been what's she's been waiting a long time—maybe her whole life—to hear.

As soon as the last closing *om* has been *om*-ed, Gary says, "Namaste."

"Namaste," he explains, "it translates to, 'the divine in me recognizes the divine in you.' "

Namaste, she thinks, and then says, as everyone else in the room says, "Namaste," too. She rolls her mat up and places it in the bin in the corner of the room. A few other people are talking to Gary, asking why he didn't do a shoulder stand with them today and he's saying something else about inversions, and so she lingers, she waits. And then the people talking to Gary are gone, actually all the people in the room are gone.

"Gary?" she says. He turns.

"Hey."

"Gary," she begins, and she thinks she can feel herself blushing, and she thinks she might be too old for blushing. "I just wanted to say, that what you just said before, *'Try easy'*? I know this might sound weird, or like I'm getting a little carried away, but it meant a lot to me. It was a really good thing for me to hear right now."

"It means a lot to me, too," he tells her. "I first heard that from Baron Baptiste, who was my first yoga teacher. It's actually one of the things that made me want to teach yoga. And doga," he adds. "I'm so glad I could pass it on to you." He smiles, so dewy and fresh and new, even if he's only, what, two years younger than her, at most three. She thinks about the restaurants she'll be eating at this week, does a quick weekly rundown in her head. She's doing all Japaneses this week (a sushi roll? Only three points! And one more survey never hurt anyone). Monday is Jewel Bako, Tuesday is Morimoto, Wednesday is G-Doga class at the Y, of course, and Thursday is a small Japanese restaurant that an involved reader, a tipster, has recommended she visit time and again. She remembers the description he wrote in about it: *"Peaceful, thoughtful, kind."* She thinks it could be a description of Gary.

"I'm a restaurant critic," she says.

"Cool," he says.

"I mean, um, I mean on Thursday, I'm reviewing this small and supposedly lovely restaurant uptown actually. I was wondering if you'd like to join me?" she asks him.

"Thursday night? I don't teach that night. I'd love to."

She gives him the address, tells him the reservation is for eight and she'll meet him there, and they can just confirm at G-Doga class on Wednesday night. "You know," she adds on, "if anything changes." Either she just asked out her yoga and G-Doga instructor, or she just filled a seat at her dinner table, she's not sure which. Except she is, because she'd been planning, for all the Japanese places, to sit at the sushi bar by herself.

"Sounds good," Gary says, nodding.

"Great," she says.

"Great, Meredith," he says, and it sounds nice, the way he says her name.

"Just one thing. On Thursday, it's Sarah. Sarah Marin."

"Okay," he says, and as his head turns slightly quizzically to one side, she thinks she should elaborate.

"Because I can't be myself," she explains. She says it matter-of-factly, confidently, without any hesitation, but once the words are said, once they seem to be hanging in the air, she does wonder if there was perhaps another way she could have phrased it.

He smiles at her.

twenty

not one gold star,
but two

At her third Weight Watchers meeting, Stephanie received not one gold star, but two. One for reaching the first five-pound goal (and even surpassing it, true story) and one for sharing her recipe for four-point popovers that take hardly any time to make. She feels positive, she feels on the right track. As she takes out her key and turns it in the door, she feels very much as if things, so many different things, are taking a turn, too; an unmistakable turn for the better.

She enters the kitchen to see Ivy, gleeful in her high chair. She wonders why Jenna doesn't have her upstairs already, and she can't help but think, *Yes. Yes, see, I was right.* Even though Jenna seems competent, and capable, and loving, and like an excellent nanny in so many ways, she's not. Even though *everyone* thought it was insane all these months to never leave Ivy alone with her nanny, it wasn't. Because, look. *Look here at my beau-*

tiful baby abandoned helpless in her high chair! Ivy reaches two beautiful arms out. She kicks her legs out in the air. That glimpse, that almost stolen view of that delicious little leg makes Stephanie forget everything for a moment; that leg filled with beautiful rolls of fat, kicking toward her, led by its little white baby-socked foot makes her sure for a moment that the world is a beautiful place. Quickly she puts her folder on the counter along with her two boxes of popcorn and her Mini Bars, and rushes over to Ivy. She unsnaps a snap, picks her up out of her high chair, and holds her, "Hello, darling!" she says.

"Hey, Steph."

She turns quickly to see Aubrey, sitting at the kitchen table, and even though it's Aubrey, it's the new, but not improved, Aubrey, so different in so many ways from the old Aubrey. Seeing him there doesn't startle her nearly as much as it makes her nervous.

"Oh, God, Aubrey. You scared me." He doesn't say anything, he cocks his head a little bit to the side and for a second he looks like he used to. For a second, he looks like a ghost. "You're home early. Didn't you have Dr. Petty?"

"Yeah. Dr. Petty called and he had an earlier opening so I took that. It was a quiet day at work so I just took it rather than hanging around at the office until seven." She looks at him and thinks of him and Dr. Petty, how they have their own relationship, their own world that is so separate from her. And she doesn't even realize she's about to ask him a question she's never asked him before.

"Have you been drinking?" She doesn't know why she asks him that when she has other questions (Where is Jenna? Did you give Ivy dinner? Is it wrong that if you say Jenna isn't here, that I'll be a little freaked out that you were here with Ivy alone?). They've never talked about it, and she doesn't really know, but if Aubrey has a substance-abuse problem, does that mean he has a drinking problem, too? Should he not drink? Who would she ask?

"No, I haven't been drinking," he says. He narrows his eyes, maybe to show he means business, maybe to show that as much as she hates him a little bit lately, he hates her a little bit, too.

"Oh, okay. I was just, you know," and she doesn't bother finishing the sentence, there is no way to end it well. "Did you feed her? Where is Jenna?"

"Jenna was feeding her when I got home and then when she was done I told her she could go."

"And she just left?"

"Yes," he says slowly, "she just left. Is there a problem, Stephanie?"

She doesn't say anything. And even with five lost pounds and two gold stars, when he asks her if there is a problem, the only thing she can think is that there are so many. He's been going to therapy for what is it, over a month? He hasn't been catatonic and he has assured her there haven't been any pills. She wonders if it would be shrew-like to say, *Yes there is a problem. The problem is that I just have no faith. I have no faith that it will last, and maybe I need a necklace, one that says* faith *or* hope *or even* love.

"No," she says.

"Where were you?"

"I went to my Weight Watchers meeting."

"Oh, really?"

"Yes, really." She thinks he's smirking. "Aubrey, what?"

"No, nothing, it's just that Weight Watchers makes me think of Richard Simmons."

"Well, Aubrey," she answers back quickly, "I don't know what you're talking about because I don't think Weight Watchers has anything to do with Richard Simmons."

"Sorry," he says. "I shouldn't have said that."

"You think?" She heads to the door with Ivy and she wants to ask him, wasn't it supposed to get better? Wasn't he supposed to stop doing drugs and then they would be happy again? She thinks all she does is support him, couldn't he say, *Good for you, Stephanie, that's really terrific you're going to Weight Watchers*. Couldn't he do something supportive rather than just always being supported? He doesn't say anything.

"Okay," she says. With her free hand, she grabs a box of Mini Bars and her Weight Watchers week three book off the counter. It's called *Be Active* and has a picture of someone wearing red striped tights and roller skates. There's a caption, it says, *Now I'm moving in the right direction*. She goes upstairs to put Ivy down, and Ivy settles into her crib, closes her eyes remarkably quickly.

When she returns to the kitchen, baby monitor in hand, she takes a seat at the kitchen table, in the chair right across from Aubrey. She looks at him again, and she sees his eyes, and she didn't notice it before because they were narrowed at her but she notices it now. They don't look the same, one looks bigger than the other, and she knows what that means.

"Oh, Aubrey."

He doesn't look up at her, and he says the same thing he's said, so many times already that it doesn't really seem to make any sense. "I'm sorry."

And she wonders if she should leave, if she should just take Ivy and go.

She has no idea, no idea how any amount of understanding, how any amount of team spirit (Go Team Cunningham!) is going to get them through this. Even though Aubrey isn't technically an alcoholic, she knows a lot of the time in AA they talk about a higher power, and she has no idea, she really doesn't, but she thinks that maybe the whole reason there *is* the higher power, and the whole reason people talk about it, isn't necessarily because they're religious, but more because no one can fathom another way. But she has no idea how to believe in a higher power, in anything. And she has no idea how they're going to get through this.

He says it again, "I'm sorry," and she wants to strangle him, she wants to throw things at him, bottles filled with Vicodin, and plates, and pictures off the wall. She wants to have a temper tantrum and scream, and say, *How could you do this? Why can't you stop?* And she wants to protect him, and to make him better, and she wants none of this ever to have happened, and she wants none of it ever to happen again.

"I just can't be perfect," he says.

"I don't want you to be perfect," she says.

"Yes, you do," he says, full of hostility and anger and venom and he spits a little bit as he says it. When did Aubrey become a spitter? When did it start? When was the day that he went from being Aubrey to being this? Was there one day that he came home and was this person, half-anger, half-Vicodin, and was she too busy, or too tired, or too exhausted, or too freaked-out to notice? Had she simply said, "Hi, Aubrey, honey, how was your day?" and then he just stayed that way until eventually she caught on? Or did it happen slowly, was it a slow roll down a hill, a pharmaceutical snowball that she could have stopped if she'd just been paying more attention, if she'd watched a little closer, tuned in a little more?

Was she supposed to have stopped him? Was she supposed to walk around and say, "Aubrey, what's in your glass?" except that that wouldn't have helped anyway because Aubrey isn't an alcoholic. Aubrey doesn't have a drinking problem. Or maybe he does.

"I'm not perfect," she says and she doesn't even know what part of what conversation she's responding to.

"No," he says vaguely. It's unclear to her if he's actually speaking to her. It doesn't seem like he is, until he says, "You're not."

A short burst of sound emerges from the monitor in Stephanie's hand and for a moment she's just grateful for it. And then the room she's in with Aubrey is filled with the sound of Ivy, one floor up, and crying.

"Aubrey," she says slowly, standing slowly and then she's looking down at him, his eyes look so glassy and demented, and she's not afraid of him but she wonders if she should be. "I have to get her. Will you stay here?" As if he's a flight risk, as if he's going to run through the house. But he could. She thinks of the time she got a root canal and they gave her Vicodin and it made her nauseous and confused and afterward ravenous, and she can't understand how anyone could take it for fun. Though it's not as if it looks like anything Aubrey is feeling right now could be called fun. And it still doesn't seem like her role in all of this, whatever it may be, is to understand.

"Just leave her," Aubrey says and when he says that the only thing she can do is hope that he *has* taken pills. He glares at her. "Perfect's somewhere else, Stephanie. It's sure as hell not here." She'd never understood before how people got divorced and hated their exes. She'd always thought of love as something that was lasting, like it was in the movies, and she'd never understood how love for some people turned into hate so easily. She thinks maybe now she does.

She holds the monitor, stares at it, takes a deep breath, and says, "There's this place." He looks up at her. "I looked into it, and I researched it and I think it's time. I think this is it." There's a part of her that's throwing the baby monitor at him, hurling it across the room, screaming, *This is it! This is it!*

"Rehab?" he says to her blankly.

"It's in Connecticut," she continues, "It's called Bonfin, and they have a high success rate. I mean, the thing is, none of these places have a really high success rate because it seems a lot of people relapse. But in terms of the relatively low success rate, theirs is high." And he stares into the fireplace as if there's a fire in there. She can't imagine bricks painted black could be so mesmerizing. And she knows she has to be the sane one here, and that it isn't sane at all to suggest he might enjoy watching *Baby Mozart*, even though she thinks at this point in time he very much would. "And you know, in French, *bonne fin*, it means good ending? I don't know, Aubrey, I think it could be a good sign."

"Yeah," he says, " 'cause you know all about things in France, right?" He smiles a little bit when he says it, and she imagines it's not because he actually thinks he's funny, and not even because he is in fact as mean as he has lately been endeavoring to be. She thinks the smile is because there is a part of him, somewhere, buried underneath a pile of Vicodin, that's trying not to be so awful. But still she clenches her jaw, sets it, and stares at him coldly for a moment. It's not that she means to, it's like the reverse of when you tell someone you love them, how it isn't always planned, how it just pops out.

"You didn't have to say that, Aubrey." He looks right at her, and she doesn't even try to figure out if it's hostility in his eyes, or hatred, or something else altogether.

"Yeah?" he says, kind of softly. "Maybe I was just trying to show you that I understand."

She doesn't say anything. She can't talk to him right now, but if she could she would want to ask him what it is that he understands. Trying to believe in something better, does he understand that? Or does he just understand that sometimes, in order to get through things, people have to lie?

On her way up to Ivy's room, she stops in their bedroom and gets a pillow, and then the comforter, the blanket, and all the sheets. She pulls everything off the bed. She carries it all with her into Ivy's room and shuts the door behind her. She locks it. There's something inside her that's getting louder, telling her she really has to leave. Ivy's crying is getting louder, too, but she doesn't go to her yet. She takes the chair and wedges it under the door. She'd been meaning for so long to get a rocking chair in here, or a glider. She is glad now that she didn't. She goes to the crib and picks up Ivy and stays there for a while holding her, whispering any number of soothing and reassuring and comforting things to her.

And this isn't something that she means to spring on you, and it isn't something that she feels apologetic about not mentioning before because if anything had been ingrained in her growing up it was that this one thing was never to be mentioned. She's sure that Meredith, for example, doesn't ever mention it; she's sure she never even thinks about it, even in her quietest moments, if Meredith has any quiet moments. But she doesn't want to think about that right now.

The thing is, their father doesn't really live in France. Stephanie just started saying that a long time ago, because she liked the way it sounded in the movie *Kindergarten Cop* when the cute little kid said his dad lived in France. That the dad who lived in France actually turned out to be some sort of villain was, to her, beside the point. Or maybe it was exactly the point. Because their dad had left, or was perhaps asked to leave, when Stephanie wasn't even three and Meredith wasn't even one. He lives in Las Vegas now, and he has a family there. It wasn't ever presented as, or seen as, a tragic single mom scenario because they lived in such a beautiful house in Bethesda, and went to the theater, and Mom had so many dinner parties, and senators and congressmen and important people were always there. Their childhood was so close to ideal, it really was perfect, everyone said so.

Stephanie had always hated that her father lived in Las Vegas, had always hated that he'd never been home. And as she got older, she thought she hated it less, but she still hated Las Vegas.

She thought Las Vegas sounded so unseemly, so bad, a place for gamblers and ne'er-do-wells. So she'd just started saying France, and she thought that was okay; she thought it seemed so much better that way.

Holding Ivy in one arm, over her shoulder, the exact position they are always in, the one that seems to be theirs, gives Stephanie comfort, even now, as she lays out the sheets, the blankets, the comforter, and the pillows onto the floor. She places Ivy gently down—she doesn't cry—and lies down next to her. There are ways in which she'd like Ivy to be like her, but not this way. She doesn't want Ivy to say, in all seriousness, "my dad lives in France."

She thinks her daughter may never know her father. Her daughter may only see her father on weekends. Her daughter may have a father who doesn't have a job, who's in and out of rehab, and that might not be an exaggeration. Her daughter may never say "my parents' house," she might have to say instead "my mom's house." Her daughter, her child, her baby, might never know her father. And she thinks there will be ways she'll spend the rest of her life trying to make up for that, to make up to Ivy for the fact that her father may live in his own version of France.

The way she feels right now reminds her so much of when she used to live in New York and take taxis. It reminds her of the feeling you get when you leave a taxi and for a moment you think you left your wallet on the seat, or the moment when you think you left your shopping bag in the restaurant, the moment on the way to the airport, about to go on vacation, when you think you forgot to pack something you needed. And everything

stops for a millisecond, but then it starts again because you realize you've got your wallet, you didn't leave your shopping
bag, you remembered to pack everything you might need. But
this is different, this feeling she has right now is so different
from that. Because there isn't any moment when everything
starts back up. Her wallet is in a cab somewhere, her shopping
bags are in a restaurant, and it doesn't even matter if she packed
her underwear because she's not ever going to arrive at the airport and she's most certainly not going on any sort of vacation.

twenty-one

oh, the heart

The restaurant is small, and while it might lack some of the shine of Jewel Bako down in the East Village, there is something very charming about it, and indeed, as the interested reader had said, something thoughtful. Gary arrived before Meredith did, and he waited for her out on the street, and when they went in to their table, it was reserved with a hand-lettered place card with *Marin* written out in beautiful letters over a line drawing of a fish.

"I like your red hair," Gary says. Meredith smiles; she's long been a fan of this particular wig.

"I wanted to say," she says after they have each ordered a Kirin beer, but haven't yet received their menus, "I really like the chant we did last night in G-Doga class."

"Rama," he says, and then adds softly, perhaps a bit conspiratorially, "Rama rama rama." She resists the temptation to chant along with him, too.

"I think the dogs really liked it, too," she says, and it's true, though the dogs do seem to inherently like just about everything Gary does, everything Gary says to them. Dogs can be so wise.

"Yeah," he says and chuckles softly. "They like it, but they don't really need it."

Meredith looks at him, slightly confused. He learns forward, his face brightening up as he begins to explain. She thinks his face brightens because he's a teacher, because it's his natural state to explain things. "Well, you know how Rama is Vishnu?" She nods, yes, even though she doesn't really know that, but she'd like to seem like she does. "And repeating *rama rama rama* means *joy joy joy*?" She nods back at him, with a bit more confidence. "Well, that mantra, that chant, *joy joy joy*, it's actually more for the people than for the dogs. Joy is so much more innate for dogs than it is for us."

"Uh-huh," she says and nods very seriously. She thinks of DB Sweeney, of all the dogs in G-Doga class, of all the dogs she notices now everywhere. Joy. There is a part of her that wants to reach across the table, just so she can touch him. She takes a sip of her just-arrived Kirin instead. She looks across the table at him; he looks comfortable, relaxed, at home. She feels weird. She wishes the menus were here because then she could make suggestions as to what it might be nice to order.

She takes a moment to do some sort of math, as all dieting surely must require math. The Kirin is two points, though it's a big Kirin, bigger than say an Amstel Light, so maybe it could be three. And if she has sake, and really, she'd like to have sake, that's another two points, or that could be three. And she's already had seventeen points today, that's more than she'd planned for, because instead of one mint cookie crisp bar, she actually had four. (Those mint cookie crisp bars are the best thing going.) At this point she doesn't have so many points left in her day, which doesn't leave a lot of options if dinner is going to consist of anything that doesn't come ready for you in a cardboard box, its name written alluringly across the front.

Having dinner at a restaurant, at any sort of restaurant (even a Japanese one, which is slightly easier) is hard when you're a Weight Watcher, harder still when you'd like to have a drink. At this juncture, Meredith would like to ask you a question, if she could. She actually doesn't care who she's even asking, she'd just really like someone to have an answer. How are you supposed to review a restaurant on six points? Especially when six points, if you haven't been paying close attention, is roughly the equivalent of two tuna rolls?

She feels the tides of her mood beginning to turn, and it's not that she would ever have described herself as completely pleasant or even cheerful, but she thinks that since she started dieting, she's become a lot more moody. Definitely more moody than skinny. She thinks it could be because she's been trying too hard. She looks across again at Gary, who still looks so at ease, so at home, and she thinks, again, *Try easy.* A dish of steaming, salted edamame is placed on the table between them. *One cup of edamame is four points, this could be two. Cups, that is, not points.* She can't count anymore. She takes an edamame and bites down, sliding the soybean out of its shell.

"So, do you live in this neighborhood, too?" she asks.

"No," he says, placing a soybeanless edamame shell next to hers. "I live in Williamsburg."

"Brooklyn?" she asks.

"Brooklyn," he says with one of his patented grins. They should be patented. "I'm a big Brooklyn fan."

Meredith takes another edamame, and takes a moment to consider this. It could be the first bad sign. They're always out there, waiting. Meredith is an admitted Manhattan snob. She is aware that there are people who adore Brooklyn, who embrace it wholeheartedly as a vital, vibrant part of New York City. She knows these people are many, that their legions are myriad and vast. She's just not one of them.

"Do you know I've never been?" she says in lieu of anything else.

"Really? How can the restaurant critic for *The NY* not have been to Brooklyn?"

"Um, well, Andrew Bamfield?" she says, referencing the critic who covers Brooklyn restaurants. "He does all of Brooklyn, and I do all of, most of, Manhattan, so I don't really ever have the time to get out there."

"You should one of these days, it's really terrific," he says enthusiastically. "It's really lovely." Meredith has never thought of it as a place that might be lovely, or as a place that might be terrific, she has really only ever thought of it as *far*.

"It's a lot quieter than Manhattan," he continues, and there's a small part of her that thinks, after ten years of living in Manhattan, quiet would be very nice. "I can't see living anywhere else," he says.

And she can't quite imagine living there, under any circumstances, and so she just says, "Yes," in lieu of anything else.

"Manhattan," he continues, "there's just too much honking,

too much noise," and she thinks, but doesn't say, *It's Williamsburg, it's not Iowa.*

"Uh-huh."

"I wake up to birds chirping every morning. What do you wake up to?"

"My Bang & Olufsen CD player," she says matter-of-factly. He stares at her blankly for a few seconds. And then the menus arrive.

"Well, great then," she says, "let's take a look," and she redirects all her focus on her menu. A few minutes, a few edamame, and a few more sips of Kirin beer later, Gary speaks up and says, "Just let me know, *Sarah*, if there's anything special you'd like to me to order."

"Well, funny you should mention it," she says, looking up from her menu and over at him. "I'm going to get the sashimi, the oysters with ponzu sauce, and the octopus and cucumber with spicy sauce to start." His eyes widen ever so slightly. She continues, "And then the Chilean sea bass as an entrée. Do you think you could order as many of the deep-fried appetizers as you'd feel comfortable? Or, let's say the tofu, the lotus root, and the crabmeat?"

"No problem," he answers. "Oh, and do you mind if I get the sea urchin, too?"

"Oh no, by all means, get whatever you want. As long as it's not the same as mine. And that's fine, because I am *definitely* not getting the sea urchin. Though if you could get some of the fried appetizers, too?" *And tell me maybe what they taste like.* She wonders how much detail she can get him to put into his descriptions of the tempura, of all the fried appetizers, so maybe she won't have to try them at all. And she knows that's wrong. As wrong as say, sea urchin.

"Sure," he agrees.

"But, sea urchin, really?" she has to ask, and just saying the words *sea urchin* suddenly makes it so hard to swallow, suddenly makes it so that she could very well be in danger of gagging. Sea urchin is not the only thing in the world that she can't abide, oh there are a few others, but it might be the only edible thing she can't bear. She thinks it might be the only food she's never eaten, and that's saying a tremendous amount, as she's eaten quite a lot.

"Big fan," he says, displaying more of his teeth, and she thinks, *Brooklyn* and *sea urchin*, and she thinks maybe it's not just that the tides of her mood are turning but that the tides of the evening are actually turning, too. Brooklyn and sea urchin (gag) might be working together to point out that this, she and a guy named Gary, a country music–loving doga instructor, might not be a match made in heaven. The waitress arrives, they place their orders, and she makes an executive decision, the kind she's good at making: she won't linger too long on the sea urchin, as nothing good can come of sea urchin. In fact she'll change the subject altogether.

"Do you think you'll always be a yoga teacher, and a doga teacher?"

"I do," he says, nodding, "Yoga, and doga, they've become things I can't imagine my life without. And I love to share that with people." She thinks there are things she can't imagine her life without, too; thinks of how hard and how long she has worked to make it so that those things would be vital, inextricable parts of her life, her career, her *raison d'être* if you'll forgive the drama. She thinks of the Zone she never got into, the carbs she couldn't do her job without, and the points she can't calculate. She has another question: she'd like to know why she is trying so hard to take away from herself the very things she can't imagine her life without? Maybe it's just what people do. But then maybe it's not.

The conversation goes on as they make their way through their many appetizers, Meredith at some point abandoning all math, choosing to forgo point counting in favor of experiencing flavors, taste, and quality. Gary asks her to talk about being a restaurant critic, and she shakes her head, no, and indicates the waitress. He nods in understanding, and she thinks he might as well have called her Meredith. But still, she leans forward and softly tells him how she really does love it, but how she'd like to do more, how her sights are set on other things, the book deal, the TV show, the film rights.

"Do you want to try the sea urchin?" he asks her.

"No, I really don't," she answers.

As they dig into their sweet potato tempura and deep fried marinated chicken, she asks him about his future plans. "Do you want to write a G-Doga: Doggie and Me Yoga book, or maybe even franchise? I bet you could franchise. And in this day and age, what with Cesar Milan being just about everywhere, I would think a TV show of your own would be completely within the realm of possibility. Ellery would be great on TV."

"I don't think so. No," he says, and she looks at him. She'd like to be able to hold on to electricity. She had thought that maybe electricity could have connecting qualities, that it could bring two things together; but maybe that's not really what electricity is for. She feels as she looks at him, as the air of contentment about him seems to morph into complacency, that there is a small robot, a small ambitious robot inside her head, tilting its metal head in confusion and repeating over and over again, "Does not compute, does not compute."

Gary leans forward conspiratorially—he doesn't yet know that they're no longer on the same team—and says to her, "That's not really what yoga is about."

"No," she says, "of course not. I just think it's such a market waiting to be tapped. I was just thinking you could have so much success at it. You could be a huge success."

"I think we measure success differently," he says to her. The sentence hangs there in the air, between them, and she reaches for a slice of baby yellowtail. She doesn't say anything and watches as he takes another clump of the disgusting sea urchin.

"You sure you don't want to try it?" he asks again between bites, slurps.

She shakes her head, no, "Really. I'm sure."

"Look," he says, placing his chopsticks on the smooth green stone that is there on the table, especially for that purpose. "To me, being able to live in the moment, in the present, is success. And with the life I've built for myself I can do that. To me, that's success right there."

She nods. He continues.

"Sure, there are other things I could do, things that would certainly be more financially rewarding, but this is what I want. The heart wants what the heart wants, and it's a really great thing to want what you have." *Want what you have*. She was sure that saying went the other way around. She nods at him, and maybe the way she nods, maybe it's a little sadly. And he keeps talking.

"I mean," he says, "I have inner peace, I have rama, I have joy, and I get to share that with people, and I get to try to bring some of it into their lives. And no, I'm not going to live in the apartments some of my clients live in, but I'm also never going to be one of those guys I see everywhere in this city, screaming into their cell phones on the street."

"That's true," she says, and she pauses for a moment. She thinks that she'd still like it if he had his sights set on a G-Doga empire, or at least a DVD. She stares at the gelatinous orange glob that is the sea urchin he has left aside for her. And there is of course a very good chance that sea urchin is delicious, that it's wonderful, and that if anyone could appreciate and enjoy the virtues of sea urchin, it could indeed be her. But there's a line that gets drawn, everyone has one, everyone has drawn one somewhere, and hers is at sea urchin.

She gets this feeling lately—when she looks into DB Sweeney's eyes and he seems to have so much in them, lifetimes of history—that she doesn't know very much at all. But she thinks she knows that she wants Gary to be something he's not. And she thinks she knows that's a terrible idea. You can't want people to be something they're not. Because that's asking too much of them. People, she's learned, can have a hard enough time of it just being themselves.

"Excuse me," she says. "I'm just going to go to the ladies' room." And he stands up when she stands up, and she has no idea in the world what to say, there isn't anything, and so she says, "Thanks."

Alone in the bathroom, she looks in the mirror, and she thinks, no, she knows, that as much as she does endeavor not to go there, she has gone not only to the ladies' room, but also to the bad place. And the only thing she can think, for reasons most practical, is that electricity, and kindness, and that smile, aren't everything. They're not enough. To ask him to be something other than he is, is as wrong as her asking that of herself. She wants to be yogic—if that's even a word—about it, and not blame herself. She wants to understand it about herself that when you've spent the past—how long has it been that she's been dating?—eighteen years, waiting for your banker, your lawyer, your junior tycoon, your somehow-more-suitable-for-you variation on the Joshs of the world, the Kevins (though perhaps with a name more like Aubrey's), that it would be a really big leap to a G-Doga instructor. It would be a leap that would be really hard to make, especially for someone who never quite learned how to deviate from a plan, whose plan always included living in nice houses and having summer homes and sending her kids, if she ever did have them, to private schools. She washes her hands quickly and turns away from the mirror. She really can't look at it anymore, not right now.

As she makes her way back to the table, she notices as she approaches that her napkin appears to be upright on the table. Upon closer inspection, as she pulls out her chair, she can see that her napkin has been folded into an origami swan.

She looks not at Gary but self-consciously around at the other tables, at the waitresses, to see if it was they who had taken her used napkin from the table where she'd left it, when she'd gone to the bathroom for a bit of a refresher on reality and self-loathing, and folded it so lovingly into an origami swan. She wants, right now, very badly, for it to have been them. But she knows it wasn't. The swan is so buoyant, so poised for flight, and there is something so personal about it that there is no way this swan is the product of something that's done for everyone, every time a napkin is left alone on a table. She knows even before she looks up at Gary, who has somehow improved upon his smile, who can, right at this instant, only be described as beaming.

She looks into his eyes, and there are things she could say, there are so many of them. "Oh," she says, uncomfortably, "you folded my napkin into an origami swan?"

He nods and he smiles and she can't think of anything except, *This is one of those things*. This is one of those things, one of those things that could go either way, if you would let it. It could be like the moment you first saw DB Sweeney, or the moment you first heard "Don't try hard, try easy" and thought it was spoken only for you. It could be the very moment that you know you are a goner. Or it could not be. And Meredith thinks, *I don't want it to be,* and so she just says, "Thanks," and attempts to take a sip from her already empty beer.

* * *

They stand together on the sidewalk outside the restaurant. But it's not a real together, it's the together that's a few feet apart. The air is springtime. *Spring really is here*, she thinks, even though she suspects it's still winter in her heart. She crosses her arms in front of her, she's never realized how often she does that.

"Well," she says, "thanks so much for joining me and for ordering all the dishes."

"It was nice, thank you," he says.

"Okay, well, I'm heading that way," she says, but she doesn't point in any direction. "If you just want to grab a cab here, that's cool." She doesn't mean to be unkind, and she hopes it isn't coming out that way. She doesn't want it to; she just wants to walk home alone, to be alone with her thoughts, even though she hates her thoughts right now.

"I think I'll just take the subway."

"Eighty-sixth Street is definitely the closest. And it's an express," she says, though he probably knows that, spending as much time as he does at the 92nd Street Y. "I'm fine to walk alone."

He looks at her for a moment; he tilts his head. He gets it. She feels awful.

"Goodnight then, Meredith," he says and as he turns and walks toward Second Avenue, she stays glued to the cement and watches his shoulders. She tells herself that his shoulders, they're upright and they don't seem at all forlorn. She wonders if she'll ever find what she wants, and if she does if it will have a smile so sweet.

As she said she was fine to do, she walks home alone, down Second Avenue. It's not a part of New York she has ever paid much attention to, even though it is, technically, her neighborhood. She passes the innocuous noodle shops, and sushi bars, and several boring bistros, the dime-a-dozen Italian restaurants.

Restaurants she wouldn't review, and probably wouldn't even eat at. *Nothing special,* she thinks and she wonders if she can even define the word. She still feels awful. She tells herself she shouldn't. *The heart wants what the heart wants,* she tells herself. But she worries about her heart. She wonders if maybe hers is the heart that wants the wrong things, wonders if hers is the heart that wants mostly a prewar classic six on Central Park West.

twenty-two

reverse your namaste

Meredith offers DB Sweeney a piece of her Thomas' Light Multi-Grain English Muffin. They're just one point for the whole English muffin. Really. Even though the proffered piece of English muffin is slathered seductively with I Can't Believe It's Not Butter Light spread (spread of what, though, that is the question), DB Sweeney will have none of it. He is not a fan of any of Meredith's Weight Watchers food, and she thinks on occasion, on occasions such as now, as she is celebrating the fact that she has conjured a snack that is, at most, a point and a half, that DB Sweeney is very likely smarter than she is.

It's Wednesday night and G-Doga Doggie and Me Yoga class starts in an hour. She didn't make a dinner reservation for tonight, just in case she decided she wanted to go. Sunday afternoon came and went, and she didn't go to Gary's yoga class. She felt like maybe she shouldn't. But she did get Baron Baptiste's yoga DVD, since Baron Baptiste was Gary's teacher, and she has, much to her own surprise, been doing (she means practicing) yoga every morning. And actually, she's been feeling quite fantastic.

DB Sweeney looks up at her, in a way that she thinks might be soulful, or even might be full of yearning, though the yearning part, that could just be her imagination. She wonders if DB Sweeney knows that tonight is G-Doga class, even though he's only been there twice? She looks down at him, right into his eyes, and thinks she needs a sign. Or not even so much that she needs one, but just, you know, she could use one.

"Do you want to go to G-Doga class tonight?" He just looks back at her. Maybe he doesn't care.

"Do you want to see Gary?" she asks and DB Sweeney barks and gets up on both hind legs. "Okay," she says, very seriously to him, "Okay." She heads back to her computer, saves her review of Hola (mediocre tapas in Chelsea, uninspired and not recommended) and e-mails it in to Douglas. Gary said he'd never be one of those New York guys who spends his time screaming at people through his cell phone. She'd had a feeling when he said it that maybe it boded ill, that if she continued in her quest for a lawyer, a banker, a junior tycoon, that maybe she'd find herself one day, even one day soon (soon and for the rest of her life!) watching someone scream at people through his cell phone. But the only person she knows who screams like that is Douglas, and this isn't one of those stories, there is no way in hell, even if hell is filled with power types on their cell phones, that she's going to wind up with Doogie.

"Okay, dahling," she says to DB Sweeney, glancing at her

watch, "give me two seconds to change, and then we'll go to Doggie and Me Yoga class." And as she turns up the volume on the iPod dock ("Wig in a Box," even though she doesn't wear a wig to G-Doga), she thinks of course DB Sweeney is right, as right as he probably is about the I Can't Believe It's Not Butter Light spread.

She should go. There's really no reason for it to be weird. She thinks it's not her fault that when he folded her napkin into an origami swan, the only thing she had to say to that was, "Oh, look, you folded my napkin into an origami swan for me," when maybe she could have said something nicer. And really, just because she feels a little bit loopy for the first five minutes after she sees him, it's not like that has to mean anything, it's not like that has to be some statement of fact, some road she just has to follow. And she really likes the G-Doga Doggie and Me Yoga class and she's sure DB Sweeney does, too. And she thinks that once you've taken the leap and admitted to yourself that you are indeed the type of person who gets quite a lot out of Doggie and Me Yoga, once you've accepted that, embraced that even, it would be a shame not to go.

She looks at her watch again. "DB Sweeney," she says, "let's go. If we leave right now we can walk, and it's a really nice night to walk."

*   *   *

As she walks into the room up on the second floor of the 92nd Street Y, she sees all the familiar faces and one of them, of course, is Gary's. He smiles over at her, and it's not a sad smile, it's not a "I folded your napkin into an origami swan and it

could have been a moment, it could have been a really romantic moment, and you just blew it off, you just took the origami
swan that could have been symbolic of so many good and
groovy things and you made it so that it was nothing" smile. It's
not like that at all. It's just a regular Gary smile, if there's anything at all about brightness and kindness that's regular, and she
doesn't think there is.

He opens his palm up, facing out to her, and closes it. She
smiles and waves back. *It's okay,* she thinks, *it's fine.* She grabs
a mat from the bin and walks to an empty spot in the circle and
unrolls it.

After the *om*s everyone does a sun salutation and then a few
other poses: a lunge, a twist, a bending forward and looking up
with a flat back. All the dogs stretch and, to tell you the truth,
some of them are a little more unruly tonight than on other
nights, but unruly in a charming way. Jessica, the tiny Boston
terrier so filled with pizzazz, keeps skipping off to the side, over
to Gary and Ellery's mat, looking up at Gary, a bit lustfully.
Gary makes eye contact with her and mouths, *Yes,* to her, at
which point she shuffles back sideways and settles back next to
her person.

"Okay, guys," Gary says next, "let's put our hands behind
our backs in prayer position." It's a little awkward, and it hurts
Meredith's arms a bit, but she manages to get into the pose. She
notices that this might not be an accomplishment of the highest
order, as all the other people are doing it, too.

"Reverse your namaste," he says, referring to what Meredith
knows is also Sanskrit for "prayer position." But she can't help
thinking that he might be referring to the other meaning of na-

maste, too. The one that means "the divine in me recognizes the divine in you." She wonders if maybe it means that what you're supposed to recognize as divine might need to get shifted? Though she could just be imagining that.

"Feel that," Gary says, "if you're new to it, it's gonna feel a little funky, a little weird, and it might even hurt a little bit. But as long as it doesn't hurt too much, just try to stick with it." And she thinks, *No, it doesn't hurt too much,* and she resolves to try to stick with it.

"Now. Straddle your legs," he instructs. "Pivot your feet and lean forward over your right leg. Try to keep your reverse namaste. Try to feel it." She tries to feel what it feels like, she listens to the rest of the room breathing in and breathing out, the panting of the dogs. "It feels good, right?" he prods. "What's good about it, I always think, is the same thing that's good about a headstand. It's a fantastic thing every now and then to flip your perspective around, quite literally, to look at the world from a different place, right?"

Everyone breathes in, everyone breathes out. No one says anything, but she imagines everyone answers him, and as everyone slowly returns to their standing positions, she thinks how eventually, after a long time maybe, she'll learn how to do a headstand. She stumbles slightly, right before she arrives at her standing position, and thinks that maybe the headstand might be kind of far off in the future, but she reminds herself that yoga, and especially doga, is not about judgment at all. She turns her attention where everyone else's attention has suddenly turned, toward the door where Jessica is showing quite a lot of tooth and growling loudly at a rather indifferent looking Havanese.

Later, after the parading of the dogs, when there's still some time left, and everyone is together breathing in and out in downward dog, Gary says, "Let's flow," and claps his hands twice. Everyone knows the routine, and everyone moves together, jumping forward from their downward dogs, stretching up with flat backs and leaning in again and then swan diving up, and back down and stepping back, all together. She feels the door open, feels Gary slipping out to turn on music. She loves the music. And then he's back in the room, she can feel it. He claps his hands together twice again, right as they are all in downward dog, about to go through the sequence again.

"Hey, El," she hears him say, "why don't you lead one more parade?" And she's at the top of her swan dive now, raising her arms over her head, and she sees Ellery get up, his tail up straight behind him, his mouth so clearly in a smile, marching along to the first few bars of the country song Gary has put on. One by one the dogs follow him. DB Sweeney looks up at Meredith, and she nods yes, and he gets in line, too. And she's still at the top of her swan dive. Everyone else is flowing without her, but she feels frozen, because she's caught up in the lyrics, the lyrics; of the song Gary put on are starting to hit her.

Well, I spent a lifetime looking for you.

And the dogs, they are all serpentining in the spaces between the people; how does he get them to do that? How does he speak to them this way? And everyone's flowing, except for Meredith and except for Gary. She's just standing at the top of her mat, Gary's looking right at her and softly singing the chorus to "Looking for Love (In All the Wrong Places)."

And how on earth could he know? Could he know about the

bankers, the lawyers, the junior tycoons? Surely not. Surely it's just a coincidence. But lately, she's starting to wonder about coincidences, if there really is such a thing.

He's looking right at her, and he presses his lips together a little bit because he's about to laugh. And she's about to laugh, too, so she does the same thing, presses her lips together to stop herself, because she doesn't want to ruin the moment in the room. She doesn't want to alter one molecule of it, the way the dogs seem to be marching in time to the tune and the words, the way the possibly deeply weird people (herself included) are all losing themselves in the yoga. And all she can think is, *Who does this?* And she looks again at Gary, who's still singing, kind of campily now, "You oh, you, looking for love," and for a moment, before she lets herself remember all the things she thinks about, she could tell you, just for a second, what happy feels like.

*   *   *

As she and DB Sweeney walk home down Third Avenue, she thinks about reversing her namaste, and she thinks about the things in her life she needs to look at differently. She thinks about dieting. In particular, she thinks that this time, like all times, she's always seen dieting as failure. She thinks that rather than try to find a way to succeed at it, the best measure of success for her might be to just stop doing it. She wants to taste everything and experience everything and be everything. She loves food, and to her food is living, and she wants to live. She doesn't want failure anymore and she thinks, wonderfully, joyously, that if she simply looks at it all just a little bit differently, if she just tilts her perspective, reorganizes her priorities, she doesn't have to have failure anymore.

Her mind goes back; it's as if something has taken her all the way back to the middle of February and she's standing on the sidewalk, looking into the window of Bouley. And the reflection she sees, she no longer thinks of it as the reflection of someone else, she no longer sees a stranger. She takes a breath and she looks again, closer, and she sees herself.

"DB Sweeney," she says out loud, and she doesn't even mind if anyone hears. DB Sweeney looks up over his shoulder at her, in the way that puts Gary in mind of corgis, and puts her in mind of Greta Garbo. "When we get home, I'm going to throw away the scale." And she feels free. She thinks maybe it's the first time she's ever felt so free. As they continue to walk, she repeats the same thing, again and again. Rama.

"Rama rama rama rama rama."

twenty-three

la bonne fin

"This is what I wanted, this is what I got. This is what I wanted, this is what I got," Stephanie repeats it to herself, over and over again, like it's a mantra, like it will help. This is, after all, what she wanted.

"This is what I wanted, this is what I got." Except she's not sure if what she really needs is a mantra, she only knows she needs something to get her through today.

She goes to the dresser, and she takes out his socks. The socks are the last things left to pack. She wonders how many pairs he needs, if it matters.

"Oh," Aubrey says, emerging from the bathroom, showered, shaved, and dressed, and whatever else, in under fifteen minutes. "You didn't need to do that."

"No, I know," she says. "I wanted to."

"Well, thanks," he says.

His eyes stay fixed on the bag on the floor, all packed, the socks on top.

"Ready to go?" she asks him.

"Ready as I'll ever be," he says and runs a hand through his still-wet hair, not meeting her eyes. His hair is longer now, longer than she's seen it in a while.

"Alright then," she says.

"Alright."

*   *   *

Ridgewood, New Jersey, is not very far from Kent, Connecticut, just two highways mostly, with a few other roads, but still it's a very long trip. As they pull up to the gate, she does so slowly, and she stops the car for a moment right outside the entrance, two brick pillars and a wrought-iron gate. The pillars are six, maybe seven feet high, and the gates are open. She thinks it's a good thing that the gates are open; she imagines they must look very ominous when they're closed. On one of the pillars, the one on their right, there is a small black plaque that says, in gold lettering, *Bonfin*. They both look at the sign.

"It's very tasteful," Stephanie says.

"Yeah," Aubrey says. "My mother would approve."

"I think," she says, because she doesn't know what else to say, and because she wants to agree on something, wants to be the same as him on something. "I think my mother would, too."

"But, you know," he says, not looking at her, "let's stick with the plan."

"Of course," Stephanie says and nods her head, perhaps too vigorously. The plan is not one of the many they haven't stuck to lately, but the plan they made at Aubrey's request not to tell their mothers, and that includes Aubrey's father, because he does in fact have a father, too. But nonetheless, Meredith's mother would approve, as would Aubrey's, they would approve of the way the sign looks, though perhaps not of what it is a sign for, not of what it really means.

"If I want someone to talk to," she begins, "about this?"

"You can always talk to Dr. Petty," he says quickly. But she doesn't want to do that, not because she hasn't, throughout much of this, thought it might be nice to have her own therapist, not because she hasn't on occasion wondered if it would be okay in the middle of a Weight Watchers meeting to say, "You know, instead of one toffee crunch ice cream bar for dessert, I actually had three. And I know that's probably not the best use of points, but you see, my husband has an addiction to prescription painkillers and I haven't told anyone, not even Meredith, and it's a hard secret to keep and even if it wasn't (but it is) it's a hard thing to live day-to-day not knowing what's going to happen next." She wonders if she'd get a gold star. But she doesn't want to talk to Dr. Petty because she has, this whole time, thought of Dr. Petty as Aubrey's, and she'd like Aubrey to have that. She'd like him to have more things that are his.

"Well, if I don't want to talk to Dr. Petty," she continues, and he turns to look at her, "would you mind, and just say so if you do, that's all I need to hear. Do you mind if I talk to Meredith? I won't if you don't want me to. I just . . ." and she doesn't finish the rest of the sentence, she's not exactly sure how to. So she just lets it linger there like blank spaces in the air, and she wonders if he can fill in the blanks.

He considers it for a moment, and then he says, "No, you should talk to Meredith, you should call her. I don't really know what's been going on with you two, and I'm sorry if it's had any-thing to do with—with what's been going on." He turns away from her as he says it, and adds on again, "You should call her."

"I don't know if I will right now," she says and they both stare out the window a while longer. Eventually, she takes her foot off the brake and lightly turns the car through the gates. As they pass through, she takes one last look at the plaque. It's as if someone's last name should be on it instead, and Aubrey's not going to rehab at all. They're going to a dinner party, or a weekend-long retreat at the Connecticut mansion of fabulously wealthy friends.

They turn up the long driveway, and the building at the end of it is more sprawling Connecticut farmhouse than it is Con-necticut mansion, but still, it's very peaceful. She wonders if that will make it easier, what he'll have to go through here, what he'll have to look at, what he'll have to face. She'd like to think it won't be as bad because it's so peaceful, because it's so pretty.

At the end of the driveway, Stephanie pulls into a spot marked *Visitors* and as she does she wishes that Aubrey was just a visitor, to so many things. She puts the car in park, and turns off the ignition and takes the key out. She holds the key in her hand and turns to look at him. She looks at his profile because he's staring straight ahead, out the front window, not looking at her.

She knows on some level that she's telling his story, that she's been telling his story all along. And she knows there isn't any way that Aubrey doesn't look horrendous in it. But he's not, he isn't. She knows that in this story she's been telling, that Aubrey is the villain. And he isn't, deep down inside, without all the Vicodin, he's really not a villain at all. It's the Vicodin, she has to believe, that is the villain. Or maybe it's 75 percent Vicodin and 25 percent Aubrey. Maybe that's how it works out. And now that she's thinking of it, she would have liked, in telling his story, to have put in more flashbacks, more images of Aubrey when he was everything that was good in her world, when he was all brightness, all light, before he was always in the basement. She thinks she should have done that, that it all would have come across better that way. But it just never seemed to fit in. The time never seemed to be right. And also, she's been so busy.

"Well," she says slowly, "just remember that Bonfin, if you spell it a bit differently, and add a *la*, the translation, in French, it means *the good ending*."

A while goes by, long enough so that she doesn't think he's going to acknowledge that she even said anything, and she's begun to feel like maybe it was a stupid thing to say at this moment. But is there a sort of thing you're supposed to say at a moment like this? She's not sure there's any way to know. There's no reference because the people who have had these moments, who could tell you how you're supposed to act, don't tend to talk about them.

"I wonder if that's the same thing as a happy ending?" he says, still looking out the front window.

"Maybe it is," she says. *Happy ending,* she thinks, just like something in a movie. Except how do you know the ending is in fact happy, if you don't know what happens after the last line is spoken, after that last scene, as the camera pulls back and an uplifting song plays in the background and everyone's laughing or smiling or kissing or some combination of the three? How can you be sure that everything doesn't just go to hell right after that?

"Should I?" she asks, "Should I come in with you? And help with the paperwork and all, you know? I'm happy to. I mean, I want to."

Aubrey unclips his seat belt and Stephanie watches it slide back up into its holder. She watches the way his shoulder shifts to free itself from the strap and the way he moves, every single one of his gestures, they're so familiar.

"Nah," he says.

She holds on to the steering wheel and stares out the front window and nods her head. "Okay."

Aubrey keeps staring, straight out the front window, too. She wishes for a moment, for maybe longer, that she could reach over to him and put his seat belt back on and drive away from here, and more than that, make it so that none of this ever happened. She holds on to that thought, that none of this ever happened, wishes on it like some burnt-out star for what feels like forever. And she imagines that's how long she'll want it to be true.

He leans over then, across the middle console, and it's so unexpected that it almost startles her. It's awkward, and they bump into each other in the same way they would have if they'd never reached out to each other before, if they'd never held on. And then he pulls away, but he doesn't go back to the windshield, he stays turned, looking at her.

"I love you, Stephanie," he says.

"I love you, too, Aubrey," she says, and she takes a deep breath, because she doesn't want to leave him here with a sentence that ends in tears. She doesn't think crying is the right thing to do right now, but then who knows. She steadies herself, and when she's sure she has a handle on herself, or rather when she thinks she does, she says to him, "And you know I'll be here."

He stares out the side window now, and she knows he heard her even though he doesn't answer. "I'll be here," she says again, and she's not even sure she's talking to him anymore, if it's a promise she's making to him anymore, or if it's now one she's making to herself, and also to Ivy.

Aubrey moves in his seat, and he says something then, and it sounds like, "God," but she can't be sure. She isn't sure she can hear properly anymore. Just as she isn't sure she can see. She isn't sure anymore if the things she sees aren't just things she imagines and things she makes up. But right now she thinks she can see Aubrey putting his hand to his face. She thinks she can see his thumb in the corner of one eye, his forefinger in the corner of the other, his palm over his mouth. She thinks she can see his shoulders moving up and down rhythmically. She thinks she can hear him breathing in through his nose, liquidy and thick. He reaches over again, with his free hand, the one not covering most of his face. He reaches behind her neck, and leaves his hand there, and gently squeezes. She hears something else and it doesn't sound like "God" anymore. It's high-pitched and full of air, and it shakes and goes in like a whistle and then out, out, and out.

And then he says, "Alright," and she hears the door handle

clicking. She hears the door open, and then she hears the door close.

She pulls the sleeve of her sweatshirt over her hand and wipes her face with it and turns to look out the side window after him. She watches him walking away, watches the way he hikes his bag over one shoulder, the way it hangs off his side. She watches the back of the man who has been by her side for all her greatest moments, the man who has been with her on all the absolute happiest days of her life. And now, for this one, too.

twenty-four

did you come here
to dance?

"Yes," Meredith says, "I'm just walking across Union Square right now. We're meeting at Blue Water Grill."

"Well, great. I think you'll have a great time. Call me after," says Leslie.

"I will," she says, and disconnects. As she makes her way over to the restaurant she thinks that although a Sunday brunch date hardly ever says romance to her, it's a good thing that she's going. She's looking forward in fact to going on a date, since she hasn't been on one in quite a while. She doesn't think the one with Gary can count, because it wasn't really a date. And she doesn't think she should think right now about Gary. She's looking forward to Blue Water Grill; she often does. She tries not to think that the only reason Leslie and Kevin have set her up on this date is because in their happy couple bliss, maybe at one point, when they were at the movies, Kevin leaned over to

Leslie and said, "You know, I always suspected Meredith liked me, and maybe we should find her someone, just someone to go on a date with, because it's been such a while."

Her phone rings again, and even though she's much more Zen now, is doing her best to embrace a more yoga-inspired lifestyle even when she isn't practicing on her mat, she thinks, *Leslie, what now,* as she flips her phone open quickly.

"Hello," she says.

"Meres, hi."

She forgets all at once that she's been angry and she forgets all at once about everything, and it's so good just to hear her sister's voice, and she thinks she has so many things to tell her, and that maybe one of those things should be "Sorry."

"Oh, gosh. Oh, Steph. Hi."

"Hi, Meres. Listen, I know you must be so mad at me. I know you must think I'm just awful."

"No, no, Steph, I don't. I don't," she says softly, and she doesn't. She can't say she has ever, throughout a lot of this, actually understood, but she doesn't think Stephanie is awful. Mostly, she wonders if Stephanie would understand if she told her that in its way, it had been a good thing, how she left her alone, how even though she missed her and thought about her so often, that she wouldn't have done some of the things, so many of the things, she's done lately if her world hadn't been shaken up, if her perspective hadn't been changed. "And I have so many things to tell you, good things."

"Meres, I don't mean to cut you off, and there's so many things I want to say, too, but," Stephanie says, and she sounds different, a little cautious and maybe a little sad, "I'm calling because I really have to tell you something." Meredith stops walk-ing, holds on to her phone tighter than she had been.

"Sure, Steph, anything. What do you have to tell me?"

She can hear Stephanie taking a deep breath. "I have to tell you the truth."

* * *

Wow, Meredith keeps thinking over and over again as she stands across the street from Blue Water Grill, staring blankly at it, focusing and not focusing on the large blue banner that hangs over the entrance from a second story window. It's a different type of *wow* she is thinking and saying over and over again in her head. It's not festive, there is no exclamation point. It's more of a horrible *wow.* She'd never thought before that *wow*s could be horrible, but it's amazing, it's almost mind-boggling really, how very many things she might not know.

"I can catch the next train," she'd said to Stephanie. And Stephanie had been so calm, so peaceful that Meredith had won-dered if it was possible that all that was good about Stephanie hadn't been affected by everything Stephanie had just told her.

"Meres, I love you for offering. And I do want to see you, so much. But I literally just got back from dropping him off, and I think I need, oh, a moment, or the afternoon. What about a lit-tle later on in the week, would that be okay?" Stephanie had asked.

Meredith wanted to argue, wanted to insist, but she heard something in her sister's voice and she felt assured that Stephanie's spirit wasn't broken, but maybe just a little bit bent, and she hadn't really wanted to, but she'd said okay. And they made plans for Wednesday. She didn't have her blind date's number on her, to call him up and cancel, and she didn't know what else to do.

She takes a deep breath, looks straight ahead at Blue Water Grill, no longer looking forward to it, and crosses the street.

*   *   *

He's standing right by the hostess station, and she knows it's him right away. He looks like Kevin, and it's strange that doesn't mean more to her. He looks tall, too, even against the strong vertical feel, the triple height ceiling of the restaurant. She walks up to him, and he notices her, and she extends her hand.

"Hi," she says, "Brendan?"

"Hi, Meredith," he says, "Very nice to meet you," and he smiles at her, a shiny, sparkly smile, and she notes that he's very dashing looking, which makes sense of course as she has already determined that he looks like Kevin. She feels numb.

The hostess emerges from behind her post, smiling broadly at them. She wonders if she's recognized, if she should have said, *No, it's Sarah,* if maybe she should have worn a wig.

As they are about to turn and follow the smiling hostess into the cavernous space that is the dining room, Brendan's cell phone rings. He reaches quickly, sharply into his pocket and flips his phone open.

"Yeah," he says brusquely and he holds one finger up to her, and says, "Sorry, just one sec." Meredith nods and looks up at the vaulted ceiling and listens to the strains of jazz music coming up from the downstairs.

"Listen, dipshit," Brendan spits a few moments later. That's what he says, he says, "Listen, dipshit," with so much venom that no matter who is on the other end of the phone, Meredith thinks it can't be an appropriate amount. Really it can't. And he actually does spit a little bit when he says it. "If I have to come all the way down to the office today, on a Sunday, to sit in your fucking cubicle with you and look at a fucking spreadsheet, there's gonna be hell to pay."

There is, thankfully, a moment of silence, as the person on the other end of the phone apparently says something. *Poor person*, Meredith thinks. She hates this right now, hates the jazz music that's playing, hates the guy, hates his cell phone, his complete absorption in it. She thinks she really shouldn't be here. She takes her iPod out of her bag.

Brendan says, "Don't give me that shit," into his cell phone, spitting again as he does, and Meredith puts her headphones into her ears. She turns the iPod on. The song that's just starting is "Let It Rain," by OK Go, and she tries to tune everything else out, everything else as best as she can, and just listen to the music.

Did you come here to dance? pipes through her headphones and into her ears, and she thinks of Stephanie.

And she thinks of DB Sweeney, how he has in his way filled all the moments. How before him, the moments were just moments, and now, they're him. And she thinks of Gary.

Through her headphones, OK Go is lyrically inquiring, *Do you feel better now?* And even though it had always been Stephanie who had always thought so much about movies, right in this moment, Meredith is reminded of *A Christmas Carol*.

She thinks of the part, right near the end, when Scrooge wakes up and realizes it's still Christmas morning, and he still has time to fix everything.

"There's going to be hell to pay. Hell!" Brendan says and flips his phone shut, utilizing as much testosterone as could possibly be utilized to flip shut a Razor phone. And even with the jazz music, even with the music still coming through her headphones, she doubts if she's ever, at any point previous in her life, heard a sentence spoken so clearly.

"I have to go," she says.

"Where do you have to go?" He asks, rather pleasantly.

"I'm sorry," she says. "There are some people I need to see."

As soon as she's gotten back uptown in a taxi, as soon as she's run quickly upstairs to get DB Sweeney, and somehow wrangled him into his Sherpa traveling bag, as soon as she's finally, at last, on her way, she opens up her cell phone, and dials.

twenty-five

king of the fairies, ruler of the elves

"Hello?"

"Steph, hey."

"Meres, hey. What are you doing? I thought you were off to brunch at Blue Water Grill?'

"Well," she begins slowly, "I had a change of plans."

"Uh-huh?"

"I'm on the train to Ridgewood. And I know you wanted time, and I want you to have time, and even though I had a change of plans, I still of course have a plan, and do you want to hear mine?"

"Okay," Stephanie says and she can't help smiling, just at Meredith, and also because even though she told her to go on with her day—because she'd really like that, she'd really like for the whole world to go on with its day and not come to a grinding halt—she would also like to see Meredith.

"I just want to see you, I just want to give you a hug and make sure you're okay, and there's a train headed right back to the city in an hour, and I'll jump right back on that. Definitely."

"That sounds just fine, Meres. Ivy and I will leave soon and meet you at the station."

"Fantastic, and thanks," Meredith says.

"Thanks back at you," Stephanie says back.

*   *   *

Twenty minutes later, Meredith and DB Sweeney emerge from the train. Meredith bends down quickly to take DB Sweeney out of his bag, and they walk together over to Stephanie and Ivy.

Once they meet up, Stephanie and Meredith reach out to each other and hold on, and only after a while do they pull apart. Meredith bends down to Ivy's stroller to get a better look at her, and Stephanie bends down, too, and looks over at Meredith and says, "Who's this?"

"This is DB Sweeney," Meredith says proudly, and laughs a little bit, too.

"The most underrated actor of our generation?"

"Of course. I kind of named him for you," Meredith says and smiles, a sad but also happy kind of smile. "Steph," she says, still looking down at Ivy, "it's been so long. I mean, it hasn't been so long, but she's grown so much. It's amazing how much they grow. It's so amazing."

"Mmmmmm," says Ivy.

"Hi, Ivy!"

"I'm sorry, Meres. I'm so sorry you missed her last few months, and that I missed yours."

"Let's not. Let's not be sorry," Meredith says. "I think maybe we needed to miss some stuff. I just want you to know, I'm here for you, I'll always be here for you."

Stephanie smiles, "I know. And now just think, we get to catch up."

"Right," Meredith says, "but we'll catch up after you've caught your own breath. I'm sticking to the plan and coming back on Wednesday."

Stephanie wants to thank her for that, but she doesn't say anything, because she's sure some things don't, after all, always need to be said.

"As long as you're sure you're okay. As long as you don't need to talk about Aubrey?" Meredith, ever the double-checker, double-checks.

"You know, I'm sure I'm going to want to talk about it soon. And there's lots of things I'm sure I'm going to want you to know, but right now I think," and she pauses and breathes, "right now, I just want you to know that I'm sticking by him."

"Of course you are," Meredith says seriously, and Stephanie thinks that in Meredith's words she can hear hopefulness. She really does.

"I know a lot of people might think I'm crazy and that I should just look out for myself and my daughter, but you know he's her father and also, he needs me. And if he's ever needed me, if he's ever needed anyone, it's right now. And I can't turn my back on him. I can't."

"Steph," Meredith begins, "I don't think you're crazy. And I wouldn't have doubted for a second that you'd stick by Aubrey. I can't imagine anyone who knows you, even just the tiniest bit, would expect an inch, a centimeter less. You stay the course. You always have. It's one of the things that I've always admired about you the most."

"Thanks," Stephanie says, "really." And she means it, she thinks it's been a while now she's been wanting to know that there were still things about her that Meredith admired. She thinks it's been longer than that she's been wanting to know that there were things about her that Meredith still understood.

"He's really lucky to have you," Meredith says.

"Thanks, Meres," she says, looking down at DB Sweeney and then up, at nothing in particular, at the air. "I just can't imagine my life without him."

"I understand," Meredith says. "I really do."

They walk for a while, arm in arm, Ivy rolling in her stroller, and DB Sweeney walking in front of them. They head over to the town, to the main street, and walk slowly past the stores and restaurants there.

After a while, Meredith says, "I wish I'd known. I would have wanted to help you. I do always want to help you, even though it doesn't seem like that, even though it seems so much more like it's always you helping me."

"We both help each other," Stephanie says, and Meredith doesn't say anything. Stephanie doesn't say anything either, and she hopes that maybe it's their way of not saying that now they're going to put it behind them.

"Okay, and can I just say, if it's okay to say, that you look fantastic. I mean, *wow*, and I mean that only in the best way."

"Yes, you can definitely say that, Meres, thanks."

"The Zone?" She has to ask.

"Weight Watchers," Stephanie says proudly. "It's the answer. The answer for me, that is," she adds on quickly.

"I tried Weight Watchers but I sucked at it. Stephanie, I decided I'm not going to diet anymore," she confesses.

"Well," Stephanie answers thoughtfully, "then good for you if that's what you want. But, Meres, you know you look so great, too. Did you lose some weight?"

"I don't think so, but you know, I can't really say for sure. I threw away the scale."

"Nooo . . ." Stephanie says with her eyes widened, faux dramatically.

"I really did."

"Well, good for you. But you know, maybe it's not weight but you look so good, so healthy."

"Thanks, I've been doing a lot of doga."

"Doga?" she asks.

"Yeah, it's yoga for dogs, but I guess for me, it's just yoga. Steph, I learned how to stop trying so hard, I learned how to try easy."

"You? Yoga? I never would have thought, not in a million years. I have a feeling we must have a lot to catch up on."

"I have a lot to tell you. But before we move on, can I just say that you're looking very pre-pregnancy."

"Well, I'm hardly there yet, but thanks. I do feel like I'm on my way though," Stephanie tells her, and for a moment

Stephanie pauses, because she will never be the same person again. Yes, she no longer stands in front of a mirror and thinks her body surely must belong to an alien, but there is still that alien sensation, as if this isn't really her life. She thinks that feeling will be with her for a while, until Aubrey gets home, and she imagines even after that. But on the other hand, she nods enthusiastically because she has lost a lot of the weight she set out to lose.

"Okay," she continues, "I have to admit, I did set my goal weight as a little higher than I actually wanted it to be, because you know, I wanted to reach it, but I think I will reach it. Not right away, but I really have faith, I really do think I'll reach it."

Meredith smiles at her proudly.

"And," Stephanie continues, "I think when you reach your goal, you get a key chain. And you know what, I'm so going to use that key chain proudly."

"That's amazing, Stephanie. You'll make your goal. You're amazing."

"It doesn't get easier though," Stephanie says, and thinks that maybe not very much does. "And there aren't any shortcuts. There are always setbacks, but that's okay because you learn from the setbacks."

"You do," Meres agrees, and thinks to herself, *You really do.*

"I mean, just last week I gained because I'd been really over-doing it with the baby carrots. I ate two bags of baby carrots without even thinking about it. And then I just said to myself, *Stephanie, stop looking for happiness in the bags of baby carrots.*"

Meredith laughs. "Ha, true. Now this is coming from a

proud Weight Watchers dropout, so take it with a grain of salt. But I'll agree with you that maybe two bags of baby carrots in one sitting might not have been the wisest choice."

"Oh, but even if it's not one sitting, I'll just walk back and forth to the kitchen getting a handful at a time, *for hours*." Stephanie adds and they both laugh. It feels good to laugh, and to laugh together, again.

"I don't know," Stephanie chuckles. "Maybe the trick is that you can't go looking for happiness."

Meredith smiles widely, at her sister, at everything. So many lightning bolts, so little time. "Or, *maybe*," she says, eyes wide, "the trick is that you actually can."

"What's that, Meres?" Stephanie asks, looking down at Ivy, twirling something shiny and plastic on the stroller's handle.

"I'll explain. Wow, I feel like I have so much to explain," Meredith says and Stephanie looks at her, kind of confused.

"What?" she asks again, as Meredith starts bouncing from one foot to the other, pulling slightly on DB Sweeney's leash. He comes right to her and looks up at her and then at Stephanie expectantly. It looks very much to Stephanie like DB Sweeney is ready to go. (And if she mentioned this to Meredith, Meredith would have explained that DB Sweeney knows everything.)

"Stephanie, I feel like I have so much to tell you. I feel like so much has happened, or maybe it's just that it's about to, but I have to go first, I have to do something first. I have to go, and then I'll be back."

"Are you okay?"

"I am. I'm good. I'm great. I promise. The bus stop is right near here, right? Do you think there's a bus?"

"Yeah, it's right up the hill. I'm sure there's a bus soon—"

"Okay, I'll call you later and explain this, all of it. But don't worry because it's all good." Meredith says, and then leans in and hugs Stephanie again. She pulls back and looks at her right in the eye, and says, very seriously, very much like the Meredith one would expect, "It's all going to be okay. You know that, right?"

"Well," Stephanie says, going somewhere else for just a moment, but then coming back, "we'll see."

"No, really. Aubrey'll pull through this with you there to stand by him. He will."

"Ah, Aubrey," Stephanie says, looking down at the ground. "Aubrey, Aubrey," and as she says it, the repetition of his name, twice in a row, it reminds her of something so concretely, so completely, even though it was so many years ago now, even though it was, now that she thinks of it, a lifetime ago. She wonders if Meredith remembers, too. She wonders if there's something about that, the *Aubrey, Aubrey, Aubrey* that has transported Meredith back to the living room in the apartment they shared on Eighty-fourth Street, so close to the river.

She looks up at Meredith, and Meredith is, almost in spite of herself it seems, grinning. She stops grinning and looks over cautiously at Stephanie. Stephanie smiles and shakes her head, it's okay, and Meredith takes a breath first, and then says joyously, "Aubrey, Aubrey, Aubrey. He of the very cool name," and laughs and Stephanie laughs, too, and then she smiles. It's a bittersweet smile, part of it is at least, because it makes her think that you have no idea of how things are going to turn out, when you're so young and so hopeful, and that no matter how much you try to make it so that everything looks perfect, so that everything could *be* a little bit perfect, it's not going to be. And there's a part of the smile, too, that doesn't have any bitterness to it at all; there's a part of it that remembers her and Meredith's apartment and how she used to feel when Aubrey used to call. There's a part of her that still believes that some things could go back to how they used to be.

"Okay. I'm gonna run!" Meredith says, looking over her shoulder to be sure a bus is not yet on the approach. "I'll call you later. And I'll explain all this running off to the bus!"

"Call when you can," Stephanie tells her. "I'll pick up on the first ring."

"Oh, argh!" Meredith exclaims. "Ugh, don't. Pick it up on the second. Or even the third." And she's almost turned around and then she pivots back toward Stephanie, gracefully pivots, Stephanie notices. Meredith leans in and hugs Stephanie one more time tightly, and lets out a joyous, "Whoop!" the likes of which Stephanie is sure she's never heard come from her sister. Meredith puts her fingers to her lips and kisses them, releasing the kiss in the direction of the sleeping Ivy. She turns and starts running.

As Stephanie watches Meredith sprinting up the hill toward the bus stop, this little wonderful dog named DB Sweeney running jauntily along at her side, she reaches her hands up, clapping them together right above her head, without even realizing she's doing it. She takes her eyes off Meredith for a moment to see if Meredith's whooping or her clapping may have woken Ivy. And look at that, Ivy indeed is awake, but not crying or fussing or anything at all. She's just staring out of her stroller, very serenely. Stephanie reaches in and unstraps a strap and pulls Ivy up to her. Together, they watch as Meredith crests the hill, right as the bus back to New York pulls into view.

She thinks about the things that she and Meredith said today. And she knows she'll think about it all more, and they'll talk about it all more, and she smiles at the realization of how very much she's looking forward to later on this evening, or tomorrow, or sometime soon, receiving Meredith's next call. She smiles also at the realization that she's looking forward to something. As she turns away from the hill, holding Ivy over her shoulder, lightly pushing the stroller with her free hand, she pauses for a moment on the image of Meredith's smile, on the image of her own, when they used to say, "Aubrey."

"Aubrey, Aubrey, Aubrey. He of the very cool name."

Meredith always said Stephanie had a special skill for meeting guys with the very cool names. And Meredith, so often lamenting the Jims, the Matts, the Joshs, had once told Stephanie that she felt she liked the Scottish names, the Gaelic names, the Celtic names best. Depending on the translation, Aubrey means King of the Fairies or Ruler of the Elves.

"King of the Fairies," Stephanie says softly to herself, "Ruler of the Elves." And the thing is, she thinks, is that there isn't any way to know it at first. Because really, how could you? But what eventually happens is that as you get older, as you learn some things, as you "grow up," as the saying goes, you figure out that elves don't really exist, not even in the North Pole. Eventually you see that fairies aren't real.

Stephanie holds Ivy close, and together they turn toward home.

twenty-six

good things come to
those who wait

It has been a festival of public transportation to say the least. The bus from Ridgewood dropped her off at the Port Authority. From there, she took a crosstown bus over to the east side, and then a subway back to Union Square where it seemed she'd just been, maybe a lifetime ago. It's actually turned out to be a very warm day, and she's been hurrying, and carrying DB Sweeney over her shoulder in his Sherpa bag. She's not looking her best.

She makes her way through the labyrinth of the Union Square station, and she has to look at a subway map, and then she's on her way, she's on yet another subway, and the announcer is saying, in a way that is helpful and informative yet also somewhat unintelligible, "Last stop in Manhattan." And she thinks that's nice that they say that, in case you weren't ready to leave, in case you weren't quite ready to go.

She scrolls through her iPod; she needs the right song. She

briefly considers David Gray's "This Years Love (It Better Last)" but even though she's a pretty big David Gray fan, there's something too sad about that song, there's too much of a hint of "No, this isn't going to work out after all" in it. And she's sure that can't be right. Keith Urban, "Making Memories of Us"? Too Nicole Kidman. Lighthouse, "You and Me"? *No,* she thinks, too Gwyneth Paltrow and Jake Gyllenhaal in the movie *Proof.* REM, "You Are the Everything"? Too something. Johnny Lee's "Looking for Love"? *Ha,* she thinks, *look at that.* And then she smiles to herself, and then she takes her headphones off, turns off her iPod, and puts it away.

When she gets off the train, she reaches into her bag again and finds his card inside her wallet. She looks at the address on the front, and stands for a while in front of a map protected behind plastic, until she locates his address. She takes DB Sweeney out of his bag and looks around, nothing is blurry, everything is clear and in focus. She makes a left on Berry Street and begins walking quickly, and then jogging, in what she hopes, what she thinks, what she's actually pretty sure is the right direction. She stops for a moment, and notices how quiet it is. *Look at that,* she thinks, *you really can hear the birds chirping in Brooklyn.*

And she's standing right outside his building.

I'll wait, she thinks, *if he's not home, I'll just sit down on the stoop right here, and wait.*

She locates 2R on the nameless list of apartments and presses it. There's a pause, a long one. And then, Gary.

"Who is it?" His voice comes through the intercom, crisp and clear and alive. And she knows that in yoga you're supposed to really concentrate on living in the present, but for that one crisp, clear, and alive second, she's pretty sure she can see her future. She can see herself looking across a room at Gary. He's separating the movie section out from the rest of the paper, opening it up, spreading it out across the floor. DB Sweeney is there, too, right next to Gary. He's pressing his two front feet into the floor, arching his back, and stretching his tail skyward. The upward facing dog. Gary is looking up at her, and he's smiling. She's pretty sure that in this future she can see, that DB Sweeney is smiling, too. And so is she.

Oh, and in the background? Pete Townshend is singing, "Let My Love Open the Door (to Your Heart)."

"Who is it?" Gary asks a second time.

She takes a deep breath, and presses the *Talk* button. And then she says, "It's Meredith."

La Fin

adopt a dog today!

A few resources if you're hoping to adopt a dog or help homeless animals:

The American Society for the Prevention of Cruelty to Animals
www.ASPCA.org

Animal Haven Shelter
www.animalhavenshelter.org

Brooklyn Animal Rescue Coalition
www.barcshelter.org

The Humane Society of the United States
www.hsus.org

Maddie's Fund
www.maddiesfund.org

North Shore Animal League
www.nsalamerica.org

Petfinder
www.petfinder.com

The Washington Animal Rescue League
www.warl.org